Away Day

David Fairley

Bright Pen

Visit us online at www.authorsonline.co.uk

ISBN 978-07552-1085-5

Authors OnLine Ltd
19 The Cinques
Gamlingay, Sandy
Bedfordshire SG19 3NU
England

"And the fourth official has indicated four minutes of added time. If Liverpool can hang on for just a few minutes more, they will be taking the World Club trophy back to England for the first time ever.

Márcio and da Sousa are lining up to take this free kick for the Brazilians. The ball must be thirty-five yards out, but both of them are well capable of scoring from that range. Christofis is yelling at his team mates, forming them up into a wall as the referee glances at his watch again and raises his whistle to his lips.

Da Sousa strikes it! And it's headed wide by Samson Mbillah at the back post for Liverpool. It was a marvellous shot, a left foot curler struck with real venom. Mbillah's team mates are patting him on the back, grateful for his quick reactions.

So it's a corner for Corinthians, and the Brazilians are wasting no time. There's a lot of jostling going on in the area as Flavio places the ball. He's swung the ball in at pace, aiming for the edge of the area. Lucão and César are both looking to strike it. It's Lucão on the volley! And a fantastic save from Christofis to deny the Brazilian wing back. He claws it away from the goal, but it's rolled clear. Alcock gets there first and smashes it away! Desperate stuff from ten-man Liverpool as their captain clears the ball to safety.

Rogerio has picked the ball up in his own half and is heading back towards the Liverpool area. Evans slides in, but it's a wild challenge and the Brazilian takes the ball past him with ease. Van Keulen is coming forward to challenge, but Rogerio has passed to Márcio, who is in acres of space on the left wing. Mbillah is there again, but the Brazilian feints to the left and goes past him. He passes back to Rogerio just outside the area. Great control from Rogerio. He shapes to shoot! But no, he's rolled the ball into the path of Ricardinho, who has come steaming in from behind. Ricardinho unleashes a rocket! It's cannoned off Hodgkins and has rolled just wide of the post. The crowd are practically silent. This is real heart-in-mouth stuff.

Another corner for the Brazilians, and Flavio is sprinting over to the corner flag as the precious seconds tick by. Even Corinthians' keeper has come forward for this one. Flavio sends in another pinpoint cross, and César connects with a looping header. Christofis is stranded! But Alcock gets there in time and heads the ball out of the danger zone.

The ball's trickling towards the centre circle, and there are no players close enough to pick it up. Wagner, the Brazilian keeper, is sprinting back again, but young Tommy Evans is also pursuing, and he certainly has the pace. Wagner collects the ball and turns, looking for a team mate. But he hasn't seen Evans, who robs the keeper at the halfway line. Evans keeps going, keeping up his blistering pace as Wagner tries to catch up with him. The keeper has no chance. Even with the ball, the youngster is gaining distance. Evans has taken a look over his shoulder as he reaches Corinthians' area, and slowed. Wagner seems to have given up, jogging back with his shoulders sagging. Evans has stopped, and has put one foot on top of the ball right at the edge of the goal line. He's looking back at Wagner, who is now walking back, holding his hands out in frustration. Amazing cheek from the youngster, but who can blame him? Evans has raised his hand to wave at the travelling supporters, and there - he's tapped the ball in for his second goal of the evening, and Liverpool's third.

All eyes are on the referee now, and it looks like he's raising the whistle to blow for full time. Yes, he's blown the whistle! They've done it! Liverpool have beaten Corinthians by three goals to one to take the World Club Trophy back to England for the first time in history!"

The two players assembled in front of the camera for the post-match interview could hardly have been more different in appearance.

On the right stood Gavin Alcock, team captain and defensive rock. Gavin was one of the few members of the squad to have been born and brought up on Merseyside and his family (at least according to his grandfather) had been Liverpool supporters since round about the time of the Norman invasion. He was a hard person to miss, at a little over six foot three, with a frame to match his height and an unruly shock of practically radioactive ginger hair.

Beside him was the familiar face of Jason Woodruff, affectionately known as "Woody" to most of the world. If not the most talented member of the team, he was by far the most well known. He looked, as ever, immaculate. Six spikes of hair had been crafted atop his golden head, a look that would have been mildly rebellious were it not for the fact that each spike was exactly symmetrical. The fact that such perfection had been attained in the few minutes between the final whistle and the post-match interview was testament to the skill of his team of stylists.

Alcock seemed restless and distracted, grinning excitedly and glancing around the interview space, while in contrast, Woody gazed directly at the camera, his warm, accessible smile and boyish good looks exuding a practised calm.

"First of all, congratulations on a well-deserved victory", the interviewer began. "How does it feel to be the first British team to lift this trophy?"

"To be honest, mate, I think we had it coming to us", blurted Gavin, who had never been known for his shy or modest nature. "All the journalists who were saying we had no chance in this competition, that we wouldn't even get to the quarter final - well, they know where they can stick their articles now."

Faint laughter could be heard from some of the other players, who were standing out of shot.

"You played most of the second half with only ten men, after Damien St Clair's sending off for his challenge on Marcelo", the interviewer continued. "What did you make of that?"

"Well, I never saw it as a red card", replied Gavin, narrowing his eyes. "Damo's gone in for the tackle. It was a strong one, but he got a bit of the ball. I think Marcelo's made a meal of it, to be honest"

"But the player's leg was broken", the interviewer reminded him.

"Yeah, but I'm not sure Damo's done that, to be fair. Marcelo most likely done that to himself while he was rolling about on the ground."

The interviewer, momentarily lost for words, changed the subject.

"So, ah, two more goals from young Tommy Evans tonight. He just can't seem to stop scoring at the moment. His first, after only seven minutes, really gave you a foothold in the game. Tell us about that."

"Well, the ball's just fallen for Tommy, he's kicked it, and it's gone in", explained Gavin expansively.

Suddenly, shouting and singing could be heard from just outside the interview area as some of the other players became more rowdy. "Come on!" shouted Gavin, raising his fist gleefully to his friends.

The interviewer moved on, pointing his microphone towards the heavily insured face of Jason Woodruff. "Damien St. Clair's goal really was something special. What's it like to play alongside someone of his talent?"

Woody's expression, practically unblinking up until now, shifted to one of self-effacing admiration. "Damien was superb in the first half, before he was sent off", he said, shaking his head slightly. "He gets some stick from the press about his fitness level and his private life, but, you know, in these big games there's no-one else you'd rather have on your side. The other team didn't know how to stop him. What was it, four or five players he went past before he scored?"

"Yes indeed, and a fantastic finish too", the interviewer went on. "Now, another person who's been in the news lately - your manager, Rudolf Emmerich. How do you think he's feeling now?"

"Well, you know, we've all got loads of respect for Rudolf. He's really changed things around here, and brought in some great talent", Woody said, his perfect smile becoming more serious. "The papers are always saying that he's doesn't show much emotion, and isn't, you know, very enthusiastic, but no-one can say that about him tonight. I don't know if you caught it on camera, but he was standing up for the whole of the last fifteen minutes."

The shouting and cheering from off-camera became louder as the interview drew to a close

"Okay, thank you, and once again, congratulations on an historic win", said the interviewer. "Back to you in the studio, Gary."

The Boeing Business Jet sped through the stormy night. Ahead in the far distance, the sky was lightened slightly by the coming dawn, spreading ghostly creepers through the dark, roiling clouds that churned below the aircraft. Here and there, the angry carpet of cloud flashed as veins of lightning were discharged. Thunder boomed like artillery fire below the whine of the jet engines as they laboured in the turbulent air.

Within the warmth of the aircraft, Damien St Clair was holding court. Whilst Gavin Alcock was the heart and body of the team, Damien was the soul. His boyish enthusiasm and irrepressible humour were contagious, and endowed the team with a spirit of collective vitality. He was also infamous for his practical jokes. Nearly everyone in the team had at some point been on the receiving end of one of Damien's pranks, and although these often got out of hand, his infectious grin and cheeky Geordie charm meant that he was almost always forgiven soon enough.

Damien was strutting up and down the aisle of the aircraft, holding a magnum of Champagne in one hand while his other hand was clenched round the waist of the World Club Championship Trophy, its globe-shaped head sparkling as he moved.

"Who's ready for a refill then, lads?" he asked. "There's another three of these still left!"

"Yeah, fill me up, mate", replied Marco Christofis, the club's huge Australian goalkeeper.

"How's about you then, Joey", said Damien, grinning at the young man sitting next to Marco. "You not joining us?"

"No." replied Joey sullenly, keeping his eyes fixed on the seat in front of him.

"It tastes just like lemonade, you know", encouraged Damien.

"I know how it tastes", Joey sighed, turning his head away.

"Oh, sorry, Jo-Jo, I forgot what time it was", said Damien in mock concern. "Shall I make you a nice hot cocoa, and tuck you in?"

Joey sighed loudly and turned towards Damien. His face was changing; his chin and his lower lip were pulled in while the skin below his eyes darkened as if he was about to cry. Damien had seen this face often enough. This was the face Joey made when he was upset, and if pushed any further, he was likely to start shouting and would then sulk for the foreseeable future.

Wisely, Damien backed off, giving Joey a comradely wink. "Only joking with you, pal", he said in a high-pitched voice as he moved on.

Joey – full name João Eugénio dos Santos Vasconcelos - was one of the few people who could resist Damien's charms. A talented and precocious young Portuguese superstar, he took himself very seriously, and expected everybody else to do the same. Of course, Damien saw this as a reason to push the boundaries of Joey's very limited sense of humour. Joey had recently been the victim of one of Damien's more crude practical jokes, which had resulted in Damien receiving a warning from the manager to leave Joey alone.

This joke had been weeks in preparation. Damien was both a vegetarian and a big eater, and hence was renowned for having a problem with wind. Damien saw this as more of a gift than a problem, and the team, with the exception of Joey, tolerated it with a mixture of amusement and resignation. Joey, on the other hand, could not abide it. He would shout at Damien, calling him "Pig" and "Animal" whenever his nether eruptions were audible, and leave the room in a huff.

Damien had previously discovered, while in the bath, that if he filled a bottle with liquid and turned it upside down underwater, he could catch his gases inside the bottle, pushing out the water to make room for the precious vapours.

Over the course of a few weeks, and many baths, he filled a sports bottle half full with his fumes, replacing the lid afterward and closing the nozzle.

The next day, straight after training, Damien grabbed a few of the bottles and handed them out to some of his thirsty team mates, making sure that Joey got the specially prepared one. As they strolled into the changing rooms, Joey opened the nozzle and took a sip of his, while a few of the team whom Damien had let in on the joke watched him surreptitiously. Surprised by the soapy taste, Joey stopped, pulled the lid off and smelled the contents.

Damien, when re-telling the story, is fond of saying that Joey's face became a lot like that of the Nazi interrogator in Raiders of the Lost Ark, when the Ark of the Covenant was opened.

Joey didn't take it well. When he finally got the full story from another team mate, he flew into a hysterical rage, screaming and cursing in Portuguese. He ran into one of the toilets and was audibly sick. When he emerged, his face was red from crying, and his chin seemed to have receded more than was physically possible. Shaking with rage and disgust, he stormed out of the changing rooms and jumped into his Porsche, revving his engine, and spinning his wheels as he sped away.

The next day, Joey was notably absent from training, and it turned out that he had refused to train or play again until he received an apology, which Damien swiftly gave him with as much sincerity as was possible in the situation.

Even months later, Joey would go out of his way to avoid speaking to Damien, and it was clear that the prank would never be forgiven.

Damien, never one to avoid a situation, still pestered Joey in his friendly manner, but always backed off when the danger signs were showing and the chin started to drop.

"Woody!" Damien said, stopping at the next seat along the aisle. "Where's your glass, man? Get it while it's still cold!"

"Oh, that's alright, mate. I'm on the water", replied Woody, flashing his famous smile.

"Come on, man, it's good stuff, you know. Not every day you win one of these", Damien reminded him, holding the trophy above his head.

"I can't, mate, I've got a photo shoot tomorrow, you know, and alcohol dries my skin out"

Ever since his marriage to supermodel, Elizabeth Meadows, Woody's career had been stellar. His talent and good looks had already made him a favourite with both male and female fans, but his relationship with his wife-to-be, the new face of Chanel, had acted like a catalyst for both of them, propelling them into the upper echelons of the celebrity aristocracy.

Their wedding had attracted record bids from a number of celebrity gossip magazines, but the besotted couple had opted for a low-key affair, hiring a luxury cruise ship which they had repainted in white and baby blue for the ceremony and inviting only their family and four hundred of their closest friends.

Woody became famous not just for his sporting ability, but also for his newly discovered fashion sense, and the contracts came rolling in. Over the next few years he had been paid ever-increasing sums of money to promote or model products ranging from pop socks to chest wax, and very soon he and his wife became one of the most recognised couples on earth.

"What's the shoot for, superstar? Reckon they need another model at all? I'll try not to show you up too badly", joked Damien, pouting.

Woody grinned good-naturedly. "It's for this stuff", he said, opening up a magazine that was on his lap. "It's like a kind of foundation for men. You put it under your eyes, you know, to hide the bags. I've got boxes of it that they gave me, if you want some"

"I don't know about that, man", said Damien, peering at the magazine. "I reckon I'd look like a bloody panda bear with that stuff on."

Gavin Alcock piped up from the seat behind. "I can't see many people being bothered if you were endangered though. Call out the hunting parties, more like!"

"They do make it in dark colours too, if you want me to get you some", Woody said, but Damien had already moved on.

"You wouldn't shoot me, would you, big man?" Damien said to Gavin, holding the Champagne bottle against his chest. "I thought you loved me!"

"Get off, you soft shite", Gavin answered. "I'd shoot you as soon as look at you."

Damien recoiled in mock horror. "Gavin Alcock", Damien said as if reading the voiceover to an action film trailer. "Big game hunter and captain extraordinaire. Part man, part machine…." He held the base of the trophy against his groin, bulbous end pointing towards Gavin. "….All cock!"

Some sniggering could be heard from the surrounding players.

"Get stuffed, Damo, you twat", said Gavin affectionately.

Suddenly the plane jolted violently, launching the trophy into Gavin's lap and throwing Damien to the floor of the plane. The lights inside the aircraft flickered twice and then died.

For a few moments there was utter panic. In the darkness, people shouted and screamed. Everyone on the aircraft could tell by the feeling in their stomachs, and the deafness in their ears, that they were losing height rapidly.

Pale lights came on, strips of luminescence running along the sides of the aisle. A moment later, the exit signs also lit up, casting an eerie red glow. People glanced about, unsure if this meant that they were any safer than they had been before.

Everyone's attention snapped forward as the cabin door opened and the co-pilot stepped out, his white uniform standing out in the half-light. He was doing his best to remain calm, but was clearly quite shaken himself.

"Everyone, please get to the nearest seat and fasten your seat belts. We are experiencing some… ah… some electrical problems", said the co-pilot, peering about in the dark. "Please stay in your seats and try to remain calm."

Damien levered himself off the floor. He was still clutching the Champagne bottle, although the contents were now gracing his shirt and trousers. As he glanced around, disorientated, he felt a hand grip his shoulder.

"Damien", said a voice, strangely soft in the situation. "Over here."

Damien swung around to see two bright eyes earnestly watching him.

"Samson", he sighed in relief, recognising the voice.

Damien put his arm out, and felt Samson take hold of it and pull him up and towards the seat.

Falling into the chair, Damien fumbled about for the belt. "What's going on, man?" he spluttered, trying to fasten the strap with his shaking hands.

"I'm not sure, brother. I was watching from the window. There was a bright flash, a kind of blue light. Then it went dark." Samson replied in his soft Ghanaian accent. "Here, let me help."

Samson took the buckle from Damien's hands and calmly snapped it into place, giving Damien a reassuring pat on the shoulder.

Both looked up as the co-pilot entered again, this time seeming more pale and nervous than before.

"Please, everyone, your attention. We're being forced to make an emergency landing. You must stay in your seats, and get into the brace position." The co-pilot glanced around, ensuring everyone was watching. "Hands on your head, please, and then place your head

8

between your knees."

There was more cursing as the passengers rearranged themselves.

"Please, do not leave your seats or change from that position until we have landed. There are life jackets under your seats if we need them." The co-pilot turned to go back into the cabin, and then added, hopefully, "Please try to stay calm."

"Shit!" muttered Damien, stuck for better words to describe the situation.

He heard whispering close to his ear, and turned his head awkwardly to look at the man next to him. Samson was bent over too, but his hands were clasped together, and he was clearly praying.

"Hey, Sams, mention me, will you?" Damien asked, forcing a grin.

Samson turned, his wide smile glowing in the gloom. Reaching out, he took Damien's hand, holding it tightly, and then closed his eyes again and continued to pray.

"Do I need to cross myself or anything?" Damien went on.

Samson's smile flashed in the darkness. "If you like", he answered.

With one hand still holding Samson's, Damien sat up briefly and crossed himself, unsure of quite how to do it. Then, feeling a bit sheepish, he put his head back between his knees.

"Don't mention this to the other lads though, eh?"

The aircraft tore through the solid bank of low-level cloud, jets screaming. Below, the tops of ancient trees split the canopy of dense jungle. A wide river snaked through the soaked forest, swollen with the storm. It was towards this pitch-black expanse that the stricken aircraft headed.

The tip of one wing scythed through the higher branches of the trees and then the aircraft hurtled into the churning river, spraying sheets of water to either side. The tail lifted, threatening to turn the aircraft upside down, but then a wing caught in the shallow water next to the bank, turning the aircraft around. With the aircraft now careering along sideways, the other wing sunk in to the murky river, slowing the plane and tipping the body on to its side.

With a deep, metallic creak, the plane righted itself, the higher wing splashing back down into the water. The persistent sounds of the rain-sodden jungle and the churning river now took over, claiming the aircraft as if it were nothing more than a drowning insect.

* * *

"Everyone, shut up!" shouted Gavin.

The last few moments had passed in panicked chaos. The passengers had groped for their life jackets in the gloom, and then stumbled towards the nearest exit sign. A bedraggled group were now splayed out on one wing of the aircraft, the flashing lights on their life jackets adding to the confusion.

Gavin was bellowing to make himself heard over the sound of the river.

"Have you all got a jacket on?"

A handful of voices shouted their agreement.

"Anyone not got one?"

A voice, cracked with fear, spoke up. "There was no jacket. I could not find it"

"Who's that?" Gavin shouted, peering at the faces near him. "Joey? Oh, for Christ's sake..."

Gavin sighed and glanced around, deciding what to do.

"Okay, just keep quiet and listen to me", he said after a moment.

"The plane's sinking, and we need to get off it quickly. The bank's over there a way." Gavin pointed into the humid darkness. "Do the belts on your jackets up tight, right?"

He paused a moment. "Now grab the belt of the person next to you with one hand. Hold on tight, okay? We don't want to get split up."

Gavin waited while the group groped for each other's belts.

"Right, so when I say, we're all going to get off this plane and swim to that bank over there. Just follow me. Swim with one hand and hold on to your mate's belt with the other. Joey, grab my belt with both hands, and keep those legs kicking. Don't let go."

Gavin glanced over his shoulder again, getting his bearings.

"Ready?" he shouted, giving his companions a few seconds. "Come on then, go! Go!"

The desperate group of young men kicked and paddled their way across the raging water, lights flashing like a swarm of hyperactive fireflies. The minutes stretched on, and coldness and exhaustion started to set in.

"I can't keep going", moaned Joey, struggling to keep his head above the water without a life jacket.

"Just shut up and keep kicking. Not far now", Gavin urged.

"If you stay still too long, the crocodiles'll have you," chimed in Damien's easily recognised voice.

"What?" Joey screamed, straining to see around himself in the strobing darkness.

Damien was too cold to laugh. "Don't worry, kiddo, they wouldn't eat you anyway, you're too scrawny!"

Nonetheless, Joey seemed to find some hidden energy reserves, and started kicking his legs with renewed vigour.

A few moments later, Gavin's legs bumped against solid ground.

"Alright, keep swimming. We're almost there", he shouted, his voice hoarse.

Gavin pulled himself up on to the muddy bank using a thick root that was trailing in the water. He turned round and helped heave his companions up, too exhausted to register their faces.

The group collapsed onto the bank, soaked and worn out. For a few minutes, they just lay on the muddy earth, breathing heavily, unable to speak.

Finally, Damien spoke. "Who's here, then? Joey and Gav. Who's that, Emil?" he peered at the man lying next to him.

"Yes, me", replied Emil van Keulen, the club's Dutch winger.

"Marco here"

"Tommy"

"Samson"

"Woody"

"Raphaël"

"That it?" asked Gavin, sitting up.

"I'm here - Rudolf", answered a shaken-sounding voice.

"No way. You alright, gaffer?" said Gavin, genuinely surprised.

"Yes, yes. Fine", replied Rudolf Emmerich, sounding anything but fine.

"So, what happened to the rest of them?" Emil put in.

"I think they went out the other exit", Gavin answered.

"Should we look for them?"

"Well, there's not much chance of finding anything until it gets light. We're best to sit tight, I reckon."

Joey, who seemed to have been lost in his own thoughts for a while, spoke up. "What are we going to do?"

After a moment of silence, Damien spoke up. "I know", he said, and then paused until everyone was listening. "Anyone got a pack of cards?"

Gavin chuckled, and glanced down. He grinned as the flashing light on his life jacket reflected back at him from the World Club Trophy, which he still had clasped in his hand.

Damien St. Clair came round from his fitful slumber to find that dawn had finally risen. The group had all decided that they would stay together until it was light, but their spirits soon dropped and the conversation ran dry as the reality of their situation sank in. Damien had tried to sleep, but the cold and dampness had made that almost impossible. Eventually, exhaustion took over, and he had drifted off into a disturbed torpor.

The first thing he noticed on waking was the difference in the sounds around him. While the storm-wracked jungle at night had been filled with the sounds of rushing water and creaking trees, the animals owned the daytime. A symphony of birdsong sounded over the background drone of insects, and a strange buzzing sound radiated from the trees overhead. To Damien this sounded like some kind of electrical short-circuit, and for a moment he hoped that they had chanced to land near a town or village.

He stood up and glanced around. Most of his friends were still snoozing in the small clearing, and he stumbled towards the river, which had receded some way since they had dragged themselves out of it last night.

As he tried to peer down the river, he heard a snapping and crashing sound from the jungle near to him. Imagining it to be anything from a crazed tiger to a charging rhino, he froze. The sounds were drawing closer. Glancing around, he saw a large, thick branch lying on the ground near him, and picked it up, wielding it like a baseball bat. The leaves at the edge of the clearing shook, and Damien tensed, ready to swing.

"Whoa!" said Emil van Keulen, bursting into the clearing. "Take it easy!"

"Christ, man, you scared us!" Damien said, dropping the branch. "I thought you were going to eat us."

"Maybe in another day or two", winked Emil, patting his stomach. "No, I just took a walk down along the river bank."

"Yeah? Nice one. Find anything?" asked Damien

"Well, I can see where the plane is. Just the tail is coming out of the water. Also, I saw some of the other guys. They are on the other side of the river."

"Oh, right. What are they up to?"

"I don't know. I think they were still sleeping. Maybe we should try to wake them up, shout at them."

"Okay, let's get the lads up then. Oh, by the way, you hear that sound?" Damien asked, pointing up into the canopy. "It sounds like an electric storm or something."

Emil looked perplexed for a moment. "Oh, the buzzing sound?" he said, realising what Damien was referring to. "They are cicadas"

"Cic... what?" asked Damien, none the wiser.

"Cicadas. They're insects, a bit like – what do you call them? Oh yes, grasshoppers. They are all singing to attract the females. Pretty loud, right?"

"Yeah, but not as loud as Gavin singing that karaoke, eh? Don't remember too many of the females being attracted by it, though."

Damien and Emil moved around the clearing, shaking and patting their friends to wake them.

"Come on, campers, rise and shine!" Damien shouted. "Sun's in the sky, water's warm."

Waking up to the heat and the sounds of the jungle, many of the companions looked perplexed, as if they had forgotten how they came to be in such an alien place. Marco glanced about, blinking in disbelief, while Woody picked a dirty leaf out of his hair, looking mortified.

"Bollocks", grunted Gavin, head in hands.

"Jungle tour starts in five minutes", Damien went on in his jaunty manner. "Today we'll be following the old river path all the way to a partially submerged aircraft. Legends tell that the plane crashed here many, many years ago. Search parties were sent out to find the survivors, but all they found were very well-fed crocodiles!"

"Look, Damo, just put a bloody sock in it, will you", Gavin said, unamused. "Seriously, mate. Just give it a rest."

Rudolf Emmerich, the team's revolutionary Swiss manager, dabbed the sweat from his eyes with the one of the monogrammed silk handkerchiefs that he always kept a supply of in his pocket. He had never been able to cope very well in humid environments. He loved the crisp, alpine sun of his childhood, but the moist, sticky heat of tropical regions made his head ache and his breathing laboured.

He patted his breast pocket, feeling for his glasses. It was empty. Trying not to panic, he bent his neck to peer at the leaf-strewn earth around him. They were nowhere to be seen, and the thought came to him that they could have gone anywhere. In the panicked rush from the stricken plane, and the night time swim across the churning river, he had no idea whether he had taken his glasses off or if they had been lost.

Rudolf closed his eyes and took a few deep breaths, trying to slow his accelerating heartbeat. He hated not being in control. His glasses were always in his breast pocket, wallet in his right hip pocket, handkerchiefs in his left. It didn't stop there, though. His life ran like the clocks of his native Switzerland. Mealtimes would always be at the same time, and would be chosen from the few types of food that he ate. He would then bathe each day after his afternoon meal, spend two and a half hours working on team strategies and studying his next opposition, then read for half an hour before turning his light off to sleep at ten forty-five. Had he been a child today, he would probably have been diagnosed with Asperger's syndrome, but growing up twenty-five years ago, he had just been branded a difficult and fussy child.

It was this partly his obsessiveness that made him such a successful manager. His tactics were always meticulously planned, and he had complex alternative strategies for almost every eventuality. This tactical precision had helped carry his team to the Champions' League final last season; skilfully navigating past all of the potential upsets of European football.

However, it was the nature of their final victory that had left him unsatisfied and full of self-doubt. It was the biggest match of his managerial career, a game that would define him and grant him a place in football history. He would be taking on Barcelona, a team famed for individual skill and flair, but he felt certain that his exhaustive preparation would be enough to stifle his opponents.

On the big night, though, his team were thoroughly out-played throughout the first half of the match, and went in at half time three nil down. His tactics had misfired, and every new approach he tried seemed to make things worse. In the changing room he panicked, unable to find any positive words for his players, and it fell to Gavin Alcock to lift the team's spirits, cajoling them out of their despondency with his usual boisterousness.

It was Damien St Clair who saved the team. Directing passes, making space and terrorising the opposition defence with his ball control and vision, he ran the game from midfield. Young Tommy Evans, who had been brought on shortly after half time to replace the under-performing Raphaël Jean-Baptiste, was given superb service from Damien, and scored his first two European goals within fifteen minutes. The game became heated, but their opponents had no answer to Damien's skill, and in the ninety-third minute he won and dispatched a penalty, taking the game into extra time.

Barcelona seemed to crumble, shocked that they had thrown away such a dominant position. Although they attacked, Gavin's well-drilled defence dealt with any threats, and his team went close to scoring again at the other end, hitting the post and the crossbar. The game finally went to penalties, and Liverpool triumphed, netting four times while Barcelona missed three of their kicks.

Amid the jubilation, Rudolf brooded. Although the press hailed his triumph, he knew that the victory hadn't been his. His carefully planned strategies had been pulled apart by the opposition, and it was only due to the team's resurgent spirit and individual talent that they had turned a comprehensive defeat into a narrow victory. For Rudolf, success almost seemed like failure.

Back among the sounds, smells and heat of the jungle, a cold feeling of fear spread through Rudolf's stomach. This was the stuff his nightmares were made of. Stranded in an inhospitable and confusing environment, without his glasses or any of the comforts he was used to, he realised that he was completely at the mercy of fate. Heart hammering in his ears, he started to scrabble around in the loose earth and wet leaves near where he sat.

His distress drew the attention of many of the other men.

"You alright, boss? What's up?" asked Tommy Evans, who was closest to him.

"My glasses..." Rudolf replied, trying to keep his voice even and composed.

"Relax, my friend. We will help you find them", said the calming voice of Samson Mbillah.

Pulling themselves round from the shock of waking up in such a strange situation, most of the men started hunting around the clearing for the missing glasses, but Raphaël Jean-Baptiste sat where he was, pretending not to have heard. A practically unnoticeable (and completely deniable) smile flitted across his face.

Raphaël had developed a resentment of his manager that had grown into something close to hatred. In his native Martinique, he was a superstar. Certainly the biggest sporting celebrity, if not the biggest celebrity altogether, he felt he deserved better treatment than he had received from Emmerich. His club had paid eighteen million pounds to Lyon for Raphaël's signature, and in his first season, this seemed justified. Scoring twenty-eight goals, he helped lift an otherwise under performing team. But then Emmerich had been made manager, and Raphaël's performances became less than scintillating. The goals dried up and his commitment was regularly called into question.

The final straw came in the victorious Champion's League final. Raphaël had been substituted for a seventeen-year-old – the previously untested Tommy Evans – and he had not gone quietly. When the substitution board had been held up, displaying his number, he had stared in disbelief for some time, after which he launched a verbal attack at his manager, declining to shake hands with either Evans or Emmerich, and then kicking a water bottle into the dugout.

Since this humiliation, Raphaël's commitment levels had plummeted, as had his first-team opportunities. Having only started two games this season, he had recently handed a transfer request to Emmerich, which had been promptly turned down. Raphaël, an arrogant man at the best of times, was appalled at this fall from glory, and refused to turn up for training, bringing a disciplinary fine from his club. He had not played for his team since then, and although he had been on the bench for the final in Japan, he had not been used.

Seeing Rudolf in such distress was undeniably satisfying for Raphaël.

Indeed, a darker part of him wished his manager had perished in the crash. Although he was never outwardly hostile to Emmerich, he would certainly never lift a finger to help him.

As the minutes passed with no sign of his glasses, Rudolf became more and more agitated. Samson and Emil waded into the river up to their waists, but it was too murky to see to the riverbed. The rest of the men rummaged around in the clearing, moving leaves and branches about and turning over the loose earth. Eventually, Gavin called the hunt off.

"Sorry, Gaffer", he said softly to Emmerich. "Maybe you lost them in the plane or when we were swimming."

"Don't worry though, mate", Marco added. "We're not gonna be here for long. I mean, people must know where we are."

An awkward silence descended. From the nervous glances a few of the men gave each other, it seemed that not everyone was as confident about their future as Marco.

The ten companions moved slowly through the jungle, occasionally having to fight their way through the undergrowth that grew wildly along the banks of the river. The heat had steadily increased as the morning grew older, and by now everyone had a sheen of sweat on their faces. Woody and Joey, never ones to be shy about their bodies, had removed their shirts, much to the delight of the thirsty local mosquito population.

"Okay, here we are", said Emil, drawing to a halt.

Following Emil's gaze, they could see the final third of the aircraft jutting out of the dirty river. About twenty metres downriver of the drowned plane, on the opposite bank, they could just make out the sprawled figures of their missing companions.

"Are they alright?" asked Tommy, squinting in the glare of the sun. "I can't see any movement."

"Probably just kipping", Gavin replied, with more confidence than he felt. "Come on lads, let's wake them up."

The louder men among them began yelling across the swollen river, while Tommy and Samson hunted around for some suitable pieces of wood to throw. Despite Gavin's yelling and Damien's impressively realistic Tarzan impression, the figures on the bank didn't stir, drawing a few nervous glances between the shouting men.

Tommy came to the bank, hefting a short, thick lump of wood. He took a brief run up and launched it towards the opposite bank. It fell woefully short, splashing down in the middle of the river. Samson returned with two lumps of wood and lobbed the first one, flinging it further than Tommy, but still at least ten metres short of the bank. Before he could throw the other piece, Marco stopped him.

"You want to give me a try, Sams?" asked the big Australian.

Marco was well known for having a long throw; he could easily throw the football from his area to the half way line. Taking the lump of wood from Samson, he took a few steps and hurled the wood over the river, producing a deep whooshing sound. The missile arced over the water, spinning rapidly, and then seemed almost to hang in the air as it slowed down. With a crash, it buried itself in the undergrowth just next to the clearing where the other group of men were sleeping.

"Shot, man!" congratulated Damien, clapping his hands.

Across the river they could see one of the men stir. As he sat up, they recognised the look of bewilderment in his body language – the same confusion and disbelief they had felt when they had woken up a short time ago.

"Who is that? Carlos?" Gavin said, and then cupped his hands to shout. "Hey, Carlos! Over here!"

Some of the other men started shouting too, and the figure across the water jerked and glanced about in alarm, as if he expected to be attacked. Noticing the figures across the river from him, it took a few moments for him to realise what he was seeing. Hesitantly, he raised a hand and waved back at them.

Ten minutes later, the men on the far bank had all been woken, and talk had turned to how it would be possible to cross the river and meet up with them, or at least to collect some of the provisions they had salvaged from the sunken plane.

"We could swim it again, I reckon", volunteered Woody.

"I don't know, mate, it was pretty hairy last night, and it's even further to the other side", Gavin said, glancing at Rudolf, who didn't even look capable of tying his shoelaces, let alone swimming across a fast-flowing river.

"Maybe we could make a kind of boat", suggested Emil.

"What, a raft, you mean?" asked Damien, miming a paddling motion.

Emil nodded. "There's plenty of wood, and those....things....should be fine for tying it together", he said, pointing at the vines hanging from some of the trees. "Also, we can tie some of the life jackets to the bottom to help it float."

"It's not a bad idea", Gavin conceded. "Give it a go, mate, if you reckon you can do it. How long will it take?"

"It could be some time, I don't know", shrugged Emil.

"I'll give you a hand, Emil", Samson offered.

"Yeah, me too, mate", Marco said. "Let's do it."

Gavin watched them as they left the clearing, scanning the floor for large enough pieces of wood.

"I don't know how long they'll last without food or water though", he said as they got out of earshot.

"Yes, I'm starving", Joey said, screwing up his face. "What are we going to eat?"

"Well, there's plenty on that plane there", Gavin pointed. "If you don't mind airline food."

"Reckon you could swim out there, Joey? Grab us a take away?" Damien asked.

Joey paused to think for a moment, deciding that in the circumstances he would forget his hatred of Damien for the time being.

"I am a strong swimmer", he said, standing up and stretching. "I think I could swim that far."

"Yeah, man", Damien patted him on the shoulders. "And you're good at diving too."

"Yes. I could probably reach the…" Joey stopped, wondering why everyone was chuckling at him. "What? He asked.

"Oh, nothing. We were just thinking about how you've got the most experience of diving." Damien grinned, nudging Joey.

Joey sighed as he realised what the joke was. "Oh, just shut up, can't you? Stop it."

"Aw, it's only a joke, mate", Damien consoled him.

But it was too late. Joey's eyes were reddening, his chin receding.

"Don't talk to me!" He replied angrily as he walked out of the clearing to join the raft makers.

It was midday by the time the raft-makers had completed their vessel, and the heat had become sweltering. Marco and Samson proudly carried the rickety-looking construction to the river, dropped it by the bank and stood back, tired and thirsty but proud.

As the morning had worn on, the mood had turned tense and fractious. Even Damien, usually cheerful and light-hearted, became quiet and introspective as the companions contemplated their situation.

A few of the men, spurred on by their thirst, had tried drinking the river water, but it was gritty and unsatisfying. Eventually, they had resigned themselves to being thirsty and retreated to the shade at the edge of the clearing where they dozed and swatted at the ever more aggressive mosquitoes.

On the other bank, two of their friends had swum out to the aircraft, a much closer journey from where they were, and had salvaged what looked to be some food packets and water bottles, which had temporarily lifted the mood, as well as the desire to find a safe way across the river.

"So, what do you reckon?" Marco asked expectantly, gesturing at their wooden creation.

A few of the men stirred, trying to muster some enthusiasm.

"Well, it's not the QE2, mate. Looks more like a big bird's nest. Think it'll float?" Gavin asked.

"Only one way to find out, eh?" Marco replied, wading into the river up to his waist.

Emil and Samson pushed the raft out into the dirty water; where Marco grabbed hold of it, pushing down to check the buoyancy. He heaved himself on board, lying flat on his stomach, but the raft lurched, and plunged deep into the water.

"I dunno about that", said Marco, shaking his head as he clambered off.

"How much do you weigh?" Emil asked.

"Bit more than a hundred kilos, last time I checked"

"Okay, well I am seventy-four. Maybe I should try it?"

"Yeah, sure. Be my guest."

Marco held the raft steady for his friend, who nimbly mounted the unsteady craft. It rocked as it sank deeper into the river, but eventually settled with a few inches showing above the water. Emil gestured for Samson to pass him the makeshift paddle.

"Are you sure you wanna do this?" Marco asked him.

Emil hesitated for a moment, and then nodded. "Yes, it should be fine. Push me out as far as you can – until it is too deep for you."

As Marco and Samson waded deeper into the river, pushing the raft, Gavin called out.

"If you can come back, mate, bring as much water as you can."

"And, please – some food", added Joey plaintively.

"Oh, and if you see a comb...." Woody added rather sheepishly, drawing some quizzical glances from his friends.

As the river got too deep for Samson, Marco struggled on alone for another few metres until he was almost shoulder-deep and then shoved the raft with its precarious passenger off towards the submerged aircraft and the opposite bank. Emil immediately started paddling, awkwardly propelling himself out into the centre of the river.

His progress was good at first, with the momentum of Marco's push and Emil's initial energy, but after a moment the stronger flow in the central channel of the river started to get a grip on the raft, pulling it downriver. Emil doubled his efforts, paddling the small vessel against the flow as well as towards the far bank.

On both banks, the other men started to cheer, spurring their friend on in his hazardous journey. Even the men who had been sulking in the shade came to the edge of the river to shout their encouragement. Emil was more than half way across now, but the flow of the river began to take hold of the raft, spinning it around and causing its passenger to lose balance. Emil toppled over, legs dangling in the water, but he managed to cling on to one of the vines binding the raft together. From the bank the other men could see his chest heaving with exertion.

"Come on Emil! Come on mate!" bellowed Marco, startling a group of birds which had been roosting in the trees along the bank.

With visible effort, Emil hauled himself back onboard the raft, using his paddle to stop it spinning out of control. Realising he was getting pulled further downriver, and away from his objective, he took up his vigorous paddling once more, heaving the raft on towards the far bank.

Once out of the central channel, the flow lessened, and Emil made good progress, finally reaching dry land about thirty metres downriver of the other camp. Dragging the raft on to the bank, he turned back to his friends and held both fists in the air triumphantly, before falling to the ground in exhaustion.

Joey sat by himself on the bank and brooded. He had dipped his t-shirt in the river and then tied it around his head, draping it over his back to try and keep cooler in the sweltering humidity, but this did nothing to help his black mood.

He felt trapped and helpless. Not only was he stranded in the middle of a jungle, but he was also stranded with Damien, the disgusting animal who made his life a misery. All of his life, Joey had been used to being looked up to and admired for his ability and his youthful good looks. But in England people didn't seem to value him in the same way. Instead they looked up to jokers such as Damien, who was undeniably talented, but was hardly a handsome man, and more to the point, was rude and uncouth. He would never understand why people put up with, and even encouraged, Damien's foolishness. If it were up to Joey, the man would be ignored and excluded until he learned some respect and decency.

It was not the first time Joey had brooded like this. In fact, these feelings surfaced whenever he was around Damien, but normally he had an escape route. He would jump in his Porsche, race back to his beautiful house, spend some time working out in his private gym, and afterwards would perhaps spend an hour or two reading through fan mail from some of the adoring female fans back in his home country.

Here, though, there was nothing to escape in, and nowhere to escape to. He was stuck in a hellhole with that revolting buffoon. Hungry, thirsty, tired, dirty and sweaty, he felt as if there was no hope left for him.

Water splashed on his legs, disturbing him from his thoughts. Most of the other men were in the shallower part of the river near the bank, messing around or keeping cool. Joey was too fed up to care who it was that had splashed him. He just stood up and dejectedly wandered towards the shade where Raphaël and Rudolph were. Rudolph was lying on his side, snoozing. Inexplicably, a large clod of mud lay on the side of his head.

"Alright?" Joey said uninterestedly, sitting down in between them.

Raphaël nodded furtively, and looked away. Joey continued to watch him, sure he had seen his jaw moving.

"Are you eating?" Joey asked excitedly. "Do you have something?"

Raphaël turned round sharply, eyes full of warning.

"Shh!" hissed the Martiniquan, putting a finger up to Joey's face. Checking that no one else was watching, Raphaël slipped his hand into his pocket and pulled out part of a large slab of half-melted milk chocolate. Begrudgingly, he pulled a few squares off and handed them to Joey.

"This is all I have. Too small for everyone. Keep quiet, Okay?"

Joey nodded quickly, taking the offering and slipping it on to his tongue. His parched mouth started to fill with saliva as the sweet chocolate hit his taste buds. Things were looking up, finally. It was not much, but this treat tasted all the sweeter because it was denied to Damien and his cronies.

As Joey swallowed the last of the chocolate, the men near the bank started to cheer again, obviously watching something in the river. Joey and Raphaël stood up and ambled towards the river to join the others, wiping their lips to remove any traces of their secret.

Arriving by the bank, they could see what the commotion was about. Emil was once again aboard the raft, and paddling back towards them, this time starting some way upriver, obviously hoping that he would end up landing closer to his target. They could just make out a light blue rucksack on his back.

Emil, now much more experienced in controlling the raft than he had been on his first crossing, paddled confidently on, rounding the visible part of the submerged aircraft. As he entered the faster-flowing central channel, he skilfully steered the raft to stop it from spinning, and then paddled on, hunching low for balance.

"Hold on, what's that?", Gavin said, pointing to the side of the raft. "Looks like it's coming apart!"

The spectators peered at their friend as he guided the makeshift vessel across the dirty expanse of water, and true enough, one of the binding vines had come loose, and was allowing pieces of wood to work free of the raft.

"Raft's falling apart, mate! Get a move on!" bellowed Marco.

Emil glanced down at the side of the raft, and with a look of panic, started to paddle furiously towards his friends. The rocking of the raft and the buffeting of the river was playing havoc. More of the wood which made up the bulk of the vessel was working loose now, and two of the life jackets came free, floating away downriver. Although Emil was still making some progress towards the bank, he was floating lower and lower with every metre he paddled.

By the time the Dutchman had managed to power the raft out of the central channel, it was almost entirely underwater, and he was finding it very hard work. Panting loudly, he paused for a moment to get his breath back. As he started paddling again, the raft suddenly lurched to the side and went under, spilling its passenger into the murky river. Emil began to swim towards the bank, but exhausted as he was, and burdened by the rucksack on his back, he was finding it hard to stay afloat, let alone make any progress.

Gavin jumped from the bank, striding as fast as possible into the river.

"Come on, everyone who can swim. Help him!" he shouted, diving in and kicking out towards his friend.

Emil, by now, was practically submerged. Choking and spluttering on the water which kept forcing itself into his mouth and nose, he took a big breath, sure now that he was going under.

Most of the men on the bank had now dived into the river, leaving only Tommy, Rudolph, Raphaël and Joey on dry land. Samson and Marco, the best swimmers in the group, covered the distance to where they had last seen their friend in a few moments, with some of the poorer swimmers splashing about rather less effectively. Taking a deep breath, Samson dived down, feeling about for his friend in the murky water.

Realising that it would be impossible to see any distance in the muddy river, Marco called out "Fan out around here! Dive down and search with your arms!"

Following Marco's suggestion, the men swam to different positions near where their friend had gone missing, and, with varying degrees of ability, plunged down into the water, reaching out for any sign of Emil.

Moments ticked by, and the faces that emerged to take air began to look more worried. Suddenly, Damien began to thrash about.

"Something's got me leg!" He screamed, trying to swim back to shore.

Thinking quickly, Samson swam towards him.

"Stop kicking!" The Ghanaian shouted. "Stay as still as you can!"

"You what?" Damien replied, looking petrified.

"Just keep still for a minute, okay?" Samson repeated as he reached him, and then dived swiftly down towards Damien's feet.

By now the other men had surfaced and were watching Damien with deep concern.

"It's a bloody anaconda isn't it? Bloody huge snake!" He moaned, trying to keep above water.

"No, mate. Not in this part of the world", Marco assured him.

"What, then?"

"Just stay still, hey?"

"Oh Christ, man! It's got me other leg!"

With this exclamation, Damien turned and thrashed about again, not succeeding in getting very far. A moment later, Samson surfaced right next to him, and his legs became free.

"Samson! I nearly pissed meself!" Damien sighed in relief.

"Nothing bad. It was Emil!" Samson gasped and pulled with his arms, dragging the Dutchman above the surface.

"Help me, please. I can't hold him for long."

Marco and Gavin swam over and relieved Samson of his burden, and then struck out towards the bank as quickly as possible. Heaving their friend on to dry land, they turned him on his side and opened his mouth.

"Anyone know what to do?" Gavin asked, glancing around. "And you", he said, fixing Joey with a stern look. "I thought you said you were a good swimmer! Where were you?"

Joey avoided Gavin's glare, looking at the ground. At that moment, Emil coughed loudly, ejecting water from his mouth and nose with a spluttering sound.

"That's it, mate!" Marco encouraged him, patting him on the back firmly to help him breathe.

Emil coughed and spluttered for a few minutes more, and then lay on his front, chest heaving with exhaustion.

"Can anyone else hear that?" Asked Tommy Evans, who been standing up, watching the sky for a moment or two before speaking.

"Hear what?" Asked Gavin.

"Listen!"

All of them men, except Emil, who was too busy getting his breath back, stopped speaking and listened intently.

Raphaël was the first to respond. "Yes, I hear something. Helicopter?"

As he said the words, the rest of the men could also make out the sound of heavy rotor blades in the distance.

"They are looking for us!" Joey exclaimed, teeth exposed in relief.

A cheer of joy erupted from the men, who started hugging each other, any rivalries of the past forgotten in their moment of relief. Holding each other's shoulders and jumping up and down while they cheered, none of them noticed that Gavin was not joining in the celebrations.

At the perimeter of the clearing, Gavin was hunched over, yanking at the undergrowth. With a crash of leaves, he fell backwards, holding the object he had been trying to free – a long, straight stick. Looking back at the cheering men, he searched for the brightest piece of clothing. Only he and Tommy were wearing their red team football shirts. He made as if to take his shirt off, but something stopped him.

During his career as a professional footballer, Gavin had kept every shirt worn in triumphant finals he had played in. His display case at home featured the shirt he had worn in his first ever senior game for the club, as well as the shirts he had worn while winning the FA and league cups. In pride of place was the grass-stained shirt with which he had captained his side to victory in the Champions' League last season.

Many players liked to exchange shirts with their opposition, but Gavin preferred to keep his own, refusing to wash them. Every stain, smell or stretch was a proud part of his history that he would treasure forever.

The shirt that he now wore was the very shirt he had played in during their recent triumph in Japan, and he was very reluctant to let go of it.

"Oy, Tommy. Give us your shirt", Gavin called, giving in to his own instincts.

"You what?" The teenager replied, perplexed.

"Your shirt – I need it to signal the chopper."

"What about yours?"

"Look, just give us your bloody shirt, or do you want a slap?" Gavin snapped, becoming frustrated.

Tommy chuckled, pulling his shirt off and tossing it to Gavin. Holding the long stick between his legs, Gavin tied the arms of the shirt securely on, forming a makeshift flag.

"You lot keep your eyes peeled!" he said, hoisting his creation into the air.

The other men quietened down, scanning the air for a sight of their would-be saviours. Damien and Marco waded out into the river so that they could get a better view of the sky. An eerie silence descended, with only the gradually loudening sound of the helicopter as a background.

Damien was the first to spot the helicopter, appearing over the trees some way upriver on the other side.

"There!" he shouted, pointing excitedly.

The other men jumped into the water from where they could see the helicopter and started waving their arms wildly, shouting at the top of their voices. Gavin held his flag aloft and waved it in wide arcs above their heads.

For an agonising few moments, the helicopter continued on its present course, crossing the river about half a kilometre upriver from them. As it disappeared behind the trees on their side of the river, a loud groan of disappointment went up from the men.

"What now?" Joey whined, looking distraught.

"We need to make a fire", suggested Samson.

"With what? By rubbing two sticks?" Joey scoffed.

"Have you got a better idea?" Gavin asked, sticking his flag into the soft mud of the bank and casting his eyes about for some suitable pieces of wood. Grabbing the first two sticks he found, he started striking one against the other.

"Does that even work?" Damien asked him, but Gavin was not listening.

After a few minutes of frantic rubbing, Gavin gave up, throwing the sticks at a nearby tree in anger.

"Listen!", shouted Tommy "It's coming back."

Sure enough, as the men stopped and listened, the sound of the helicopter grew louder than ever, until it appeared high above the trees at the back of the clearing. It hovered there for a moment while the men again waved their arms and shouted. Very slowly, it moved directly above them and hovered over the river, dropping down gently until it was twenty or so metres above the water.

Screwing his eyes up against the fine spray of water which the helicopter was whipping up, Gavin saw a sliding door open in the side of the aircraft, and a man move to the opening, holding on with one hand to the inside of the helicopter. The man was wearing a khaki jump suit and a white helmet, and appeared to be looking directly at him. Slowly, the man's arm reached out and waved to him, pausing as if waiting for a response. Gavin put his own arm up and waved back. Once again moving slowly and deliberately, the man motioned expansively with his arm, pointing repeatedly at the ground where Gavin and his companions were standing. He then held his hand out in a thumbs-up signal and paused again.

"Wants us to stay put, I reckon", Gavin said, although no one would be able to hear him above the din of the helicopter.

Tentatively, Gavin replied, holding his own thumb up. The man nodded and held his thumb out again briefly before retreating back into the helicopter, closing the door. The pitch of the rotor blades rose as the helicopter ascended above the tree line. Spinning to point in the direction it had originally come from, it dipped its nose and moved off, still rising as it advanced. The men watched it as flew off, too relieved to speak.

The helicopter had travelled about three hundred metres when they heard a sharp metallic sound followed by a hiss. A thin plume of smoke shot rapidly from the tree line some distance away towards the helicopter. As if in slow motion, the men watched in shock as the smoke trail reached its target, and exploded loudly against the back of the aircraft.

Obeying their natural reactions, most of the men had fallen to their knees, watching wide-eyed as the helicopter faltered. The body of the aircraft seemed to be largely intact, but most of the tail had been blown away. As they looked on, the pilot seemed to lose control, the body beginning to rotate as it fell gradually and agonisingly toward the trees.

The doomed helicopter stuck the jungle with a horrendous noise. There were no explosions, but the deafening cracks and whizzes as the fast-spinning blades cut through and then broke against the ancient trees was excruciating. Finally, with a crunch, the aircraft hit the jungle floor, leaving only a high-pitched whining sound that gradually dropped in pitch and died away.

For a moment, the men were too shocked to speak. Rudolph, unable to see properly without his glasses, broke the silence.

"What was that?"

"I don't know, man. Rocket launcher?" Damien shrugged.

"I think you're right, mate", Marco replied. "Shit!"

On the other side of the river, panic was spreading. From their position on the opposite bank, their friends would have been unable to see anything. All they knew was that there had been some sort of accident on their side of the river, not a great distance away from them.

"What happened?" Someone shouted across the river to them.

For a moment, Gavin was lost in thought. Whoever had fired the weapon had clearly intended to bring the helicopter down. It followed that their intentions towards him and his team mates might not be much better.

"Keep quiet", Gavin yelled back across the river. "And try to hide!"

"What?" a voice yelled back.

"Shut up! Hide!" He yelled again at the top of his voice.

The message seemed to get through, because the panicked voices of their friends soon subsided, and they gradually disappeared into the undergrowth.

"Us too", Gavin demanded. "Get in cover!"

Emil, still weak from his ordeal, dragged himself towards the trees at the edge of the clearing.

"My bag", he called weakly.

"Gotcha", Gavin said, taking the heavy rucksack from him and putting it on his own back. "Here, give us your arm."

With Gavin's help, Emil made it into the line of thick trees and bushes by the side of the clearing where the rest of the men were hiding. Through the thick foliage, it was just possible to make out what was happening on the other bank.

For what seemed like at least half an hour, the men sat practically motionless in their hiding place, occasionally whispering to each other. Very faint voices could be heard from the other side of the river.

"Who's that speaking – our lads?" Whispered Tommy.

"Doesn't sound like them", Marco replied, trying to keep his booming voice down.

Before they could speculate further, shouts rang out from across the river. The tone was angry and authoritative, and spoken in a language that none of the men could comprehend. In reply, a fainter, pleading voice spoke up, seemingly in English, but too quiet to be understood.

The companions watched in shocked silence as a brightly clothed man stood up from his hiding place and retreated backwards towards the river, holding his arms up in the air. In his garish yellow tracksuit, the man was instantly recognisable as Kevin Murray, one of the team physiotherapists. He was followed by a stranger. This man was dressed in combat trousers, a camouflage vest and a peaked khaki cap. In his hands he carried a rifle, which was pointed menacingly at Kevin's stomach.

"That's an AK", Damien exclaimed in horror.

"Shut up!" Gavin hissed back at him

Once more, the armed man started shouting at the terrified Physiotherapist, who pleaded again at an increasingly higher pitch. Without warning, the stranger stepped forward and struck Kevin in the face with the butt of his rifle. Kevin crumpled soundlessly to the floor, where he lay still and silent.

Looking over his shoulder, the armed man called out in his unknown language. Three more men stepped into the jungle, all dressed similarly to the first stranger. They wore combat trousers of various colours and designs, a military vest or jacket, and some type of hat. Two of the men carried rifles similar to that of the man who had struck Kevin, and one hefted a long metal tube over his shoulder – clearly the rocket launcher with which they had taken down the helicopter.

The soldiers started speaking to one another, seemingly in a heated exchange. After a moment or two of bickering, the first soldier raised his voice above the others, silencing them. He strode over to where Kevin was laying, and stood above him. Turning towards the jungle again, he shouted again, repeating a short phrase as if calling to the area around him. He pointed his rifle in the air and let off a shot, then once again pointed it at the prone man, who had now regained consciousness and was sobbing pitifully.

"Shit. We've got to do something!" Damien muttered.

"He doesn't know we're here. Keep quiet, keep still", Gavin whispered, shooting him a warning glare.

The soldier began to shout again, short one- or two-syllable phrases with a few seconds pause in between, as he menaced the injured man with his rifle. It was clear he was counting. After the sixth or seventh shout, other voices spoke up, in the same pleading tone Kevin had used. One by one, the other team members who had been stranded on the opposite bank emerged from their hiding places. The soldiers grabbed them roughly, pushing them down so that they were all on their knees, grouped around the groaning physiotherapist, holding their hands on their heads.

The soldiers began chattering again, pointing at their prisoners, at the sky and into the jungle. The man carrying the rocket launcher suddenly stopped bickering, looking intently at the opposite bank, and then shouted, silencing the other soldiers. He raised his free arm and pointed across the water at a point about fifteen metres upriver from where Gavin and his companions were hiding. With a sinking feeling, they looked round at the place which the soldier was indicating. There, proudly sticking out from the muddy bank, was the hastily made red flag.

"Oh, bollocks!" Marco swore. "What now?"

As he spoke, the first soldier raised his rifle, aiming near the flag, and let off a short burst of automatic fire, making the bank close to the flag erupt with small showers of water and earth.

"Run!" Gavin exclaimed, no longer bothering to keep his voice down.

The men turned and bolted, running in the opposite direction to their attackers, dodging trees and crashing through foliage in their hurry to get further from the soldiers. More shots rang out from across the river as the other soldiers started firing.

Gavin, taking position at the back of the group, shouted his encouragement.

"Keep going! Stay together!"

Rudolph, just in front of him, was holding his arms out, unable to see properly without his glasses. As Gavin caught up with him, he stumbled on a fallen branch and fell, sprawling on the leafy ground. Gavin stopped, quickly helping him up.

"You alright, gaffer?"

Rudolph nodded, glancing around, obviously unsure which way to run. Suddenly, Gavin gasped as he remembered something. He would have to go back to the clearing.

"Tommy! Stop!" he shouted.

Tommy, who was still visible but a fair distance ahead of them, glanced back, and then slowed, reluctant to stop his flight.

"Get over here, kid!" Gavin shouted again.

Sighing, Tommy sprinted back to his captain and his manager.

"Listen up. Boss, grab hold of Tommy's shirt, and try and keep up. Tommy, look after him, and keep the others in sight.

"Can't you do it?" Complained Tommy.

"I've got to go back"

"Go back?" Tommy repeated incredulously.

"I forgot something. I'll catch up with you. Get a move on!"

Tommy shook his head in confusion, but jogged on, leading Rudolph through the obstacle course of the jungle. Taking a deep breath, Gavin turned around and ran back towards the clearing, hunched as low as he could be while still keeping any speed. Occasional shots were fired from across the river, and Gavin winced as the bullets passed near him, making a tearing sound as they ripped through leaves and branches.

He made his way round to the opposite side of the clearing to where he and his friends had hidden, using trees and bushes as cover. The soldiers had finally stopped firing and he could faintly hear them bickering again.

Gavin threw himself to the ground as he reached the spot he was looking for. Groping under a bush, he pulled the World Club trophy out from where he had hidden it earlier. Allowing himself a quick smile, he knelt up, taking the rucksack which Emil had filled with provisions from the other camp off his back, and opened its drawstring. He stuffed the trophy into it, pulled the string and swung the bag onto his back.

Ready to flee again, he glanced quickly up towards the other bank, and turned cold with fear at what he saw. The three soldiers with rifles were still arguing, but the soldier with the rocket launcher was gazing directly at him, clearly not fooled by Gavin's bright red camouflage. Gavin, frozen with dread for a moment, watched as the man pulled a metal object about the size of a wine bottle from his belt and began to attach it to the end of his rocket launcher.

Adrenalin surged through Gavin, and he took off like a shot, vaulting a bush in his path and crashing through some low branches. More rifle shots were fired, tearing through the jungle near to him as he sped away, but a few seconds later came the sound he feared the most. As the sharp metallic sound came, followed immediately by an ominous whoosh, Gavin's instincts took over and he threw himself to the ground, rolling behind the scant cover provided by a rotten tree trunk.

Gavin's senses were assaulted as the explosion rocked the jungle around him. Deafened by the blast, he was first hit by the searing heat, and then covered by warm earth and wood chips. For a moment, he lay there, unsure of what had happened. He picked himself up, spitting out a mouthful of earth, and wondered whether he was hurt.

Gingerly, he tested his legs. Still dazed and deafened by the explosion, he looked around himself and tried to get his bearings. Suddenly, he was filled with a feeling of exhilaration. He was alive, and apparently unharmed. Resisting the urge to whoop with joy, he harnessed his new-found energy and sprinted off into the jungle at breakneck speed, expertly dodging and hurdling the hazards which the jungle put in his way.

He raced on, oblivious to anything but his sprinting. After many minutes of running, he remembered that he was not sure exactly where he was going. He needed to catch up with his friends, but was not certain that he had been running in quite the same direction. He slowed down, listening for any sounds, but the ringing in his ears made it impossible to hear anything but the hammering of his own heart. He finally decided he would zigzag his way through the jungle, making himself more likely to come across the other men. Choosing a direction, he set off again at his adrenalin-fuelled pace. Glancing from side to side as he ran, he continued for a few minutes and then turned around and sped off again at roughly a forty-five degree angle to the direction he had just been running.

Three more times he stopped, turned and ran, and just as it was dawning in him that he was probably completely lost, he charged through a wall of leaves into a slightly more open area, and bundled straight into Raphaël. The other man's head bounced off Gavin's shoulder as he was thrown to the ground. The rest of the men were all there, staring at him in alarm.

As the adrenalin wore off, Gavin realised how utterly tired he was, and bent over, panting furiously and trying not to laugh with relief.

"Soz", he said between gasps, holding his hand up to Raphaël, who was still lying where he had been knocked over, unsure whether to be angry, scared or relieved.

It was then that Gavin realised why everyone was looking shocked. He was blackened all down one side from the explosion, covered in earth, and had leaves and twigs pointing out from his shock of hair. He must have looked like he'd just crawled out of his own grave.

"Gavin?" Said Marco hesitantly. "You alright, mate?"

Gavin studied himself for a moment, still heaving with exhaustion. Finally, he looked up at his friends.

"Splinter", he said, grinning as he pointed to a small drop of blood that had formed on his forearm.

The group gathered in a tight circle around Gavin as he opened the rucksack. First of all, he removed the trophy, which was still glittering brightly in the dappled sun even after its ordeal. A few of the men gasped in surprise as he pulled it out.

"You brought it with you?" Woody asked, visibly impressed.

"No chance I was leaving this behind", Gavin replied, grinning proudly.

"Nice one, mate", Marco congratulated.

"Yeah, man, good going!" Added Damien.

"Is there any food and water?" Asked an irritated Joey, clearly less impressed than most of his companions.

"Yes, I took some of both", said Emil, still recovering from his near drowning and the subsequent hectic flight through the jungle. "There is not a large amount though, I thought it was for only a short time."

"You did well, mate, don't worry", Gavin reassured Emil as he began to tip the contents out of the bag and line them up on the ground.

There were fourteen small bottles of water, five tubes of chocolate biscuits and eight small tubes of crisps.

"This is not enough even for one day", Joey moaned.

"Well it'll just have to do for now. We've not got much choice, have we?" Gavin replied, hardly able to conceal his own disappointment. "Everyone take one bottle of water for starters."

The men needed no more encouragement. They eagerly picked up and opened their water bottles, threw their heads back and drank deeply. The water was like a blessing to their parched throats, and a few of them grunted happily as they drank.

"Rudolph, I brought something for you", Emil said, finishing his water and rummaging in a side pocket of the rucksack. "Bill gave me his spare glasses."

The Dutchman pulled out some mangled-looking spectacles. The frame was smashed on one side, and the lens had fallen out. Wincing, Emil fished out the lens and tried to fit it back, but it was an impossible task. Shrugging, he handed the broken glasses to Rudolph.

"Sorry, boss", Gavin apologised. "I must've fallen on them."

Rudolph took the glasses eagerly, straightening them out as best he could before placing them on his nose. Covering one eye, he blinked through the single lens, a slight smile spreading across his lips.

"Yes, it is better", the Swiss manager nodded. "Not great, but I can see some more."

While the attention was on Rudolph and his glasses, Joey had opened a packet of the biscuits and started to munch his way through them.

"Hey, steady on, mate!" Marco said, drawing the attention of the rest of the men.

"But I'm hungry!" Joey replied indignantly, continuing to eat.

30

"Hold on, Joey, for Christ's sake!" Gavin said angrily, confiscating the packet and putting it back alongside the others. "Wait for the rest of us!"

Joey sighed loudly and muttered something in Portuguese, folding his arms and looking down to avoid Gavin's warning stare.

"We need to keep some of this for later", Gavin went on, addressing the group. "It's only early afternoon, still."

"I dunno, mate", Marco replied. "I'm bloody ravenous. We've got to find civilisation soon, surely? Or if not, couldn't we look for stuff here? Kind of live off the land."

"Who are you – Crocodile Dundee?" Damien joked.

The conversation went back and forth, each man with his own opinion on how best to manage their meagre food supply. Meanwhile, Rudolph had been gathering his wits about him. The one-lensed spectacles, although they weren't a good fit and the magnification was slightly off, nonetheless gave him a strand of control on which to pull himself up. A combination of the heat, wildness and loss of proper sight had been devastating for Rudolph, who normally prided himself on his ability to deal with any situation calmly and logically. This small boon - being able to see better out of one eye - jogged him out of his bewilderment. He was not used to being the weak link. Usually, he, not Gavin, would be calling the shots. His captain was competent and strong-willed, but Rudolph was the real brains behind the team. It was time to step up on to his throne once more.

"We will ration the food", he said in his calm and quietly authoritative way.

It had been so long since Rudolph had spoken that the group was shocked into silence. Every man turned towards him with an expression of surprise and expectation.

"What's that, Gaffer?" Damien asked.

"We could be a long way from civilisation", Rudolph began after a moment's pause to make sure he had everyone's full attention. "And we have no idea if there is anything edible here. We have to assume that we will be here for a matter of days."

At this statement, a sigh went up from his players, but none of them challenged his opinion.

"Also, the men who were shooting at us will probably come to find us, and we will not be hard for them to locate. We have to keep going, and hope that our head start gives us a small advantage. My strategy is that we will divide two of the packets of biscuits between us now, pack up and move on in the direction we have been heading so far."

"The boss man's right, lads", Gavin said, tipping out the contents of the open packet and one of the full ones. "Alright, that's about two and a half biscuits each. Hey, leave off it, Joey! You've already eaten more than that yourself."

Joey turned his back and stalked away, muttering under his breath. The other men, although clearly dismayed about having to trek through the jungle with a couple of biscuits as fuel, kept their silence, appreciating that their manager was correct. Most took small bites of their biscuits, chewing slowly as if that would somehow make them feel more satisfied.

Gavin bolted his portion down and packed the rucksack up again, shouldering it and pausing to get his bearings.

"Come on, lads, let's get moving. Eat on the way if you like. We don't want those soldier boys breathing down our necks."

"We are walking in circles!" cried Joey, tired and exasperated.

The companions had been walking for over four hours in the sweltering heat, stopping occasionally to get their breath back, but always hurried on after a short time by Gavin, who was becoming increasingly agitated. It had been hard going, with the jungle flora always seeming to hamper their progress and make navigation almost impossible.

"This tree", Joey went on, gesticulating angrily. "This big one that is on its side. We walked past this an hour ago!"

"Alright, calm down, mate", Marco said amiably. "You're not helping, are you?"

"I'm not helping?" Joey shouted, starting to turn red. "This is not helping", he gestured around at the jungle, and then pointed at Gavin. "He is not helping!"

"Right, that's enough!" Gavin said, looming over Joey. "You keep your voice down! If you haven't got any useful suggestions, then just keep your mouth shut!"

Joey lowered his voice, looking warily back at his captain. "Well, we are not going anywhere. This is pointless!"

"So, which way we should go then, clever bollocks?"

"We could find the soldiers. We have plenty of money. We could pay them to help us."

"You saw what they did to Kevin!" Gavin replied, shaking his head in disbelief. "And what are you going to say anyway? You speak their language, do you?"

"Perhaps they speak English. Anything is better than this."

Joey looked around at the other men, as if willing one of them to agree with him.

"We should vote on it", he said finally.

"Vote? What do you think this is, Pop Idol?" Gavin said incredulously.

"Fine then, let's vote. Anyone who wants to go and speak to the nice, friendly lads with the AKs, raise your hand!"

Gavin remained staring at Joey, while the Portuguese looked round at the other men, who greeted his gaze with expressions ranging from annoyance to apathy. Not one of them raised their hand.

"Raphaël?" Joey implored, but the Martiniquan sneered and shook his head.

"Fine. I am leaving!" he hissed, turning on his heel and striding away. Before Joey could walk more than a few steps, Gavin had caught up with him and laid a firm hand on his shoulder. Joey swung round, fists clenched as if he was going to strike out. Gavin pointed his finger at Joey's face and spoke in a quiet but threatening tone.

"If you take one more step, I'll punch you out and drag you along by your foot!"

The two men remained practically motionless for what seemed like more than a minute, Joey shaking with what may have been rage, fear, or a mixture of both. Suddenly, Gavin lowered his hands and glanced about, a worried expression on his face. He raised his finger to his lips, looking first at Joey and then back at the other men, obviously directing them to be silent.

For another minute, the men remained silent. They could hear a faint, rhythmic sound from roughly the direction they had come from. The sound stopped for a few moments and then started up again. It sounded like the undergrowth being beaten repeatedly. The men stood wide-eyed, hearts beating with adrenalin.

"Behind the tree!" Marco whispered, pointing towards the large, toppled trunk that lay by the side of the small clearing they were standing in. The companions stepped as silently as they could towards the tree, rounding it one by one and crouching behind it. Gavin came last, once again motioning everyone to remain silent.

The men crouched there for what seemed like many minutes, trying to ignore the itching of their sweat as it trickled down their faces and necks. The intermittent sound grew closer until it seemed to come from a few metres away. Gavin leaned round carefully, peering out from between the knotted roots of the fallen tree, from where he could see the small clearing.

A slim man came out of the jungle close to where he and Joey had confronted one another. He was holding a machete, which had clearly been responsible for the slashing sound that had alerted Gavin and his companions to their danger. The man was young, not much older than Tommy, and had Oriental features. He wore a wide-brimmed khaki hat and was naked to the waist. He sported a patchy beard, and a rifle was slung over his back.

The young man stood there for a moment, catching his breath, and then looked back the way he had come, saying something in a tone of complaint. A deeper, gruffer voice replied, and presently another man stepped into the clearing. This man was a lot older than his companion, with pockmarked skin and a patch over one eye. One hand rested on the rifle that was slung over his shoulder and his other hand held a cigarette. His clothing was much smarter than his younger companion's, a full set of identically coloured and styled combat fatigues, and a tight peaked cap.

The younger soldier spoke complainingly again, shrugging and proffering the machete. The older man laughed sharply, took a puff of his cigarette, and then spoke again, looking at the younger man with amusement before throwing his cigarette towards him and walking onwards. The younger man sighed dejectedly and then followed.

As the men reached the other side of the clearing, the older man held his hand up, speaking more rapidly and seriously. He knelt down, studying the forest floor for a moment. Standing back up, he barked some orders at the younger man and then took up his rifle in both hands, walking on as if with a purpose.

Keeping completely silent for a few more minutes, Gavin then turned back to look at his companions, sighing and shaking his head.

"What?" Whispered Woody, concern written all over his perfect face.

"They saw something - picked up our trail, I think", Gavin replied in hushed tones. "They'll be back round here in less than an hour. We've got to get moving."

Motioning once more for silence, Gavin stood up warily and came out from behind the tree, waving his companions forward. They looked comical - wide-eyed and stooped, tip-toeing their way between the dead leaves and twigs on the forest floor.

Choosing an onward direction that was different to that taken by the soldiers, Gavin led his team further on into the inhospitable jungle.

As dusk fell, the companions slogged their way through the jungle. They trudged on in a kind of silent trance, the noises of the jungle and the rumbling of their stomachs providing a monotonous soundtrack. The last of the water had been finished hours ago, and their mouths were dry and tacky. Mosquitoes landed on them and drank their fill, as none of the men had the energy or impetus to swat them away.

As they stepped wearily over a tangled shrub, Rudolph caught his foot and fell. Marco, the only man behind him, stopped and held his hand out. Rudolph, ignoring this, continued to lie on the leaf-strewn floor, panting and blinking his eyes. Marco summoned up all the energy he could find, and grunted loudly. A few of the men near the back of the group stopped and turned towards him, also grunting to get the attention of those ahead.

Assembled around their manager, the men seemed unsure of what to do for a moment, before Samson bent down, putting one hand under Rudolph's arm. Marco reacted, picking up the other arm and helping Samson to pull the collapsed man upright, and lay his back against a tree.

Gavin swallowed with difficulty, trying to clear his mouth of the glue-like saliva that coated it.

"Boss…. What's wrong?" he managed to verbalise.

Rudolf shook his head weakly and closed his eyes, still panting heavily. The other men glanced at each other, too weak and thirsty to speak. As if by unspoken agreement, they all slowly knelt, sat and then collapsed on their backs, gazing up vacantly at the jungle canopy.

For many minutes they lay there in silence, enjoying the feeling of not having to keep struggling on. At that moment, none of the men cared about their pursuers. They didn't have the energy to keep going, to keep fighting their way through this inhospitable maze of nature. Between the gaps in the canopy, the sky gradually darkened.

"Oy, who's spitting?" Damien demanded weakly, having just felt a large lump of liquid land in his eye.

"Wish I could, mate!" Marco replied.

As Damien raised a hand to wipe his eye, a new sound started to emanate from the roof of the jungle. It was a faint but constant sound, rather like the white noise that an untuned television set makes. The sound grew gradually louder as the drone of the cicadas faded.

The first raindrops hit them at precisely the same time that the thunder began. The drops were large, having collected on the canopy and then been released earthwards. Within seconds, the companions' faces were covered with rainwater. Not caring in the slightest about getting soaked, they remained on the floor, opening their mouths as wide as possible to let the water cure their parched throats.

As they lay their luxuriating in the warm rain, a few of the men laughed with relief as the water invigorated them, washing the dried sweat from their dirty faces. Samson could be heard offering an audible prayer of thanks. After a few minutes of rehydration, Emil sat up, looking around himself thoughtfully.

"I have an idea", he said presently.

"As good as your raft idea?" Damien asked with a grin.

"Even better", Emil replied good-naturedly. "Gavin, we kept all the water bottles, I think, yes?"

"Yes, mate, in the bag. Didn't want to leave anything to track us by."

"Good. Tommy, help me pick some of these leaves. The big, wide ones."

Emil and Tommy picked themselves up from the muddy earth and pulled handfuls of leaves from the branches of one of the shorter trees nearby.

"We need lots, about thirty or forty each, I think. And take some of these longer twigs, too. The soft ones."

After a few minutes, Emil and Tommy sat back down again, Emil opening the rucksack and removing all of the empty water bottles.

"Everyone take some leaves", Emil continued, absorbed in his idea. "About five or six. And some of these soft twigs. Also, a bottle."

With puzzled looks, all of the men except Rudolph collected the items

Emil had named.

"Okay, so what we are doing is making a kind of funnel for the bottles. Line up the leaves, like this."

The Dutchman arranged his leaves next to each other, in a roughly arched design.

"Now you can use the twigs to join them together. See, you make a hole in the leaf and pull the twig through, a bit like when you are sewing."

"Never sewed anything in my life!" Tommy said, watching Emil with a kind of amused fascination.

"No problem", Emil replied, grinning. "Look, it is not hard."

After a few minutes, Emil fitted one side of his arch of leaves to the other, fashioning a rough conical shape. He placed the bottle under a nearby bush and then arranged the leafy funnel in the branches just above it, with the narrow end of the funnel above the opening of the bottle. The other men gathered round, and watched as raindrops collected on the wide funnel, gradually accumulating and dropping into the bottle.

"You're a bloody genius, mate!" Marco congratulated Emil, patting him on the back.

"Yeah, man, you should be on Blue Peter!" added Damien.

The men got to work on their funnels with varying degrees of success, happy to have something to take their minds off the more worrying concerns they had been absorbed by up until now. As Woody set up the last of the funnels, he looked upward, wincing.

"It's getting dark", he said, looking at Gavin questioningly.

"Yeah, we can't carry on with no light. The good news is, neither can the soldiers, most likely. This rain should bollocks things up for them, too." Gavin responded.

The men nodded, glancing at each other with relief. None of them wanted to walk any further today.

By now the rain had died down to a steady drizzle, but with the absence of the sun, the sticky heat of the daytime had given way to an uncomfortable chill. The men pulled what little clothing they wore tighter around themselves and some sat with their knees pulled up to their chests, wrapping their arms around their legs.

"We need fire", Raphaël said, suppressing a shiver.

"A fire would be tops, mate, but even if that wasn't like handing ourselves over to those solders, there's still no way we'd light one here in this rain, with no matches or dry wood." Gavin said, wincing up at the sky. "Best bet is if we try and get a bit of kip here, and then move on first thing in the morning."

"Yeah, and what about my shirt that you nicked?" Tommy spoke up, shivering as he leant against a tree, topless.

"Sorry, kiddo. I wasn't expecting us to get shot at. Anyone got any extra bits of clothing that Tommy can have? Poor lad's freezing", Gavin asked the men.

"I've got a vest on underneath my shirt", Woody answered.

"Didn't know anyone still wore vests these days. Bit old-fashioned for you, eh?" Damien asked him.

"It's made from lambs wool. Elizabeth brings them back for me when she goes shopping in Italy. They're really trendy over there."

"Nice one, Woody. You want to give Tommy your shirt then? Or the vest?" Gavin asked, ruffling Tommy's hair.

Woody took his shirt off, and was just about to remove his vest when he had a change of heart.

"Here, Tommy, you have the shirt. The vest's tailor-made so, you know, I want to keep it nice-looking."

"You're sitting in the middle of a bloody muddy jungle, man!" Damien grinned at him. "How long do you expect it to stay white for?"

Woody looked a bit sheepish. "Well, the shirt's warmer too, so Tommy'll be alright."

"Good man", Gavin said, picking up the rucksack and fishing out the remaining provisions. "We'd better have a bite to eat then."

"We must keep some of the food for tomorrow", Rudolph, by now recovered from his collapse, spoke up. The companions groaned loudly at his suggestion. "We will eat the crisps, the biscuits we will save."

Gavin, as hungry as anyone else, grudgingly agreed. "Alright, you're the boss. That's almost a packet each then."

Pulling a few crisps from the top of each tube, he handed the remainder to a friend until everyone else had a tube and Gavin himself had a small pile of crisps on a leaf.

The group gathered around in a rough circle, contemplating the meagre rations in front of them. Damien, the last to receive his crisps, regarded his friends with a puzzled expression.

"What are we waiting for – someone to say grace?"

Disturbed from their contemplation, the men started to dig into their tubes of crisps.

"No, wait", Samson said. "I will say grace."

"I was only joking, Sams", Damien back-pedalled, worried how long this might take.

Samson folded his hands together, looking expectantly at his companions. Joey, Gavin and Tommy, although not religious, had both had religious upbringings, so settled comfortably into a position of prayer. The other men glanced at each other with amused expressions, shrugged and put their hands together as Samson began to speak.

"Oh lord, we thank you for the food which we have been given, and for blessing us with water. We thank you for keeping us safe from harm, and from those who would do us harm. We ask you to watch over us tonight, and also to watch over our friends who have been taken captive. Give us the strength to keep moving, and guide us towards safety.

Amen."

"Amen", the companions replied.

"That was beautiful, man", Damien said, sniffing and wiping an imaginary tear from his eye.

Late that night, Rudolph lay awake, feeling miserable and lost. The rain had carried on drizzling up until an hour ago, and the ground was muddy and cold. The younger men had all ended up huddled together for warmth, and had managed to doze off.

Sleep was impossible for Rudolph, though. As if the discomfort of being cold and wet, and lying on a muddy and uneven ground weren't enough, his stomach had started to ache with hunger, and a couple of the younger men had started to snore loudly. He had tried his best to hold things together during the day, but the total darkness of the night-time jungle and the strange animal noises had started to prey on his thoughts, conjuring up images of strange and malevolent beasts in his mind's eye.

He sat with his back against a thick tree trunk and tried to think soothing thoughts. Surely, someone would come to their rescue soon. By this time tomorrow he would be safely tucked up in the comfort and silence of his own bed, having spent more than an hour soaking the dirt from his body. His chef would have prepared his favourite meal – plain grilled chicken breast with no seasoning, served with new potatoes and French beans. As Rudolph sat there with his eyes closed, his hands moved back and forth, as if cutting and feeding himself this imaginary meal. For just one second, a thin smile spread across his face, before his stomach was wracked with a violent hunger pang.

Doubled up with his head between his knees, tears finally came. His sobs were loud and pitiful, but the cold jungle swallowed them without a care. He needed something - food, heat, light, cleanliness – anything that could help lift him out of his despair.

Almost without thinking, he felt his way over to where he remembered the rucksack to be, shuffling on his hands and knees in the mud. He would just take a few of the biscuits now, and he would not eat tomorrow. Besides, they were to be rescued tomorrow. They *had* to be.

Still sobbing, he located the rucksack, and dug one of the packets of biscuits out. Ripping the top off, he stuffed the first one into his mouth. He felt despicable. Soaked, smelly, caked in dirt, with snot and tears running down his face, he was eating like a pig, bolting down this nutritionless food that he would normally avoid with contempt.

He closed his eyes tightly, bent over and crammed another biscuit into his mouth, as if this would somehow shut out his dark thoughts.

Dawn crept up on the sleeping men surprisingly quietly. While daytime had been full of the buzzing of insects and night full of the eerie calls of nocturnal animals, dawn was a peaceful time, only disturbed by the occasional birdcall from high in the canopy.

Damien was the first to stir. After his initial shock at waking up on muddy ground in the middle of a tangle of men, he extricated himself and stood back to look at his friends. He chuckled quietly at the way they had ended up huddled together, some of them with their arms around each other. There was not much he wouldn't have given for a camera.

Yawning and scratching himself, he glanced around, looking for a suitable place to perform his morning motions. His eyes settled on a large grey lump that seemed to be attached to the base of a nearby tree. At first he took it to be a giant fungus, but moving closer, he realised that it was actually a person – Rudolph, to be precise. He was sitting with his knees pulled up, leaning back against the tree with his jacket hung over his head, covering his legs all the way to the ground.

"Gaffer?" he called out.

Rudolph remained motionless. After a short pause, Damien shrugged and turned, heading away from the camp.

"Hey, Damo!" Someone called out.

"Morning, Tommy", Damien replied, turning and grinning sleepily at his friend. "Marco kept you warm, did he?"

"Get stuffed. Where are you off to?" Tommy asked, blinking.

"Need a dump."

"Hold up, then. I'll come with you."

The two friends wandered off, kicking a short piece of rotten wood between each other. A moment later, they disappeared behind a thick wall of foliage.

Gavin was the next person to wake up. Removing Joey's arm from around his waist, he stood up and stretched loudly.

"Come on, wake up lads!" He said, shaking a few of his friends by the shoulder. "Last one up makes breakfast."

The other companions stirred and sat up, nodding reservedly at whoever they had ended up wrapped around during the night. Gavin knelt down by the rucksack and fished about in it, his search becoming increasingly desperate. Eventually he turned the bag upside down and shook it vigorously. Giving the bag one final pat all over, he turned back towards his companions, his expression a mixture of regret and accusation.

"They've gone!"

"What's that?" Replied Marco, scratching his stubble.

"The food. It's gone."

"You're joking, mate."

"No, I'm not bloody joking. Someone's had it!"

"Hold on. Perhaps an animal has taken it." Emil suggested, trying to calm the situation down.

Gavin seemed to mull over this idea for a minute, while the other men groaned and swore.

"Good point, Emil", Gavin conceded. "Everyone, split up and search the area. If it was an animal it might've eaten some and left the rest."

The companions wandered around close to where they had slept, sighing as they considered the possibility of having to march on without any food. After a few minutes, Samson called out to Gavin, beckoning him over to where he stood near the hunched form of Rudolph.

"Is he alright?" Gavin asked as he reached Samson's side.

Samson gave a small shrug and then somewhat reluctantly pointed toward the pocket of Rudolph's jacket, which hung from the top of his head. As Gavin bent down, he immediately saw what Samson was referring to. The top of a crushed blue tube was poking out of the suspiciously lumpy pocket. Reaching out, Gavin pulled until the whole of the tube came out. Fishing about in the pocket, he pulled out two more crushed and empty tubes.

"Oh shit. Are you awake, boss? Did you eat all these?" Gavin asked, more with sadness than anger.

The sodden lump that was Rudolph seemed to shrink as he pulled his knees tighter against himself, and a pitiful sobbing came from beneath the jacket.

"I am sorry!" spoke Rudolph's muffled voice.

Samson winced at Gavin, who was shaking his head, a hand covering his eyes.

"What shall we do? Do we tell the others?" Samson asked after a moment.

Gavin sighed, still shaking his head.

"Yeah, we've got to. They're not going to just forget about the food."

The two men walked back towards the muddy ground where they had slept, heads bowed.

"Okay, everyone, give it up!" Gavin shouted.

"You have found them?" Joey asked, striding purposefully back.

"No. They've gone."

"What do you mean, 'gone'?"

"They've been eaten. Calm down."

"Eaten?" Joey's chin started to recede as he looked around the clearing, noticing the empty packets next to Rudolph. "By him?"

"He was desperate. Try not to be angry", Samson said softly, putting his arm around Joey's shoulders.

"Not angry? How, not angry?" Joey screamed, his English becoming less comprehensible as his face got redder and more livid. He began picking up pieces of sodden wood and hurling them at a nearby tree, a constant stream of Portuguese coming from his grimacing lips.

"He must be punished!" Raphaël demanded, pointing at the hunched form of Rudolph.

For a moment, Gavin paused, incredulous.

"Punished? Who do you think you are? No-one's going to be punished."

"Yeah, Raph, get a grip, mate!" Marco put in. "So, what *are* we gonna do then, eh?"

Gavin sighed loudly, hanging his head in despair. "Have a drink and then get ready. We'll move on in five minutes", he said dejectedly.

The group readied themselves, taking small sips of water and moaning occasionally. Emil finished half of his bottle and went to sit beside Samson, who wad just finished praying once more.

"Water?" The Dutchman offered.

"Thank you, brother", Samson replied.

"You have been praying a lot recently", Emil said, passing the bottle over.

"We have needed a lot of strength recently."

"Do you really believe we will live?"

"Yes, I believe. Things will get better."

"I wish I felt the same. For me it seems like things are only getting worse."

Samson nodded and patted Emil on the shoulder, offering his friend a smile of encouragement. At that moment, Emil heard a soft thudding sound behind him. Turning round and scanning the ground, he froze in surprise.

"Samson", he said softly, pointing towards the fallen object.

Samson turned, also reacting with shock. On the ground about two metres away lay a small, ripe banana. The two men looked upwards, trying to see where the fruit had fallen from, but the high canopy above included no bananas or banana trees. As they were staring upwards they heard the soft thudding sound again, and another small banana had appeared just in front of Samson. Emil looked at his friend incredulously, as if wondering whether his prayers could have been answered so instantly. As he opened his mouth to speak, another banana hit Emil squarely on the shoulder, bursting and spraying pulp over his neck and chin. A second later, laughing started to come from behind a large bush some distance away from them.

"Shot and a half, man!" Damien's voice called out as he appeared from behind the bush, grinning widely. He was carrying a large branch of bananas under one arm, and was followed by Tommy, who was holding his fist aloft, a banana poking out of his mouth.

The other men gathered round, momentarily silenced by the sight of food.

"I thought there was someone missing!" Gavin said, a relieved smile spreading across his face.

"May I interest Sir in some breakfast?" Damien said, pulling a banana from the branch and laying it across his hand as if offering a fine wine.

"Bloody right you can." Gavin said, peeling the banana and tucking into it as Damien offered the rest of them around.

"Where did you get these?" said Gavin through a mouthful of mashed banana.

"There's a few banana trees over there, about two minutes away", Damien replied. "Watch where you're stepping, though!" he added, winking at Tommy, who grimaced.

"Marco, grab that rucksack", Gavin ordered, swallowing the last of his banana. "We're going fruit picking!"

As morning wore on into midday, and then early afternoon, the companions trekked deeper into the jungle. The heat was even more oppressive than it had been the day before, and their eyes stung with a constant stream of sweat. After gorging themselves on bananas, as well as filling up the rucksack and their shirts with more of the fruits, they had roused Rudolph from his cocoon of guilt and set off, following Gavin's lead.

After the group's initial good humour at having chanced upon an unexpected breakfast had faded, and the water supplies once more ran low, they fell again into an indolent kind of trance, wordlessly following the man in front, lost in their own thoughts. Their diet of bananas had given them all varying degrees of indigestion, and an occasional moan or bout of wind were the only sounds to impede on the jungle's background noise.

The terrain had changed subtly at around midday. Where the jungle floor had been generally flat, it became more hilly and rocky, making the going harder. A few times they came across pits or ravines partially filled with muddy water, and had to navigate their way around these before they could continue on.

After two or three hours of walking through this new terrain, Gavin called a halt and sat down on a moss-covered rock. He fished out the remaining two bottles of water, took a sip and then passed it on.

"That's the last two. Share them out fair, okay? We'll be drinking mud from now on."

The other men groaned and took their turn drinking the warm rainwater which they had collected the night before.

"Anyone for another banana?" Gavin asked, producing a bunch from the rucksack.

"No way. I feel like a bloody monkey already." Damien said, as the other men shook their heads.

"You smell like one too, mate." Marco answered.

"Cheers, big man. I love you too." Damien replied, squeezing the Australian's knee.

"Okay lads, take ten minutes break and then we'll get moving again", Gavin said as he moved on to the floor, leaning his head back against the rock and closing his eyes.

The other men followed suit and lay back to relax and gather their energy. After a few minutes, Woody sat up again, brushing off some biting ants that he had the misfortune to have lain in. Cursing, he walked a bit further on until he found a suitable tree to rub his back on. He sighed in relief as he scratched the itchy bites left by the ants. As he finished scratching, he became aware of a new sound coming from vaguely the direction they had been travelling towards. It sounded very much like noise of the river they had crash-landed in.

"Hey, guys. I think there's a river up ahead", He said, returning to his friends.

"Yeah? Where's that?" Gavin asked him, sitting upright.

"Over that way, kind of. I was just scratching my back on a tree over there, you know, and I could hear it. Not too far off, it sounds like."

"Alright, let's check it out, hey lads?"

The party wearily got to their feet again and continued on. After ten minutes, they had still not reached the river, although the sound had become increasingly loud. The ground had also become rockier, slowing their progress to a crawl.

"Must be a bloody big river", Marco commented.

"Yeah, right. Sounds like an express train", Damien replied.

After almost another ten minutes, they found the source of the sound. The dense forest trees and shrubs ended, giving way to open, rocky ground which led down to a large, shallow pool of water. To their left, a small waterfall, perhaps four or five metres high, and three times as wide, fed the pool with water. The loudest sound, though, came from the other side of the pool, where a much narrower edge funnelled water over a higher drop. From their vantage point, they could not see how far down it fell, but the volume of the noise it made suggested that the water fell from quite some height.

Covered in sweat and sore from trudging through the jungle, some of the men whooped with joy and ran towards the natural pool, jumping in when they reached it. The rest, apart from Rudolph, removed their shoes and various pieces of clothing and waded in to the cool, fresh water.

For some time, the men splashed about, laughing with a light-heartedness that they had not felt since the crash. Marco, swimming near the wide waterfall, pulled himself up onto a ledge and removed the rest of his clothes.

"Anyone for a shower?" He shouted out.

The other men swam or waded through the waist-deep water towards Marco. Reaching the waterfall, they stripped off and stood under the cool, clear water, washing the sweat and dirt of the last two days off their bodies. Woody, who always used a separate cubicle to shower in after a match, kept his trousers on.

"You sure you don't want to wash yourself all over, mate?" Marco asked him. "It's a bloody godsend after all that sweating, honestly!"

"No, I'm alright, cheers", Woody replied, glancing about nervously.

"Promise we won't take the piss!"

Woody looked around again, seeing that all of the other men under the waterfall were looking at him, grinning expectantly.

"Yeah, alright. Okay", he said, blushing noticably.

The rest of the men carried on washing themselves as Woody took the rest of his clothes off, folding them and placing them carefully on a ledge under the waterfall.

"Don't worry, mate. I've seen smaller," Gavin reassured him as he took his boxer shorts off.

"Yeah, Gav", Damien added. "Your old man used to breed hamsters, didn't he?"

Woody stood there, mortified for a moment, while his friends chuckled at Damien's joke.

"His left bollock's probably insured for more than you're worth, Damo", Gavin countered, feeling sorry for his friend.

"Yeah, you know I'm only joking with you, superstar", Damien told Woody, slapping his back.

The group continued washing themselves under the natural shower for a few minutes until Tommy grabbed their attention.

"Hey lads, what's up with the gaffer?" the teenager asked, pointing towards Rudolph.

Their manager had taken off his trousers and shoes and was standing, wearing just his shirt and jacket, at the other side of the pool, just a foot away from the edge of the higher waterfall.

"Oh, Christ", Gavin said, picking up the rucksack. "We'd better go and check on him."

As the men made their way over to the other side of the natural pool, a few of the men tried calling out to Rudolph, but he remained motionless, staring down over the edge of the waterfall.

"What you up to, boss?" Gavin asked as he reached his manager, putting his arm around Rudolph's shoulder and leading him a few steps further away from the edge. "Admiring the view?"

"It is quite a drop", Emil said, standing next to the edge. "Maybe twenty metres."

"Yeah, okay", Gavin replied, looking concerned. "Don't get too close."

As Gavin spoke, two loud gunshots rang out, making everyone crouch a little lower in the water, turning round in shock.

At the edge of the jungle, where the companions had emerged a short time ago, stood the two soldiers who they had hidden from the day before. The younger man was pointing his assault rifle at them, while the older man had his pistol pointed upwards, presumably having fired the two warning shots they had just heard. Returning his pistol to his holster, the older man started shouting.

The men instinctively put their hands in the air, perhaps a little unnecessarily, seeing as they were all naked apart from Gavin, who had his team shirt tied around his neck, and Rudolph, who still wore his jacket and shirt, but stood with his back towards the solders, gazing over the edge of the waterfall.

The soldiers began walking forward slowly, the young one still training his weapon on them while the older one continued to shout and point.

Gavin, keeping his hands in the air, turned towards his friends and spoke in a voice which he hoped the soldiers were too far away to hear.

"After three, everyone jump over the edge. We'll be okay."

"Jump?" Joey hissed. "It is too far!"

"Look, I'm not taking my chances with these nutters." Gavin replied, trying not to shout. "We're jumping, right? And if you don't jump, they'll most likely shoot you!"

"Alright, mate, do it!" Marco encouraged.

The soldiers reached the edge of the wide pool and had just started to enter it when Gavin started counting.

"One, two…" Gavin paused for a second, noticing the younger soldier stumble in the shallow water. As the soldier put his hand down to stop himself falling, Gavin shouted.

"Three!"

The men nearest the edge jumped almost immediately, leaving only Joey, Tommy and Rudolph left at the top of the waterfall.

"Go!" Gavin shouted at them, face red with impatience. He wasn't going over until the others had jumped.

Tommy threw himself off at Gavin's command, and Joey followed him after a second's hesitation.

The older soldier was shouting more loudly as he pulled his pistol out of its holster, while the younger one recovered his footing and levelled his rifle at the remaining two men. With a deafening crack, the younger soldier started shooting, his lack of balance causing him to shoot slightly wide of the two remaining men. Tall, thin plumes of spray jumped up from where a few of his shots struck the water to Gavin's right.

Gavin seemed to view things in slow motion as the older man levelled the pistol at his chest. Without pausing to think, Gavin darted to his left, catching Rudolph's legs in a rugby tackle and throwing himself towards the edge of the waterfall. He heard the pistol fire as he tumbled over, his limbs flailing wildly.

As he fell, Gavin lost all sense of direction and speed. His view switched between rushing water and treetops at a confusing rate, and he could not tell whether he was falling headfirst, feet first or somewhere in between. The noise of the falling water and the wind rushing by his ears cancelled out any other sounds, adding to his disorientation. As he fought to stop himself tumbling, he suddenly saw the churning water at the bottom of the fall rushing up to him. It was too late to change his orientation, and grabbing a quick gulp of air, he hit the water face and body first, in a similar pose to that of a skydiver.

The breath was instantly knocked out of him as he hit the surface and plunged deep into the water. Still disoriented, he flailed about, trying to fight his way to the surface, but he had no idea which direction was upwards. As he fought against the water, the pain started to hit him. His face, chest, thighs and arms had taken the full force of his impact, and now ached as if he had been hit by a bus. Resisting the impulse to cry out, he lay still for a moment, even though his lungs were desperate for air, and after a few seconds he broke the surface of the water.

Gavin gasped and opened his mouth, trying to breathe, but his lungs didn't seem to work. The long fall and awkward landing had winded him, and all he could do was make a desperate croaking noise as he tried to fill his lungs. His aching legs and arms were thrashing, trying to keep his head above water, but he was becoming weaker with lack of oxygen, and white spots were starting to fill his vision.

Unable to fight any longer, he started to fall back, his nose and mouth filling with water. As he began to give up hope, he felt a hand grab his forearm and pull him upwards. Surrendering himself, he allowed his saviour to drag him to the surface and fling an arm round his chest, holding his head above the water. Gavin spluttered and took a long, painful gasp of air, still winded and unable to breathe properly. Glancing around at the man who had helped him, he saw that it was Samson, once more saving a friend from watery doom.

Samson was breathing hard as he struggled to keep himself and Gavin afloat in the churning water. Gavin's breathing was becoming slightly less laboured, but he still lacked the energy to keep himself above water. As the pair were swept out of the churning pool beneath the waterfall, they heard a shout from close by.

"Samson! Over here!"

Looking over his shoulder, he saw Marco hanging on to a large, floating tree trunk with one hand, reaching out to Samson with his other hand. Samson struck out with his legs and his one free arm, trying to reach Marco before the rushing water carried him too far downriver. When the pair came in range, Marco reached out and grabbed Gavin's arm, relieving Samson of his burden.

"Sams. Grab him, can you? Quick!" Marco yelled, pointing back towards the waterfall's base.

A few metres upriver, Rudolph was struggling against the river, coughing as he swallowed a mouthful of water. Samson allowed himself a couple of seconds to catch his breath and then he struck out again, swimming powerfully towards his manager. Holding Rudolph around the chest, as he had done with Gavin, he hauled the older man above water and struck off again towards the tree trunk where the other men were gathered. Once again, Marco took his burden from him, and then Samson was able to grab hold of the trunk himself, breathing heavily after his exertion.

The tree which the ten companions found themselves hanging on to was long and thick, and judging by the healthy branches which stuck out from it, had been alive until recently. It was being held back from its journey down the river by some rocks that jutted up from the river bed in the shallower part of the river, to the side of the pool at the base of the waterfall.

Hanging on to the broken branches that jutted out from the trunk, the men caught their breath and glanced about, looking for a suitable escape route. To their right, the river bank was overgrown with weeds and bushes, while to their left the central channel of the river churned and frothed after its hectic journey down the waterfall. As they were contemplating this, a shot rang out from above. Looking up, they saw the two soldiers standing at the top of the waterfall. The older man shot again, then turned to his companion, who was levelling his assault rifle at the group below.

"Look out!" Marco screamed, ducking low behind the tree trunk.

The assault rifle barked angrily as it showered bullets down at the stranded men. A series of loud cracks erupted as some of the bullets tore into the thick trunk. When the racket stopped, Marco poked his head up, taking a quick peek at the gunman.

"He's reloading!" The Australian confirmed.

"We've got to do something. We're like target practice for him", Gavin said, wincing. "Let's try and stall him for a bit, right?"

Saying this, he raised one hand above his head, calling out to the soldiers above.

"Don't shoot! We surrender!"

The other men followed suit, putting one free hand in the air. Seeing the group's gesture of defeat, the older soldier put his arm out to stop his companion, and then started to scream at the men below. He repeated the same phrase three times, shouting so loud that it was clearly audible over the roar of the waterfall. With each order, he jabbed his finger at them.

"Think he wants us to stay put", Tommy suggested.

"Yeah, well we've not got much choice right now", Gavin said with a sigh.

Having finished shouting and pointing, the soldier disappeared from view, leaving the man with the assault rifle watching them intently.

"What's he up to, then?" Asked Tommy.

"Probably looking for a way to get down to us", Emil replied.

"Hey, can anyone else touch the bottom?" Marco asked.

"Yep, just about", Gavin said after a moment's testing.

The other men shook their heads. Marco looked thoughtful for a short while, and then spoke up.

"I've got an idea. If we can get this tree trunk dislodged from whatever's holding it, we can float away down the river. Gives us something to hide behind too."

"Not bad", Gavin conceded. "But we need to do it without that goon up there getting suspicious."

"How's about we pretend we're being attacked by crocs? I reckon that's a good enough reason for us to be struggling!" Damien suggested.

"Okay, mate, I like it!" Gavin said after a moment's consideration. "You up for taking the starring role?"

"You just tell me when, Mr. Spielberg."

"Any time now. Go for it!"

Damien let out a blood-curdling scream and disappeared under the surface of the water. As the water churned, his companions tried to put on a decent performance of distress. Moving away from him, they panicked, shouting and trying to pull themselves out of the water and on to the tree trunk. After about twenty seconds, Damien re-appeared, screaming at the top of his voice and shouting, "Help me!" as he thrashed about with his arms.

Gavin took a surreptitious look at the gunman atop the waterfall. Distracted, the man was looking off to his right, cupping his hand to his mouth as if shouting for his companion. Deciding that this was as good a chance as they were going to get, Gavin turned to Marco.

"Now! Pull!"

On Gavin's command, Marco grabbed the tree with both hands and leaned backwards, trying to use his weight to dislodge the trunk. It moved barely an inch, but Marco went under as he lost his footing. Surfacing once more, he turned to his friends.

"Give me a hand, hey, guys. Grab a branch and pull!"

The men did as suggested, taking hold of the tree and trying their best to budge it. This time the tree responded, rolling slightly and shifting towards them. Gavin took another glance at the soldier. His head was again turned to the side, mouth moving as he spoke. With one hand he trained his rifle on Gavin and his companions, and with the other he was pointing towards them. The other soldier was back, Gavin concluded. They had to get out of there now.

"Right, fellas, one more big push. Give it some! Go!"

Damien, who had now surfaced, also grabbed the tree, and with grunts of effort, the men heaved at the trunk. Again, it rolled over, and for a moment seemed to stick, before finally letting go of its moorings and being taken by the flow of the river.

"Hang on!" Gavin had time to shout as the tree rapidly accelerated.

There were shouts of surprise from some of the men as the tree trunk built up speed, and some of them had their heads forced underwater, only visible by their hands that stuck out, holding desperately on to the branches.

Suddenly, the roar of the assault rifle began once more, making each of the men who were above water instinctively duck down low behind the tree. Again, some of the bullets ripped into the tree with a deafening crunch. A moment later, the firing ceased and Gavin peeked out from the side of the tree. The soldier was reloading his rifle, but by now the companions had put about forty metres of extra space between them and their attacker, and were still accelerating. By the time the soldier had reloaded, they should be well out of range.

"Everyone okay?" Gavin asked, turning to his friends.

The men who had been dragged underwater had now surfaced, some of them coughing and spluttering. The others nodded back at Gavin, eyes bright with adrenalin.

"Well, best get comfortable, lads, I reckon we're staying aboard for a while. We'll make excellent time down the river, and they'll never catch us up through the jungle."

As the sun fell behind the tangled tree line, a glorious sunset painted the clouds orange, pink and yellow. These colours were reflected vividly off the surface of the river, giving it the appearance of shimmering liquid gold.

The men were still clinging on to the tree, chatting idly to one another, half of them having moved around to the other side of the trunk to even out the weight. The mood had improved greatly since earlier. With the river keeping them cool and safe from mosquitoes, they were no longer constantly sweaty and under attack. Where before they had to keep pushing themselves onward with little water to drink, now they were being carried at a much faster pace than they could ever walk, and were surrounded by fresh water.

"Do you reckon there's any piranhas in here?" Tommy Evans asked reluctantly.

"I don't think so", Emil replied calmly. "They are only in South America, and we must be somewhere in Asia."

"Okay, what about those fish which swim up your piss?"

"I don't know." Emil admitted, chuckling. "I doubt it."

The men, who, except for Rudolph, were all naked from the waist down, subconsciously took one hand from the tree and used it to cover their more vulnerable appendages.

"So, where are we, do you reckon, mate? You're good at geography",

Marco enquired.

"I am not sure. There are a lot of jungles in the south of Asia. Perhaps we are in Cambodia or Vietnam, or maybe the south of China."

"What does that mean?" asked Joey, who had been uncharacteristically calm for the last two hours. "Will anyone come to take us home?"

"Well, all of those places are a lot more civilised that people often think," Emil went on. "I cannot believe that they would leave us here, or try to stop our countries from helping us."

"What's with the goons and guns then, eh?" Marco asked.

Emil shrugged, sighing. "Maybe some sort of private militia. They did not look or act like they were soldiers of the government."

"Well", interrupted Damien. "I can at least confirm that there's nothing which swims up your piss."

"Oh, sort it out, mate!" Grimaced Gavin, who was positioned opposite and downstream from Damien. "I was wondering why the water was getting warmer."

"I'll hold on to the number two for now then, shall I, skipper?"

"Unless you'd prefer to swim, yeah!"

"Hey, boys!" Tommy called out. "I can see the bottom."

Shifting their positions to look down through the river, the men could make just make out the bottom of the river. It was a mottled colour, partly sandy and partly muddy, with weeds and various debris standing out from it. Looking ahead, they saw that the river widened and grew even calmer ahead. Within a few minutes, the tallest of them were touching the riverbed with their feet.

"Lads, I'm thinking that this might be a good place to park up and find a place to sleep. I don't really fancy trying to kip while hanging on to a tree. It looks pretty peaceful here too", Gavin suggested.

"Yeah, okay, mate. We'll try and push ourselves towards the bank then, yeah?" Replied Marco, who was now walking on the riverbed, keeping pace with his floating friends.

"That's the plan!"

By now even the shorter men could touch the bottom, and they managed to steer their tree trunk to the bank with little trouble. Pulling part of the trunk on to the low bank, they looked around at their home for the night.

The area of the forest where they now found themselves was much less wild than the previous terrain they had battled through. The forest canopy was lower and not so dense, and the ground was clearer of the spiky and tangled undergrowth they had contended with that morning.

Looking up at the darkening sky, shot through with colourful clouds, and listening to the calls of exotic and unseen birds, Gavin took a deep breath through his nose and sighed happily.

"Not bad, eh, lads? Things are looking up!"

As the day drew to a close, the companions were gathered in the wide clearing that would be their home for the night, eating the last of the bananas they had gathered that morning.

"I didn't want to say anything", Damien said, looking around at his naked friends with distaste. "But you lot are really putting us off me banana!"

"Yeah, we really need to find something to wear", Woody agreed.

"Could we make something out of leaves? Adam and Eve-style? Emil, you're the leaf master, got any bright ideas?"

"Hmm", Emil replied, sucking his teeth for a moment. "Perhaps some larger leaves and some thin twigs would make something. But it would be uncomfortable and I don't think it would last very long."

"Well, actually, I was thinking", Woody said, looking somewhat reluctantly at his manager. "Rudolph's got some Y-fronts, so he's alright. I thought we could borrow his shirt and jacket, you know, and tie some pieces of those around ourselves."

Rudolph, who had been staring at his feet, apparently in deep thought, glanced up when he heard his name. All the other men were looking back at him expectantly. He raised his eyebrows questioningly.

"Rudolph? Mate?" Woody began in an amicable manner. "Can we borrow your jacket and shirt? Please, Mate?"

Rudolph gazed back hopefully for a moment, as if he expected someone to admit that it was just a joke, but then his face fell into a resigned frown. Sighing, he inclined his head slightly, took off his jacket and unbuttoned his shirt, and then threw them into the centre of the group.

Woody picked up the shirt first and made a few tiny cuts in the material with his teeth. Ripping the shirt carefully, he divided it into four pieces. He wrapped one of the pieces around his groin, tying the material together at the sides to fashion a makeshift loincloth.

"Nice threads, man!" Damien applauded. "Give us one then!"

Woody handed out the other pieces of the shirt and then set to work on the jacket. He unpicked some of the stitches between the jacket and the lining with his teeth, and then gradually pulled the lining free.

"I dunno if this will make more than two or three pieces", Woody said, examining the lining material.

"Don't worry about me, mate", Gavin said. "I'll wrap my shirt around my boys."

Woody nodded, biting a few more tears in the lining and then ripping the material apart to form three more loincloths.

"Here you go, Boss", he said, handing the lining-less jacket back to Rudolph, who looked thankful to be receiving anything at all.

As the last of the light faded from the sky, the men made some final adjustments to their loincloths and then looked around for a place to sleep. It was a dry evening, and a warm wind blew gently through the trees, so the men felt no need to huddle together for heat, and instead staked their own claims to some of the more comfortable spots around the clearing.

Within a few minutes, it had become so dark that the men could hardly see their own arms in front of their faces. The cicadas and the night birds created a soothing blanket of sound.

Gavin lay down, one arm behind his head. He tried to make plans for the coming day – How would they eat? Which way would they travel? – But within a minute of closing his eyes, he felt himself dropping off to sleep. The last sound he heard was the soft whispering of Samson's prayers.

4

Gavin must have slept deeply, because when he awoke the day was in full swing. The drone of insects and the shifting melodies of birdsong were so loud and clear that they sounded as if they were being made just for his benefit. The river - wide, shallow and slow at the point where they were camped – made a soft, tinkling sound, and the gentle breeze shifted the jungle canopy every so often with a lazy hiss. The sun, high in the sky now, had heated the atmosphere up to a just-bearable swelter, and Gavin found that he was covered in a sheen of sweat.

An unusual scraping sound made him turn his head towards the river. Sitting with his back to Gavin, feet dangling in the river, was Damien. A long stick poked out behind him, moving rhythmically as he fiddled with the other end. Getting up and stretching, he sidled over to the river bank.

"What you up to, mate?" He asked Damien.

"What? Oh, morning, skipper", Damien replied, shocked out of his concentration. "I was making a spear."

"A spear, right? Are you gonna throw it at the guys with the guns?"

"Eh? No, don't be a dickhead, man. It's for the fish. Look!"

Following Damien's pointing arm, he spied two more of his companions – Samson and Emil, as far as he could tell – in the river, far out from the bank. They were waist-deep in water, their top halves naked, of course. He could just make out that each of them had a stick similar to Damien's in his hand, and they appeared to be standing very still, concentrating on the water.

"Oh yeah, nice one! They having any luck?"

"Not yet, but there's plenty of the little buggers out there, so it's worth a go, right?"

"Yeah, too right. How did you make this then?" Gavin asked, studying the end of Damien's spear.

"You just need a long, straight stick. I've been shaving a spike on the end with this rock. It's pretty easy."

"Did you notice any more good sticks when you were looking?"

"I'll tell you what, Gav. You have this one. It's pretty much finished. And I'll make another one. It's no problem."

"Alright. Cheers, mate!" Gavin said as Damien handed the makeshift spear to him, grinned and walked off into a shadier area outside the clearing to look for another stick.

Gavin hefted the crude spear, feeling the weight of it. It certainly didn't inspire much confidence, but Samson and Emil seemed to think it would work, judging by their apparent concentration. Looking back at the few men who were still sleeping in the clearing, he wondered whether they were wasting their time, and should be moving on as soon as possible, but the location seemed so peaceful after the trials of the last two days that he decided it couldn't hurt to spend a few hours relaxing. Besides, they would need to find some kind of food soon enough.

Wading out into the river, Gavin found that the water came up to round about his waist, and was pleasantly warm. He slowly pushed on, heading towards his two spear-fishing friends. After a few minutes, he had come within fifteen metres of Samson and Emil. Noticing him, Samson held his hand up, gesturing to Gavin to stay where he was. Looking down, Gavin could see a few fish, the larger ones about twice the length of his feet. Their top sides were roughly striped with dark grey and brown, and they swam about lethargically, stopping now and again to pick up some morsel from the riverbed.

As Gavin was watching the fish, he heard Emil call out, and looking up, Gavin saw the two men jab their spears violently into the water. The fish that were swimming near them startled, picking up speed and swimming further upriver.

"Damn. I almost caught one of them", Emil sighed.

"Does this work at all then, lads?" Gavin asked.

"We have only been trying for a short time. I think we have learned the better way to do it now, but you have to be very calm."

"Okay then mate, tell us what I have to do"

"The water is very clear" Samson said, taking over from Emil. "If you duck under it you can see for some distance underwater. It's possible to notice where the fish are. They seem to always stay together. Have a try"

Nodding, Gavin knelt on the riverbed and leaned forward, taking a deep breath before his head went under the water. As he opened his eyes he expected them to sting, but in this fresh water, untainted by salt or chlorine, the sensation was actually quite refreshing. He scanned the river around him for movement, and noticed the movement of a number of fish further ahead and to the right of where they were now.

"Over there", Gavin announced on surfacing.

"Good. We need to move towards them slowly. If we are careful we can get right into the middle of the group. When we are ready we will all pick a different fish, and line up our spear with it. Wait until Emil says go, and then spear it!"

Gavin nodded and then moved off slowly with his friends. They waded cautiously on, forcing themselves not to rush. As they approached the edge of the group of fish, the first ones darted a few metres away from their legs. They men slowed down even more, inching forward bit my bit.

A moment later, they stood as close to the middle of the group of fish as they felt they could. Nodding at each other, they took up their positions, spear tips below the water line, with the haft of the spear poised in their tensed arms. Gavin chose his target, a fairly large fish which seemed to be floating in one place, fins gradually turning it around. He felt like a snake ready to strike, waiting for Emil to give the order.

After another second, Emil shouted, and Gavin powered his spear towards his prey. The commotion that followed took Gavin completely by surprise. Immediately after he struck, the water in front of him frothed and his spear jerked about wildly. Gavin stumbled backwards, losing his footing and almost letting go of his spear. Samson reacted quickly, grabbing Gavin's spear and pulling the sharp end out of the water, with its struggling and thrashing captive skewered on the end.

"Feisty little bugger, eh?" Gavin said, grinning.

"Amazing, catching one on your first try. You are very lucky!" Emil remarked.

"Lucky? I'm a natural, mate!"

"Okay, okay", Emil laughed, clapping Gavin on the shoulder. "Well, you must catch us some more, then."

For the next two hours, the men moved up and down the river in search of their prey. Gavin had no more luck, but Samson caught two fish, with Emil adding one more. Damien, who joined them about half an hour after Gavin came, had no luck at all, his spear coming up empty every time. They waded back to the camp, feeling like Stone Age hunter-gatherers with their loincloths and primitive spears.

In the camp, all the other men had risen and were either exploring the area close to the camp, or sitting in the shade talking. They looked up as Gavin and the other fishermen heaved themselves on to the bank.

"Anyone for sushi?" Damien asked, holding aloft the fish he had been given to carry.

The other men seemed shocked at first that the men with their crude weapons had actually managed to catch any fish, but then cheered as they realised that they were about to have their first proper meal since they had been stranded in this unforgiving jungle.

They gathered round expectantly as Gavin picked up the sharp stone which Damien had used earlier to make the spears, and started to try to cut the fish into pieces. He managed to cut into the soft belly easily enough, and washed the innards out in the river, but the stone was not sharp enough to make much impression on the flesh. After a few minutes of struggling, Gavin managed to cut a small flap of skin away, with a meagre amount of flesh attached. Putting his mouth to the fish, he bit the flesh from the skin and chewed, an expression of distaste spreading across his face.

"It's really tough", he said, spitting out the chewed pieces of fish. "Tastes bad."

"They must be cooked", Joey said with a despairing expression. "It is not meant to be eaten raw."

"Yeah, I know, mate." Gavin replied, looking frustrated. "Only, I forgot to pack the barbecue."

"Let's give it another try with the sticks, eh?" Marco said. "I've seen it done on the telly. You just have to have some sort of really dry grass to catch the spark and then drill a stick into another bit of wood, kind of like sharpening a pencil."

Gavin sighed. "We can give it a try. One thing we have got a lot of is wood. Right, lads, collect all the dry bits you can find near here, and Marco, you look for the grass or something else that'll do the job, right?"

The men nodded and moved off, studying the ground around the edges of the clearing. After a short time a fair pile of kindling had been deposited in the middle of the clearing. Marco eventually returned, studying a pile of light yellow dust in his hand.

"You find something, big man?" Damien asked him.

"Yeah. There's no grass really around here, but I found quite a bit of this moss, and it's very dry. Should be alright."

Marco got to work, gouging a small hole in one piece of wood with the stone, and then rounding off the end of a tough, stubby stick. He started slowly, rolling the stick between his hands as it poked into the hole in the wood, and then built up speed until he was frantically rubbing at the wood. After a few minutes of this he gave up, face dripping with sweat.

"Bloody hell", he said, shaking out his aching wrists. "It's hard going. Anyone else want to try? I can feel it getting warm."

"Yeah, man, I'll give it a go", volunteered Damien.

Picking up the pointed stick, Damien took over from Marco, energetically rotating the stick in the hole. Marco sat with the dry moss in his hand, poised to catch any sparks that might be produced. Damien worked at it for a few minutes, concentration and fatigue showing in his face. As he threw the stick down in defeat, Raphaël walked back into the clearing, carrying a small pile of round objects.

"Mangoes!" he declared, a small grin escaping his usually austere face.

"Wicked!" Tommy exclaimed. "Give us one!"

Raphaël deposited his burden on the ground, throwing a fruit to each of the men. Tommy caught his mango first, and set to work trying to make a cut in it and peel the skin off.

"Not like that. They are very soft, sweet", Raphaël said, picking up a fruit for himself. "Best is if you can bite the end. See? Then you can squeeze. Juice and fruit you can suck from the hole."

The companions did as was suggested, biting a hole in the end of their mango and squeezing the juice and pulp into their mouths. Noises of appreciation spread through the group.

"There any more of these?" Asked Tommy, juices dribbling down his chin.

"Yes. Two trees, through there", Raphaël pointed. "Many on the floor also."

"Of course!" Marco suddenly shouted, interrupting. "Why didn't I think of that?"

The Australian was kneeling up, watching Rudolph, an expression of excitement on his face. Rudolph had been trying his best to clean his glasses on his Y-fronts, and looked back at Marco somewhat fearfully.

"Rudolph, mate", Marco continued enthusiastically. "Can I have your glasses, just for a minute or two?"

Rudolph, who was still unhappy about having his shirt and jacket lining taken away, seemed ready to protest, but then handed his glasses over with a small sigh.

Taking the spectacles, Marco grabbed the handful of dry moss and jogged over to the river bank, where there was no shade form the overhanging trees. He placed the small pile of moss carefully on the ground and squinted up at the sun, getting his bearings. Opening the glasses out, he spent a minute adjusting the angle and distance of the glasses to the moss, and then knelt there in motionless concentration as the rest of the men gathered round to watch.

The group remained silent and still in anticipation as Marco trained the tiny beam of light on the moss.

"It's working!" He whispered, still focused intently on his task.

An excited clamour rose from the watching companions as a small wisp of smoke rose lazily up from the moss.

"Someone grab the smallest bits of wood and make a pile just where you lot are standing, will you?" Marco asked without looking up.

Half of the men reacted, racing back to the wood pile they had collected earlier and hurriedly selecting the smallest twigs. By the time they had returned to the river bank, the moss had started to smoke more as tiny sparks lit up under the glare of the glasses. Marco blew gently on the moss, causing the sparks to spread and brighten.

"Gangway!" Marco said, picking up the smouldering moss and carrying it towards the pile of kindling.

Laying down the moss, he rapidly selected some of the sticks and laid them on top. Leaning down with his cheek almost touching the ground, he started to blow on the moss, starting gently and then more forcefully as the sparks caught.

A cheer rose from the companions as the first flame erupted form the pile of twigs, and a few of them hugged each other in delight. Marco carried on blowing gently until some of the twigs had caught the flame.

"Alright!" he said, standing up and looking very pleased with himself. "So, who brought the shrimps?"

A short while later, the fire had been built up into a fair-sized blaze. Although the weather was hot anyway, the men gathered round the fire, seemingly fascinated by its crackling heart and shimmering fumes. They sat in silence, sweating profusely with the extra heat from the flames, but each man looked comforted by the fire, perhaps because its presence made them feel slightly more civilised than the desperate, hunted animals they had recently become.

Woody eventually broke the silence.

"Are we going to cook these fish then? Isn't that why we made the fire, you know?"

The other men reacted as if shocked from a trance.

"Yes, you are right", Emil answered. "So, I suppose we need to break the fish into pieces and then hold it over the fire with a stick?"

"I dunno, mate. They're bloody tough", Gavin said. "Might just have to chuck the whole thing on."

"I know a good way for fish, for cooking", Raphaël put in.

The other men, taken aback at the usually quiet and surly Raphaël's recent input into the group, listened avidly to him.

"It is a way for cooking we used on the beach, at parties. Very good for fish, cooking it soft. If the fire is straight on the fish it will be dry, not tasty."

"Alright, sounds awesome, mate. Need any help?" Marco offered.

"Yes, the fire must be big. Put more wood. I need to get something. Not very far."

Raphaël walked purposefully out of the clearing while a few of the men hunted about for more fuel. After about five minutes, the fire had been fed with plenty more wood, which it was furiously devouring, while another large pile of wood sat a few paces away, ready to add to the blaze. Raphaël came sauntering back to the group, a few long, thick leaves under his arm. He sat down near the fire and began to gouge lumps of flesh out of one of the remaining mangoes, heaping this on to one of the leaves.

"What have you got there?" Marco asked him.

"Leaves from banana tree. You can cook fish inside it. Is much better." Raphaël replied.

Picking up one of the fish, he used Damien's sharp stone to cut open the belly, eventually opening it wide enough to remove the guts. He repeated this with the other three fish, laying all of them out on one of the long banana leaves. Picking up a small handful of the mango pulp, he stuffed it inside the open belly of one of the fish. When he had put as much of the fruit inside as he could, he picked up a fresh banana leaf and began to wrap the fish in it.

"Ah, I see what you are doing. This is a good idea!" Emil enthused.

"The juice from the mango. It cooks fish from inside. Makes it soft. Tasty."

Raphaël finished the parcel off, using the stalk of the banana leaf to tie it up. He placed it among the hot embers around the edge of the roaring fire.

"After fifteen minutes, turn over", he said, starting work on the next fish. While the other fish were prepared, the men around the fire found their gazes fixing on the cooking fish, mouths watering in anticipation as they sat in fascinated silence. After what seemed like an interminable amount of time, Raphaël had placed the next three fish in the glowing embers, and after piling some more wood on the fire, turned over the first fish with a stick.

"How long now?" Asked Tommy eagerly.

"Fifteen minutes" Raphaël replied, and then saw Tommy's look of despair. "Ten minutes."

Silence descended again as the companions, entranced by the fire and the prospect of proper food, got caught up in their own thoughts. Every few minutes, Raphaël moved the fish parcels around on to hotter new embers, watched eagerly by everyone.

Eventually, he prodded the first fish out of the fire and, fingers smarting from the heat, gradually unwrapped the package. Fresh fish-scented steam rose as he exposed the tail section, causing a few stomachs to rumble. When the fish was entirely unwrapped, he broke it into two pieces along the belly, placing one piece on another banana leaf. Taking a large pinch of the now white flesh and mango pulp, he tasted it. All eyes were fixed on him. After chewing and swallowing, he gave an approving nod, passing one half of the fish to his left and the other to his right.

As the fish was passed round, each of the men took a lump and passed it on, grunting in pleasure as they tasted what was, in their current situation at least, a gourmet meal. By the time the fish had been passed all the way round, most of the flesh had been eaten, but the men still kept hunting, prising small pieces of meat from the bones or skin and then passing the modest offering on again.

"I could eat the head too", Tommy said, looking a little sheepish.

"It is okay, this one should be cooked", Raphaël said, rescuing the next fish from the fire.

As they worked their way through the second and third fish, the men started to become more animated, laughing and joking in a relaxed and comradely way, just as if they were on a night out together back in Liverpool.

As they worked their way through the last fish, Marco looked quizzically at Damien for a moment before speaking.

"Hey, Damo, I thought you were a vegetarian."

"Here we go. I was wondering when someone'd start this one up", Damien responded, shaking his head good-naturedly. "I may be a veggie but I'm not a bloody idiot. I won't starve myself to death, will I?"

"But what about the poor little fishy? He probably had a wife and kids depending on him!"

"Don't be a fool, man. It's had a good life, swimming about here. It's not like it's lived all its life in a cramped shed, is it?"

"So it's alright to eat the poor little bugger if you're a bit hungry?" Marco continued, grinning.

"Okay, for the benefit of the more mentally challenged among us", He pointed to Marco. "I shall explain once more. When I'm in England I have a choice of what to buy. I can get stuff without animal flesh in it or I can get stuff with. Either of them are going to be nutritious and tasty, so why should I support an industry which I disagree with? The more people who stick up for what they believe, the more chance that people will take notice."

"He's Ché bloody Guevara." Gavin cut in, motioning towards Damien. "Anyway, we weren't always so high up on the food chain, you know. *They* used to eat *us* once upon a time."

"Who used to eat us? The bastard sabre-toothed tigers or something?" Damien replied, becoming more worked up even though he knew he was being goaded.

"Yeah, them, for one."

"So, the evil sabre-toothed tigers ate a few cave men. I don't remember anything about them capturing us, locking us up and breeding us in captivity. I must have missed all the cave paintings of the human-farms kept by our enemies, the evil sabre-tooths."

"Yeah, well they do say that not eating meat is bad for the brain, mate"

"Don't be a daft shite, man. Let me eat my food."

Damien grabbed a large lump of the fish meat, as if to show that he wasn't squeamish or ashamed of eating it. As he put it in his mouth, Marco picked up the head of one of the other fish and pointed it towards Damien, waggling it as he spoke in a high-pitched voice.

"Oh no! Don't eat me, Damien! Stop! That hurts! No! No!"

The other men laughed even harder as Damien attempted to chew and swallow his food while trying not to laugh himself. Eventually he forced the food down, shaking his head and grinning as his friends continued to mock him.

"Yeah, bollocks to you lot, and all."

"I've had a thought", Woody said after the mocking had subsided.

"Hold the front page!" Marco said, punching Woody's shoulder good-naturedly.

"No, seriously", Woody said, narrowing his eyes. "You know what day it is?"

"Pay day?"

"Yeah, always!" Woody grinned. "No, I mean I just worked it out – it's Christmas day today"

"You sure?" Tommy asked.

"Well, the final was on the twenty-first, right?" Some of the men nodded. "Well, that was four days ago, I make it."

"He is right", Samson confirmed.

The men sat quietly for some time, lost in thoughts of home. Only in such a chaotic and alien situation as this could they have forgotten Christmas day. In a way it reassured them to be reminded of previous Christmases, bit it also brought home to them just how far away they were from the people and places that they loved.

"What are you thinking about?" Damien asked, to break the morose silence.

"Roast spuds!" Tommy answered immediately, to the agreement of all of the Englishmen.

"Singing in the streets", Samson offered.

"I'm thinking about my kids, and the misses", Gavin said, looking sorrowful.

"Yeah, me too", Woody agreed, placing his hand lightly on Gavin's shoulder.

"Come on then, lads", Damien said, kneeling up. "Shall we sing a carol?"

"Okay then, mate", said Marco. "Which one are we gonna sing?"

"I dunno. Any suggestions?"

"I have a suggestion", Samson said with a smile. "We can sing 'Once in Royal David's City'"

"Sounds good to me. Want to start us off?"

Samson nodded and then began to sing, softly at first and then louder as more people joined in. No one apart from Samson knew all of the words, but everyone contributed something, even if it was just a tuneless humming. When they finished, a warm glow of comfort and companionship remained between the men.

"That was great, Sams", Damien congratulated. "Know any more?"

"I know very many!" Samson answered, a broad grin lighting his face.

"Take it away, mate!"

Samson began again, singing carols that everyone had heard as well as more obscure ones that he remembered from his childhood. The other men sang with him when they could, or hummed and clapped where appropriate. The cooked food and the singing gradually brought them out of their depression and for a short time, at least, they found themselves feeling content and even positive towards the future.

As the day wore on into mid afternoon, their conversation turned to plans for when and how they should continue.

"Well, I think we should be moving on tomorrow. We're just wasting time here." Gavin opined.

"But we have good things here", Joey replied earnestly. "Food, fire, water. A comfortable place to sleep."

There was a murmur of agreement from many of the other men.

"Yeah, mate, but we can't stay here forever. Don't you want to get out of here?"

"We could be anywhere", said Emil, wincing. "It may be hundreds of miles to the nearest town. We do not even know which direction to take."

"So, we just stay here and cook fish for the rest of our lives?"

"Maybe we will be rescued soon. It cannot be too long before we are found."

"Well I'd love that to be true, mate, but how do we know they're even looking in the right place? That chopper was shot down two days ago, and we've heard nothing."

Emil gave a wincing nod and kept his silence.

"I was thinking if we keep travelling along the river, we should make good time. We're more likely to find a town or village along the river too, right?"

"That is true", Samson said, nodding. "People do prefer to live by the water. But maybe we should stay at least for a few days in case there are people coming to help us."

"I think we'd be wasting time. Shall we vote on it, then?"

Everyone nodded at Gavin.

"So, who thinks we should leave tomorrow morning?" Gavin said enthusiastically, putting his own hand up straight away.

Not a single person voted with Gavin, drawing a pronounced sigh from him.

"Okay then", he shook his head. "Who wants to stay here for a while, and hope someone comes for us?"

All except Gavin and Rudolph put their hands up.

"How long then? Another day? Two?"

Silence.

"Three days?"

Most of the men nodded, making positive noises.

"Bollocks. Three days, then", said Gavin, clearly unhappy with the decision. "We need to keep that fire going, and someone else can catch the bloody fish this time."

5

As it turned out, they ended up staying at the camp for only two more days, but this was due to the weather rather than by choice. As the men slept off their two hearty fish meals that night, the heavens opened once more. The men were woken up to a cacophony of violent thunder, and watched in awe as great streaks of lightning criss-crossed the sky. The rain, when it came a moment later, was hard and heavy, forcing them under the cover of nearby trees, and it didn't let up until close to dawn, when it died down to a slimy drizzle.

When the first men woke up after managing to catch a few more hours of disturbed sleep, they found that their tree trunk had been washed away by the now swollen and churning river, and the fire was well and truly sodden and lifeless. The depth and ferocity of the swollen river, combined with the fact that it was now dark with disturbed mud, made fishing impossible, so the men sat around silently for the most part, feeling sorry for themselves.

Raphaël and Gavin trekked off in the mud and filled the rucksack with fruit from the trees Raphaël had found the day before, but their friends greeted their return with little enthusiasm.

The day proceeded in a similar fashion, with the rain dying off for a few hours now and again, but the river always remaining too disturbed for fishing.

Towards the end of the second day, as the consistently grey sky started to turn a shade darker, Emil stood up in shock where he stood on the bank of the river. He stared downriver, unable to decide whether he was imagining things or not.

"Hey, guys, come here – quick!" He called out.

Samson and Marco came jogging over, grateful for any distraction.

"Do you see that?" He said, pointing upriver.

"Yeah. What is it? Marco asked.

"A boat, I think. Coming our way fast. Nobody is in it." Emil replied.

The three men stared at each other in disbelief, as if to say that something so unlikely and fortunate could never be happening to them, until Samson jogged them out of their thoughts.

"We must get it. Take my hand, we will wade out. Someone stay next to the bank", the Ghanaian suggested.

Linking hands, the men waded out into the river as quickly as they could without being swept away. Samson was at the end of the chain, with Emil hanging on the river bank with one arm. The boat, a grey and khaki military-style inflatable dinghy, was coming towards them at some pace, and drew level with them swiftly.

Samson grabbed at it as it reached them, just managing to get his arm over one side, but his arm slipped off the wet plastic as the dinghy slid past them. With a shout of frustration, Samson let go of Marco's hand

and swam off after the speeding boat, but it seemed impossible that he would catch up with it.

Suddenly, Samson stopped, pointing towards the dinghy and making an unusual splashing motion with his arm. Thinking he had given up the chase, Emil and Marco relaxed, but when Samson turned round to them, his eyes were wide.

"Rope! Help me!" He shouted at them as he started back towards them, swimming with only one arm.

Not sure what was happening, Emil and Marco edged out further into the river, Marco reaching out his hand for Samson to grab. As they came within a few feet of each other, Samson was suddenly jerked backwards downriver, and it became clear what was happening. A long rope was attached to the dinghy, and had been trailing behind it. Samson had grabbed hold of this with his left arm, and had been trying to swim, but the momentum of the dinghy was dragging him away from his friends.

Without thinking, Marco let go of Emil's hand and swam after his friend, catching up with him as he struggled against the pull of the boat and the river. Linking hands, they slowed the boat's passage somewhat with their weight, as they tried to dig their feet into the barely-reachable riverbed.

"Hang on, mate!" Marco encouraged.

By now, all of the other men had come to see what the commotion was, and some had joined Emil in the river near the bank, linking hands to allow the Dutchman to wade out towards his stranded friends. Grabbing Marco's arm, he turned around and yelled at others to pull them in. With much slipping, grunting and cursing, the men managed to pull Marco and Samson on to the bank, from where Gavin took the rope from the exhausted Samson and began pulling in the dinghy.

Half an hour later, as the last light was dying in the sky, the companions sat around the dinghy, perplexed. They had searched it thoroughly for any clues as to its origin, but were still none the wiser.

It had a flat wooden bottom and rear plate, with a metal fixing for an outboard motor, but no motor was present. The thick inflatable plastic sides were grey and had been painted haphazardly with khaki paint. A thick rope was attached all the way around the sides, and it was from one section of this rope that the longer rope Samson had grabbed was fixed. This longer rope measured at least twenty metres.

"Nobody else thinks this is a bit strange, then?" Gavin asked, standing with one hand on his hip, looking suspiciously at the dinghy.

"Yeah, mate, but we were due a bit of luck, hey?" Marco said cheerily.

"This is just weird luck, though. Seems a bit too convenient for a boat like this to drop out of nowhere."

"I have been thinking the same", Emil said. "I think it could be bad news."

"How d'you mean?" Marco asked.

"Well, this is a military boat. And I think the most likely people to have military equipment here are our friends from before." He motioned back up the river.

The men sat silently for a moment, digesting Emil's thoughts.

"You mean they're still after us?" Gavin said with a sigh.

Emil gave a shrug as if to suggest that there was no other explanation. "They probably brought this boat so they could follow us. Maybe they fell in to the river or the boat was swept away."

"You've got a point. Well it's almost dark now. I reckon we need to leave here first thing in the morning."

Gavin looked about at his friends. No one moved to contradict him.

"Right, we're gonna drag it right over there, away from the river. We don't want this one being washed away."

Gavin woke shortly after dawn and reluctantly forced himself upright. It was no longer raining, but the air was thick and moist, and mist hung over the river and swept between the trees in an eerie manner. Taking a minute to stretch, scratch and compose his thoughts, he walked around the clearing, poking and cajoling his friends out of their slumber. Picking up the rucksack, he barked grumpily.

"Someone come with me and help fill this up with fruit, will you? The rest of you get ready to leave."

Ignoring his friends' moaning, he clapped Joey on the back and steered him out of the clearing towards where the fruit trees grew.

"Why me?" Joey said irritably.

"You're a tall lad, so you'll do. Besides, you don't need your beauty sleep, do you, mate?" Gavin smirked.

Joey looked at Gavin suspiciously for a moment, trying to work out whether he was being insulted or not. Eventually he decided that Gavin had paid him a compliment, and nodded cockily as he walked on.

After a few minutes, they arrived at the small grove of mango trees which Raphaël had discovered a few days earlier.

"Pick some of the hard ones as well, mate", Gavin said, putting down the rucksack. "We don't know how long these'll have to last."

The two men busied themselves, pulling down the fruits that hung low, and using sticks to shake some of the higher fruits down.

"What is in here?" Joey asked as he returned to drop his first load of mangoes into the rucksack.

"The cup", Gavin replied.

"Cup?"

"Yeah, you know. The trophy."

"How do you have this?" Joey looked shocked as he pulled the trophy out of the bag.

"Brought it with us. I wasn't gonna leave it behind, was I?"

"But why? It is not worth anything here!"

Gavin stopped and stared at Joey as if he had said something blasphemous.

"Not worth anything? We bloody won that. I'm not letting those knob heads back there get their hands on it, am I?" Gavin gestured in the general direction of their distant pursuers.

"Why not? It is worth some money, surely. Perhaps they will help us if we give it to them."

Gavin looked as if he was about to lose his cool, but then shook his head despairingly.

"Just put the cup back and shut your gob, will you, mate. Pick some bloody mangoes."

Back at the camp, the other men had roused themselves. Most were sitting about, bleary-eyed as Samson trimmed the twigs off a long branch he had found.

"What you up to, Sams?" Gavin asked him

"It is to push the boat. To steer it." Samson replied.

"Good thinking, mate. Nice one."

"We should take the spears as well. Maybe we will find some fish on the way."

"Yeah, right. You almost done there?"

Samson nodded as he broke the last of the twigs off his pole and tested its strength against his knee.

"Listen up, everyone", Gavin said, raising his voice and addressing his sleepy companions. "It's gonna be hard enough to fit us all in that boat, so no messing about, right? Wait down by the bank and get ready to get on it when you're told. Marco, give me a hand carrying it, will you?"

The two large men lifted the dinghy with ease, and walked it over to the bank and into the river, with Marco standing chest deep as he held it steady. Gavin ordered people in one by one until everyone but Marco and himself had crammed into the little boat.

"Right, I'm gonna jump in now, get yourself in as quick as you can after, okay?" Gavin shouted to Marco above the bickering of the other men.

"Aye, aye!" Marco called back with a grin.

Getting his balance, Gavin heaved himself over the edge of the dinghy and tumbled into the mass of limbs inside. Without Gavin to hold it steady, the boat began to rock and turn with the flow of the river, and Marco quickly jumped up, trying to haul himself into the dinghy. As he lifted his leg to try and throw it over the edge, he slipped, submerging himself in the river as the boat started to move away with the flow of the water.

The boat rocked worryingly as a few of the men plunged their hands over the side, reaching for their friend.

"Got him!" Tommy shouted, grabbing Marco's arm and trying to pull the big man out of the water. "Give us a hand!"

Raphaël and Woody, the two men closest to Tommy, leaned over and grabbed hold of Marco. His head and shoulders came above water and he wrapped his free arm around the side of the dinghy. Looking panicked, he started trying to heave himself over again, causing the opposite side of the boat to tip up out of the water.

"Woah! Careful!" cried some of the men across the boat as they started to slip towards the others.

Gavin leaped up, throwing his body half over the edge of the boat across from the side Marco was hanging on to, forcing that side of the boat back down onto the water with a slap. Crawling back to the edge, the men on Gavin's side leant on the hard, rubbery edge of the dinghy, counterbalancing it so that Marco could pull himself on board. After much heaving and splashing, and a little help from the men who were holding his arms, the big Australian clambered over the edge and lay dripping on the solid bottom of the boat.

By now the dinghy was travelling down the river slightly faster than normal walking pace, and without a rudder or oars to steer it was revolving slowly as it went. As the passengers had no particular destination other than downriver, they weren't concerned about their orientation, and instead busied themselves trying to find enough space in the cramped boat so that they could all be at least passably comfortable. This proved difficult, with ten men in an unsteady and rotating boat all jostling each other as they moved. Eventually, they found a satisfactory formation, with two men sitting on the soft, inflatable back of the dinghy and one more at the pointed front, while the other seven sat lengthways across the boat, alternating the direction their feet were pointing. In this way, they could all see each other and had enough space so that they didn't feel too uncomfortable.

"You guys look like a tin of sardines", commented Marco, who as the tallest man, had been given the place at the front of the dinghy.

"Yeah, well it's alright for you, ain't it?" Tommy replied testily. "Sitting on your bloody throne!"

"Aww, it could be worse, mate. At least you're not next to Damo's feet."

"Hey, leave it out!" Damien said in mock outrage as Tommy began to choke theatrically.

As the day wore on, tempers frayed. It was a humid, cloudy day, and the lack of wind made the river a happy hunting ground for mosquitoes. The men sat in their cramped boat, sweating and beating off hungry insects as they made their way downriver.

Although everyone had become somewhat snappy, the biggest row, unsurprisingly, had been between Damien and Joey. A diet consisting exclusively of fruit and fish had given everyone digestive problems to some degree, but Damien, unused as his body was to eating fish, had suffered the worst. After a bout of stomach cramps, Damien had eased the pressure loudly and aromatically. This being Joey's pet hate, a confrontation was inevitable.

"What was that?" Joey asked, staring at Damien as if he wished death upon him.

"Better out than in", Damien replied tiredly.

"'Better out than in'?" Joey repeated, raising his hands agitatedly. "What is this? Who says this?"

"Look, just chill out, can't you? You're like an old woman!"

"Old woman? And what are you like? A dog? A pig?"

"I'll be anything you like, Jo-Jo, if you'll stop bitching for five minutes!"

"Because I am a decent person, now I am 'bitching'?"

"Alright, give it a bloody rest, you two", Gavin cut in. "You'll drive us all mad!"

"I can't be near that man", Joey shouted back, his face flushed with temper. "I would rather swim!"

"Suits me, prissy boy!" Damien said, folding his arms.

"You too, Damo", Gavin warned, starting to raise his voice. "You're not helping!"

"Well, he keeps winding us up, making a big deal out of nothing."

"Nothing?" Joey screamed, his voice harsh with frustration. "Oh, this is not nothing, this is something!"

"Shut up!" Gavin shouted at the top of his voice.

The ferocity of Gavin's shout made everyone in the dinghy flinch, and the two bickering men were shocked into silence.

"You're a pair of bloody kids!" Gavin went on. "Joey, if you swap places with me and sit here, away from Damien, will you stop moaning for a while?"

Gavin, as the second tallest man, had been given a place at the back of the boat where he could sit upright.

"Yes, this will be better", Joey said after a moment's consideration. "If he does not speak to me, I will not say anything."

The two men swapped places, manoeuvring themselves awkwardly in the crowded boat.

"Don't fall in, mate!" Damien said sarcastically as Joey took his seat at the back of the dinghy.

Joey, still looking ready to explode, turned on Damien, eyes wide, but his wrath was interrupted by Marco, whose voice had a worried tone.

"Guys", Said the Australian, who had turned his body to look down the river ahead of them. "What does that sound like to you?"

"What, mate?" Gavin asked, giving Joey a warning glance.

"See there, just ahead, the river curls round out of view?" Marco pointed downriver. "Can you hear that rushing sound? Remind you of anything?"

The other men strained to listen for a moment, and then glanced nervously at each other as the realised what Marco was getting at. Samson was the first to vocalise their suspicion.

"Waterfall?"

"That's what I thought, mate", Marco replied. "Wanna give me that stick?"

Samson hurriedly passed the long stick to Marco, who plunged it in the water, trying to steer the dinghy towards the nearest bank. The stick sunk in the river almost entirely, and Marco almost toppled in as he tried to push the boat with his limited leverage.

"It's deep!" Marco said, looking concerned. "Can you guys paddle with your hands too?"

The dinghy rocked as its occupants leaned over the edge, thrust their arms into the river and paddled, trying to coax the boat towards the bank on their right. Their efforts had little effect other than to destabilise the dinghy, causing it to revolve and point towards the far bank. Marco tried to straighten its course, but he could feel that the boat was now speeding up, being pulled along more strongly by the water which was steadily picking up speed as they drew closer to the bend in the river.

"That's having no bloody effect at all!" Marco told his friends. "If it's a waterfall we'd better jump and swim, eh?"

"We don't wanna lose the boat, Marco." Gavin replied, wincing in frustration. "We'll be back to square one again."

"Yeah, mate, but we don't know how big the fall's gonna be, do we? Can't just go over it blind."

"Alright, fair enough", Gavin nodded begrudgingly. "We're almost up to the bend now anyway. Get ready, lads!"

The men watched in tense silence as their dinghy steadily gained more speed. After a few moments, they began to round the bend in the river, and the way ahead gradually revealed itself. Roughly half a kilometre ahead, the water became disturbed and frothy, and a number of bulky rocks broke the surface.

"Is that a waterfall or what?" Tommy asked, squinting.

"Steady now, guys", Marco said as he stood up, spreading out his arms for balance.

After a brief pause, he turned back, frowning.

"Shit. Rapids. We jumping, then?"

"Hold on, mate", Gavin said, peering down the river. "You reckon we can make it? People go down rapids for fun, don't they?

"What, ten people in a piece of crap like this? With no life jackets?" Marco shrugged. "I dunno, mate. Sounds a bit dodgy to me."

"I'm not just chucking the boat away, it's our best way out of here", Gavin shook his head. "I reckon we hang on and try our luck on the river."

Gavin glanced around at his friends, but any opposition to his suggestion was half hearted.

"It's too late now anyway, boys." He said after a minute. "If we jump in we're still going down the rapids, but on our arses rather than in a boat."

"'Fraid you're right, mate", Marco replied, "Everyone better hold on tight to the ropes on the side here. It's not gonna be a pleasure cruise."

"I hate to say it, lads", Damien piped up. "But it looks like we're literally up shit creek without a paddle!"

"On the plus side", Gavin shouted above the increasing roar of the turbulent water, "At least you and Joey've stopped banging on."

The companions had a few seconds to brace themselves before the white water took hold of them. The dinghy sped up, vibrating with the rushing of the water beneath it, and seemed to charge onward, towards the heart of the rapids.

"Rock!" Gavin shouted, barely audible above the sound of the river as he pointed ahead of them.

A large rock was jutting out from the river, directly in the path of the little boat. Nudging Damien, Marco knelt up, and reached out toward the rock as it loomed nearer. Damien followed suit, and the two men pushed off against the rock, barely managing to ease their vessel past it. The side of the dinghy rubbed against the rock, jerking the vessel and its occupants violently. This collision sent the boat spinning as it sped down the first slope in the river.

The feeling of weightlessness as they rushed sideways down the slope was quickly finished as the dinghy splashed down into the churning water at the bottom, jarring the men's' bones and drenching them with water. The boat stayed upright, but was spinning out of control and picking up even more speed as it headed on down the raging water.

Disorientated by the boat's erratic motion and the water in their eyes, the men barely had time to brace themselves before they careered over the next slope. This time they slid for longer, the dinghy scraping against outcroppings as they descended. They hit the water with the back of the boat first this time, and Joey, who was now sitting in the back, toppled over into the water.

With his hand tightly gripping the rope around the edge of the boat, he held on as the boat span around again and he was dragged behind it. The two nearest men moved to help him, but at that moment the dinghy struck another rock, throwing everyone towards the front. The boat whipped round violently, and the back of the boat was thrown upwards as it struck a rock that was hidden under the water. With a look of terror, Joey was catapulted away from the boat and into the churning river.

The men looked at each other in shock, unsure how to react. Almost by instinct, Samson knelt up as if to jump in after Joey. He stopped himself, looking about at the churning river with an expression of hopelessness, and then closed his eyes, lips moving as he muttered a few words under his breath. He then launched himself over the edge of the boat and disappeared beneath the frothing river.

The other men turned back in shock, looking to Gavin for guidance. Gavin was shaking his head in horror. If they all jumped now, they would probably all drown. Samson was a strong swimmer, and if anyone could survive this it was him. He decided that their best bet was to stay in the relative safety of the boat and hope that Samson was successful, as well as that the worst of the rapids was over.

"Just hang on!" Gavin finally yelled, strengthening his grip again on the rope.

The next few minutes became a blur. The dinghy was thrown about the river like a kite in a storm, buffeted by unpredictable swells and battered by unyielding rocks as it continued its hectic journey at the will of the angry river.

As the boat approached a turn in the river, it got pulled violently to the side, caught in an unseen current. The men barely had time to brace themselves as a large rock loomed out of the water ahead. The dinghy struck it head on, the force of their collision lifting the front of the boat clear of the water, half on and half off the rock. As the water buffeted them, the boat was pushed up against the rock until it was vertically on its side. The men held on as best they could, but one by one they were pulled from the dinghy by the raging water.

Damien was one of the last to fall, but he quickly got dragged under the foaming water. He fought his way to the surface and gasped for breath, getting a mouthful of water in the process. Unable to see around him, he was forced to struggle for a minute just to stay afloat. Forcing his body upwards, he whipped his head about, taking in his surroundings. He found that he was fairly close to the bank on his left hand side, and immediately struck out in that direction, panic and exertion making his limbs heavy.

For a few minutes, Damien struggled against the water as he tried to make his way to safety. Suddenly, he caught a glimpse of something large out of the corner of his eye, and turning to his right he could see that he was rapidly approaching a flat rock that protruded a foot or two from the river. Abandoning his flight to the river bank, he twisted round in the water so that he was facing this new obstacle. In a few seconds he was upon it, stretching out his arms to hug the rock, and receiving a painful blow to the cheek. He struggled to find purchase on the rock, but it was smooth and slick with water. As the river buffeted him from behind, he reached up and managed to grab hold of the top edge of the rock.

Before he had a chance to relax, Damien heard a spluttering sound coming from close behind him. Whipping his head round, he saw a flailing arm in the water a few metres upriver, moving rapidly towards him. Without thinking, he thrust his free hand out and grabbed the arm by the wrist as it came past him. The mystery hand immediately grasped Damien's wrist, clutching it so tightly that the nails dug in, causing Damien to yelp. With a strength lent by pain, he dragged his catch out of the river.

The face that emerged belonged to Tommy. He had his eyes screwed up and was spluttering and spitting, reaching out with his other hand to grab on to his saviour. Damien, still suffering from the pressure of Tommy's grip on his wrist, guided the other hand towards the top edge of the rock, where it grabbed on tightly next to his own.

"Tommy! Let go of my bastard wrist, will you?" Damien shouted above the roar of the river.

Tommy opened his eyes wide. They were panicked, the pupils dilated. He glanced around, disorientated, and then focussed on Damien. Slowly, he relaxed his grip.

"Are you alright, man?" Damien asked his friend.

Tommy seemed to consider the question for a bit, coughed a few times and then nodded.

"Okay, well I'm getting on top of this rock, out of the water. Hold on for a bit, right?" Damien suggested, slapping Tommy on his shoulder.

Turning to face the rock, Damien grabbed on with both hands, readying himself to leap from the water. Letting himself sink down to his chin, he kicked with his legs and pulled with his arms, just managing to get his torso over the edge of the rock. Rolling over, he pulled his legs up and lay panting for a moment.

"Oy, Damo!" Came Tommy's cry from below.

"Yeah, alright, I'm coming", Damien replied, shifting round to the edge of the rock.

Looking down at Tommy, scared and with all his usual cheeky bravado gone, Damien was reminded that his friend was really still a child.

"Grab my arm tight, like before", Damien said, offering his arm.

Tommy spat the last of the water in his mouth and then held on to Damien's arm with both hands. Damien mustered the last of his energy. Pulling with his dangling arm and pushing against the rock with his other, he managed to hoist Tommy up to safety, and then collapsed back, exhausted. He lay there with his eyes shut, breathing deeply, but after a moment was disturbed by Tommy, who was nudging his shoulder urgently.

"Leave off, man. I'm knackered." Damien complained.

"Look!" Tommy replied, still nudging his arm.

With a sigh, Damien raised himself up to sit again, and followed Tommy's line of sight. Near the centre of the rapids, the Dinghy had worked itself loose, and was once more hurtling downriver. To their astonishment, a man still remained in the boat, held in place by his arms, which were firmly entwined in the ropes at the front end. As the dinghy drew level with them, they could see that it was Rudolph who still clung on. Their manager sat motionless in the boat, shirt and ragged jacket soaked with water, skinny bare legs splayed out beneath him. He stared back at them with a blank sort of expression, concerned but calm, as the river carried him past them and spun the boat around. Damien and Tommy turned to look at each other, incredulous.

"Gaffer!" Damien shouted, but Rudolph didn't turn. A minute later the boat and its occupant were out of sight.

Further upriver, two more of the companions were also stranded, but this time on dry land. Samson had dived in to help Joey, but the current had proved to strong for him to reach the Portuguese, and it was all he could do to fight his way to the surface and remain afloat. After a minute, he had sighted his target, a little way downriver from him and further towards the left bank. Joey was splashing wildly, but seemed to be making some progress towards the bank, so Samson had breathed deeply and set out towards him, trying desperately to keep himself on course in the disorientating and hostile water.

For a few minutes, Samson had kept up his stroke, his muscles burning with the exertion. Pausing for a moment, he had looked up and seen that he was close to the edge of the river, and could make out a slim, rocky section of river bank beneath a tall cliff. This cliff continued downriver, but fell straight to the water. Joey was nowhere to be seen. Thinking quickly, Samson had set out again, redoubling his effort to reach the tiny bank. If he had missed the bank, he would have been swimming towards sheer rock, and he had no idea how far down the river the cliff ran.

As he had begun to worry that he would not make the bank, his feet grazed against the rocky floor of the river. Powering himself forward, he had touched the floor with all four limbs and continued to crawl out of the unruly river. As he reached the bank, he had noticed Joey, and also realised why he had not been visible earlier. Joey was lying on his front, his lower body submerged in the water, while his head lay just upon the bank, his back emerging from and disappearing into the water as he took huge, panting breaths.

Relieved, Samson crawled over and patted him on the back.

"Come on, my friend, we must pull you out of the river" Samson said, but got no reaction from Joey.

Samson put hands under Joey's armpits and began to try to drag him to safety. Without warning, Joey lashed out. Screaming words that

Samson didn't understand, Joey flailed his arms back, fists clenched, and caught Samson on the mouth with the back of his knuckles. Samson let go, stepping back and putting his hand to his mouth, to find blood flowing from where his lip had been split. Joey turned around now, wild-eyed, fists still clenched, and for a moment he looked as if he was about to attack the Ghanaian.

Gradually, Joey's red mist faded, and he looked about himself, taking in the churning river, the sheer cliff and the small rocky bank they had escaped to. Turning back to Samson, he seemed as if he was about to speak, and then turned away, sitting down facing the cliff with his head buried between his arms. A soft sobbing sound came from the hunched figure as his shoulders heaved.

Samson licked the salty blood from his lip as he stood there, perplexed. His natural instinct was to comfort the other man, but Joey seemed unbalanced and erratic. He decided to leave Joey to himself for a while – hopefully the younger man would feel better after letting his pent-up emotions out.

Bending down, Samson washed his mouth in the river, the cold water stinging his cut. The pain was strangely exhilarating, pushing the tiredness and gloominess from his mind and replacing it with a cool kind of clarity. Crouching there with his hands in the water, watching the river race by, he was struck by a vivid memory.

In his youth, he and his older brother, Daniel, had spent many a hazy Sunday afternoon playing in the river near where they grew up. After the morning service at their church, the two of them would change out of their good clothes as fast as possible and race down to the river which lay two or three miles from their home, where they would paddle, swim and dive in the cool waters. When the afternoon began to fade, they would walk home, tired but happy, singing the songs they had learned in church that morning.

Samson grinned. Although the river he was currently surrounded by was far more wild and dangerous than the river of his youth, he could almost picture himself and his brother splashing and laughing in front of him. Overtaken by nostalgia, he began to sing a hymn to himself, quietly at first, but then growing as his strong tenor voice was given full reign. By the time he reached the second verse, his voice was louder than the rushing of the river.

"Shut up!" Joey screamed suddenly, his voice cracking with temper.

Samson, shocked out of his reminiscence, turned around incredulously. Joey was breathing heavily, his face pale and blotchy. His chin had receded almost entirely into this throat and his eyes were wild and unfocused.

"Why singing?" Joey continued to rant. "What is good here? Nothing for singing!"

"We are still alive!" Samson replied, confused by Joey's outburst.

"Alive? This is not being alive. This is worse than being dead. I would rather not be alive than to be here."

"You do not mean that, brother." Samson replied, trying to calm the other man down.

Joey showed no signs of calm, though. If anything, Samson's words seemed to enrage Joey further.

"I am not your brother! I do not even care for you! I would care for some proper food, food for human people. I would care for some clothes to wear. I would care to be sleeping not in mud. I would care not to be always too hot or too cold. But you? You I do not care."

Samson was silent for a moment as Joey sat there, shoulders heaving. He felt angry. If he had not dived in to this river to help Joey, he would still be aboard the boat, or at least with his other friends. Samson had done nothing other than try to raise Joey's spirits, but the younger man just spoken to him with contempt and disrespect. Anger was not a common emotion for Samson, but the more he dwelled on this, the angrier he became. It was not a good feeling. Samson felt a knot building in his throat as he sat there, frowning. He had to stop himself feeling this way – it was upsetting his spirit.

Taking a deep breath, Samson began to sing again, as loudly as before, but this time he was deaf to Joey's protests. And protest, Joey did. He began by telling Samson to be quiet, but when this had no effect, he started to scream in his native Portuguese, a constant stream of what were most likely insults. Samson carried on singing, oblivious to Joey's ongoing tantrum.

After a few minutes, Joey was horse with shouting, and finally became silent, literally quivering with outrage. He glanced about deliriously, and seemed for a moment to be considering jumping back into the river, but his eyes settled on the cliff behind him. It was about eight metres high, and practically vertical, although a few outcropping stones and dry roots suggested that ascent might be possible.

Joey took two strides and then leaped upwards, catching hold of an ancient root that stuck out of the hard, dry earth of the cliff. Feeling with his toes, he found a foothold and pushed himself higher, towards another root which curled out of the cliff and back in again. Swinging with his arm and pushing with his leg, he sprung up and caught on to the natural handhold. He steadied himself again, finding another foothold and looked up for his next target.

This would be harder. The next clear handhold was almost a foot further up, and he would have to pull himself up there with just his arms. He took a few breaths, trying to block out Samson's infuriating voice, and strained with his arms. Gradually he levered himself up until he could let go with one hand and grab on to the small ledge just above.

The physical activity was clearing Joey's mind of the rage he had been consumed by a moment before. He found himself admiring his own athleticism and courage. It was a shame, he thought, that no one important was here to witness this, or to take photographs. He must look impressive with his bare, lightly muscled physique as he fought against the perilous cliff. It would prove wrong the people who spoke badly of him, who said that he was fragile and somewhat effete. He looked sideways, watching his shoulder tense as he pulled himself up to the small ledge.

Without warning, the dry earth that he had been hanging on to crumbled beneath his fingers, and he fell, barely having time to yell before he hit the rocky shore below.

Samson recognised the serious tone in Joey's voice as he screamed, and stopping his singing he turned around sharply. Joey lay on his back, head twisted towards Samson as he lay still and silent. Samson rushed over immediately, putting his fingers to the unconscious man's throat to test for a pulse.

"Alive", he said to himself in relief.

Carefully turning Joey's head so that it faced upwards, he noticed a livid cut just above and to the side of the right eyebrow. Dark blood trickled out of it and dripped on the pale rock beneath Joey's head.

"I am sorry, my friend." Samson said softly, feeling sick with himself.

Half a mile downriver, four more of the companions finished their hectic journey down the rapids. Marco, Woody, Raphaël and Emil had all fallen from the dinghy soon after it had collided with the rock, and rather than attempt to swim towards the distant river banks, had focused all their energy on staying afloat and avoiding collisions with rocks or other obstructions. At one point, the dinghy floated by a few metres away, and Marco struck out to try and catch hold of it, but it was travelling faster than them and was soon out of their range.

The five minutes they spent fighting to keep their heads above water seemed like much longer as they were pulled this way and that at the will of the river. At roughly the same time, they came to a drop in the river, where the water fell a metre or so into a wider, calmer stretch of river, and haphazardly they flew over it one by one. Plunging deep into the water, they hit the rocky bottom, each receiving a bruise or two.

Now that the flow of the water had eased off, they put their feet to the river bed, finding that they were able to stand about chest deep in the water. Hearts still racing from their perilous experience, they quickly waded towards the right-hand bank of the river, where the water became shallow enough that they were only waist-deep.

"Fell right on my bloody arse!" Marco grimaced, rubbing his bruise.

"Yeah, I got my shoulder." Woody said, holding his hand around a nasty-looking graze.

"We are very lucky, I think", said Email, arching his back painfully. "Everyone is alright."

All of the four men, except for Raphaël, nodded. It was then that they noticed the Martiniquan's distress. Raphaël was taking short, laboured breaths, and was wearing an expression of worry and queasiness as he lightly held his left arm, which was hanging by his side.

"What's wrong, mate?" Marco asked.

"My arm", Raphaël replied shakily. "When we fall. At first not pain, but now.... It is bad."

"Can you make it to the bank?" Marco said, wading over to help. "Lean on me if you like."

Raphaël reached out with his right arm, holding on to Marco's shoulder as he shuffled slowly toward the bank. As soon as they reached the edge of the river, the injured man sat down, eyelids fluttering as if he was about to faint.

"Okay, take it easy", Emil said, kneeling next to Raphaël. "Have big breaths, it will be better."

Raphaël nodded weakly and closed his eyes, trying to control his breathing.

"Let me see your arm", the Dutchman went on, supporting the weight of Raphaël's injured arm as he gently ran his other hand along it.

"Ah, putain!" Raphaël screamed as Emil's hand touched a swollen area of his arm a few inches above the wrist.

"Sorry", Emil said softly. "Please try to take the pain while I feel this bad area."

Raphaël nodded again, clenching his teeth and looking away. His breathing came in shuddering gasps as Emil ran his hands carefully around the inflamed area of the arm.

After a moment, Emil took his hand away, frowning.

"What's up, mate?" Marco asked. "How bad is it?"

"This one bone here, at the top", Emil replied gravely. "I think it is broken."

Raphaël turned to face him, fearfully.

"Is there anything we can do?" Woody asked. "You know, like make a stretcher?"

"Well, he can walk okay, but we must keep the arm straight. We must make – I am not sure how you call it – a 'spilk'. Some pieces of wood that are tied to keep the arm straight."

"Oh yeah, a splint", Woody prompted.

"Sure. We will need something like string or tape to make it strong. If you will stay with Raphaël, make sure he is safe, and Marco will come with me to look for things to make the...."

"Splint", Woody prompted. "Yeah, no problem. I'll stay here with him."

"Just give us a holler if you need us, mate", Marco added as he and Emil rose and set off into the undergrowth nearby.

For a few minutes, Woody listened to the rustling of their friends as the moved about nearby, occasionally shouting to one another.

Turning back to Raphaël, he became nervous. The injured man was lying with his back to a tree trunk, eyes closed, and breathing shallowly. A heavy sheen of sweat covered his brow. Woody was nervous. Unsure of whether he should disturb Raphaël, and possibly make him more uncomfortable, or whether he should keep the man focussed and conscious, eventually decided to speak to the man.

"You alright, mate?" Woody asked softly.

Raphaël didn't stir as the seconds went by. Woody decided to raise his voice.

"Raph! Wake up!"

With a sudden intake of breath, Raphaël opened his eyes, glancing about disorientatedly. Eventually his gaze settled on Woody's face and remained there.

"It hurts!" He said, weakly.

"Yeah, I know, mate", Woody replied, searching for some words of comfort. "Well, it'll get better soon, okay?

Raphaël contemplated these words for a moment.

"It will? How do you know this?"

"Well, you know", Woody paused, lost for words. "Things always heal up, don't they?"

The injured man nodded slightly, looking away, but then turned back to Woody with a frown.

"Here? In this place?"

"What's that, mate?"

"It will heal, here? In this wild place? I am not sure."

Woody scratched his head, looking for something to say to cheer his team mate up.

"At least it wasn't your leg, you know? You won't be out for long!"

"Out? Oh, you mean I will play football again. I hope you are right, but I think I will not live for much time out here."

Woody reacted by clasping the other man gently on the shoulder. He was lost for words that would comfort his friend. Raphaël closed his eyes for a few minutes, and then opened them once more, turning to Woody with an earnest expression on his face.

"Ten thousand people!" He said, pronouncing each syllable precisely.

"You what?" Woody replied, confused.

"Ten thousand people, I had to greet me from the aircraft, last summer when I return. They were filling the streets. You know how many people we have in Martinique? In the whole country?"

"No, mate. Tell me."

"Four hundred thousand. One person in every forty was there to greet me, in the streets. They carry banners, like it was a carnival!"

"Yeah, there's no feeling like it! It's like, you know, when you're in a magazine, and you're reading it, and you're thinking 'There's thousands of other people out there reading about me!'. You know what I mean, right? You've been in magazines?"

"Only once. But it is a great feeling. I would like it again!" Raphaël paused for a moment, frowning. "But I do not think it will happen again. I do not think I will ever get out of this place."

Raphaël's pessimism had started to depress Woody's naturally buoyant nature, but after a long pause for thought, he replied. "We'll all get out of here. And just think, you know, we'll all be heroes. Even more than normal! Specially you, mate." Woody was grinning now, and gesturing with his hand. "Imagine the headlines. 'Caribbean Star Survives Jungle Trek With Broken Arm'. What do you reckon? You'll be like a legend!"

Raphaël gave a quick snort of laughter, and then gazed out at the river, a faint smile playing on his mouth.

"Thank you, friend. I hope you are right."

The two men sat, gazing ahead, each happily lost in their private world of fame and glory. After some time, they heard approaching footsteps, and presently Marco and Emil emerged from the tree line a short way downriver from them, clutching various pieces of dried plant matter.

"You alright, guys?" Marco asked, surprised to find the two of them in fair spirits.

Woody nodded, moving aside so that Marco and Emil could get close enough to Raphaël to tend to his injury. Laying down the pieces they had collected in a small pile, Emil started to sort through for the most suitable ones.

"This will be good for tying with – where did you find it?" The Dutchman asked

"Oh, that's some old dried-out ivy or something like that, mate", Marco replied. "It seemed pretty tough and flexible so I brought a load of it."

"Yes, it will work, I think. We will need the four straightest pieces of wood we have. Not too thick, but maybe thirty or forty centimetres long. This one is good."

Marco helped size up the pieces of drier wood that they had collected. After a minute, they had selected the most suitable pieces, and with some trepidation, Emil turned to Raphaël, who had been watching them warily as they worked.

"This will probably hurt quite a bit, but I will try to be as quick as I can", Emil said in what he hoped was a reassuring voice.

Raphaël leaned away slightly as if he was going to refuse, but after a moment he nodded slowly and turned away, leaving Emil to begin work on the injured arm.

Gently, he picked up Raphaël's arm and laid it flat on top of his leg. Placing the first piece of wood against the outside of the arm, at the bottom.

"Marco, please hold this here", Emil requested.

As Marco held the long, straight pieces of wood in place, Emil added them one by one, until the four pieces were pressed evenly around Raphaël's arm, starting just below the elbow and finishing just past the wrist. Raphaël had his eyes closed and was wincing, but had not yet cried out.

"Good. Marco, keep those pieces there and I will try to tie them. Raphaël?" Emil waited for the injured man to turn and look at him. "This may be the most painful part. Please, you must try to stay still even if you are having pain."

Raphaël grimaced, nodding resignedly, as Emil lifted the arm slightly and passed the makeshift twine under it. Tying as strong a knot as he could, he continued slowly along the arm, wrapping the twine around the arm and splints, tying it off when he reached the end of the twine and starting again. As he came level with the break, Raphaël started to whimper softly.

"I am sorry. Only a few minutes more now and we are finished."

Emil continued to secure the splints while Raphaël drew shuddering breaths.

"Hold on, mate!" Marco said, nodding towards Raphaël's face. The Martiniquan was sweating profusely, his head and shoulders covered in moisture, and his eyelids were fluttering, while his eyes seemed to be rolling back.

"Raphaël!" Emil said forcefully, but there was no response. "Woody, go to the river and collect some water in your hands, please. Quickly!"

Woody reacted without question, plunging his cupped hands into the cool, shaded water at the edge of the river and carrying it back with visible concentration.

"On his head, please", Emil directed.

Woody carefully released the water on to Raphaël's face, watching it run down his forehead, into his eyes and down his cheeks. Raphaël shook his head in surprise, but his eyes were back in focus. He was now taking slow, laboured breaths and looking directly into Emil's eyes with an almost outraged expression.

"More water?" Emil asked, warily.

Raphaël stared fiercely at Emil for a few seconds more, then shook his head.

"Finish it!" He said hoarsely.

Emil nodded and set to work again, trying to finish off quickly but carefully. After another agonising minute, Emil tied off the last piece of twine and sat back, sighing.

"It is done?" Raphaël asked.

Emil nodded, wiping the sweat from his own eyes.

"But it still hurts. More than before."

"It will hurt for some time, I think. But this will keep your arm straight, so you cannot move the wrist. Maybe then it can heal. You must try to keep it very still also", Emil advised as he went to the river himself to splash water on his face.

"Okay", Raphaël said, and then after a long pause, "Thank you."

"You are welcome", Emil grinned.

"Looks like you're turning into a tree, mate!" Marco joked, trying to cheer Raphaël up.

Raphaël smiled weakly, looking down at his heavily strapped arm.

"Don't worry, Raph", Woody said, sitting by his side again. "We can take it off before the press get there, you know, when we're rescued."

Gavin came back to consciousness with a start. A hideous smell assaulted his senses and his head throbbed as if it was about to burst. He was facing upwards, face and shoulders held above the water by something soft yet slimy, while his legs dangled to the river bed. Unsure of how he had got to where he was, he splashed himself upright and turned.

The first thing he noticed was soft, slimy object which he had been planted in up until a second ago. It was some sort of jam on one side of the river, just next to the bank. Debris had collected there – leaves, branches, dead fish, weeds and various other objects – and had rotted there, like a floating compost heap. It was from here that the obnoxious smell was emanating.

Gavin's natural reaction was to gag, and as his head throbbed again, he could feel bile rising in his throat. Fighting this reaction, he waded as fast as he could upriver, away from the stinking mess, and plunged his head and shoulders into the river to wash off the stinking slime that he could feel clinging to him.

Surfacing again, he turned back with a grimace to look downriver. Two large rats had made their way down on to the rotting mass and were foraging in it for any scraps that were still vaguely edible. Gavin swore, turning away to avoid having to look at the filth that he had recently been slumbering among. Fighting back his compulsion to vomit, he waded further upriver, keeping close to the bank on his right-hand side.

After a few minutes he turned back, and the compost has thankfully hidden from view by some overhanging shrubs. Finally able to think straight, he realised that he was still carrying the rucksack on his back, the arms straps held in place by the strap across his chest. Making his way to the bank, he sat down against it and tried to piece together what had happened to him.

He remembered being in the dinghy, and colliding with a rock. He had been thrown out of the boat and had fought against the angry river to stay afloat. The next part seemed like a blur, but he distinctly remembered noticing that he was coming to a sharp drop in the river, and worrying that it was a waterfall. This was his last memory, but the throbbing in his head suggested that he had been knocked unconscious.

He raised his left hand to his head slowly, gradually and gently probing his scalp for damage. He yelped as he found the source of his pain, a swollen lump towards the back of his head, which throbbed warmly. Pulling his hand back, he saw that it had red streaks of blood where he had touched his wound.

With his other hand, he reached around to touch his back. There was blood there, too. The cut was clearly a large one, considering all the blood that had seeped from it in such a short time. With a cold feeling of disgust, he realised that his wound had been buried in the rot for all the time he had been there, however long that may have been. He was no expert on medical things, but he was fairly sure that an open wound shouldn't be exposed to filth like that. With a shiver, he took the rucksack off and pushed himself back into the river to lay his head back in the water, shaking it around gently in an attempt to clean it.

The coolness of the water seemed to help, and after some time, the throbbing subsided to a bearable level, although Gavin realised with a sense of unease that if there were any creatures in the river which meant him harm, he would have sent out a beacon to them by now, what with all the blood he had shed into this water. This thought preyed on his mind for a few minutes more until he decided to retreat to the safety of dry land.

Touching his head once more, he could feel a lump about the size of a fried egg yolk, with an inch-long cut splitting it. It was still painful but was no longer making him feel queasy. Taking his hand away, there was still a small amount of blood, but this did suggest that the bleeding was at least dying down.

It was then that he realised just how alone he was. He had no idea whether his friends were upriver or downriver from where he was, or even if they were still alive. Assuming they were alive, he wondered whether they were even looking for him, or if they had left him for dead. He could have been unconscious for any length of time. If the rest of the men had continued without him, they may be a long way away by now. He was, perhaps, the only person for miles around. Chilled by this thought, he looked up and realised that it would only be an hour or so until sundown. The thought of having to spend a night alone here made him shiver.

Standing up, he began to yell. Some of the time he called the names of his friends, and sometimes just a wordless shout. After a few minutes of shouting, he heard a rushing in his ears, and started to feel faint. Forced to sit against a tree, his breathing became laboured. The rushing sound in his ears increased and sweat began to form on his face.

In his confused state, Gavin tried to think. Perhaps he was still concussed from the blow to his head. Maybe he had lost more blood than he thought. The exertion of shouting, as well as his realisation of how alone he was had probably magnified these things, so that he now felt like he was about to pass out. Perhaps, he wondered grimly, he had injured himself worse than he thought. Gradually, his head lolled back and his arms went slack.

Samson and Joey gazed out over the forest canopy before them. The last half hour had seen Joey regain consciousness, and have Samson tend his wound. The bruise around Joey's temple had swollen painfully, and was in the process of turning a rich, dark purple. Joey was sullen and silent, ignoring Samson's apologies and attempts to cheer him up, and had only reacted with a slight nod when Samson volunteered himself to climb the cliff. Moving slowly and carefully, Samson had eventually scaled the obstacle, and proceeded to help Joey climb up.

They stood on a rocky slope, which fell gradually away on all three sides to the forest below. Dry grasses and small shrubs poked out from between the rocks and stones that covered the slope. To the left and right, along the river, the jungle continued as far as they could see, and ahead of them, it fell away into a huge valley.

"Enormous", Samson commented, overawed and intimidated by the panorama around him.

Joey continued to stare ahead of himself, arms folded.

"We should try to find our other friends, yes?" Samson suggested, and was answered with a shrug by the tight-lipped Joey.

"Yes, well we need to stay close to the river, they will have stopped the boat and waited for us, I hope."

Samson waited for an acknowledgement, but when none was offered, he pointed to his right, where the rocky slope led into the jungle as it followed the water downriver.

"This way, I think."

The two men picked their way carefully among the sharp rocks and stones and were soon under the cover of the jungle canopy once more. Staying on the river bank was not always possible due to the wild undergrowth, and often Samson found himself leading them in a zigzag pattern so that they kept the river in sight most of the time.

It was hard going. The last time they had walked through the jungle, they had all had footwear. Now that they were barefoot, they had to pick their way carefully, and often ended up hurting their feet on sharp stones and twigs or stinging plants. After half an hour, they had made very little progress, and Samson halted, grimacing.

"It is hard work. Maybe we will not even see them in this jungle." Samson said, stretching his back. "I will try shouting, maybe they are near."

Joey shrugged again and leaned back against a tree, turning his head to look away. Samson sighed, cupped his hands to his mouth and began to shout. His voice seemed dead and dampened in the claustrophobic jungle, and after a few minutes he gave up. Slumping down against another tree, Samson closed his eyes and tried to relax his mind. His exertions in the river and climbing the cliff, as well as the oppressive, sticky heat, had made him exhausted, and he felt himself slipping into sleep. Glad of a short break from the drudgery of the day, he let himself slip further.

After what seemed like a few seconds, he was shaken awake by a clearly agitated Joey.

"Wake up! There is something here!" The Portuguese was saying to him, as he glanced about nervously.

"What? What do you want?" Samson asked, groggy and disorientated.

"Listen!" Joey replied, gesturing towards a thick area of tall shrubs roughly fifteen metres away.

The two men crouched in silence, straining their ears for any sound, but only the background noise of the jungle could be heard. After a few minutes, Samson turned to Joey, trying not to let his exasperation show.

"What did you hear?" He asked.

As soon as Samson had spoken, a strange roaring, snorting sound came from the bushes Joey had pointed to earlier. Both men sprang up, eyes wide with shock.

"What is it?" Joey whispered hoarsely.

Samson shook his head, trying to think. It didn't sound like any animal he had heard before. To him, it sounded more like some kind of demon or evil spirit.

"Should we run?" Joey whispered, poking Samson's ribs top get his attention.

"Run where?" Samson whispered back, trying to shake the supernatural kind of fear that was growing in him. "We have bare feet. We cannot even walk fast. This thing may not be dangerous. It may not have heard us. Stay quiet."

The two men remained motionless for a few more minutes, their heartbeats gradually returning to normal. Suddenly, the noise started again, louder this time, and also seemed to be coming from another position behind them. Joey stared at Samson imploringly, as if hoping for some ingenious solution to their peril. Samson shrugged, and began to pray under his breath, while Joey turned this way and that, trying to catch a glimpse of the beasts. The noises continued on and off for another minute, sometimes one side becoming louder and sometimes the other. Both men were visibly shaking with fear and adrenalin by now, and when suddenly the bushes began to rustle violently, their bodies sprang into action.

Samson bent his knees and elbows into a fighting stance, glancing left and right with wild eyes, while Joey emitted a high-pitched screech and bolted, running off in the clearest direction that led away from the beasts.

Almost immediately, the sounds changed to mocking laughter, which disquieted Samson even further, until Damien crawled from the bushes ahead on his hands and knees, face creased with amusement. Relaxing and looking behind him, Samson saw Tommy emerge from the other bush, pointing his finger in the direction Joey had run off, doubled over in laughter.

The two men made their way over to Samson, who was shaking his head with relief

"Not funny!" he scolded, but was clearly making an effort not to laugh himself.

"Not funny? Did you see Joey?" Tommy asked between guffaws.

Samson looked in the direction Joey had run off, and after a few seconds, saw him return. Joey was striding purposefully back, eyes stormy and chin receded.

"Christ, it's the bloody Elephant Man!" Damien exclaimed, pointing to Joey's disfiguring bruises.

By now, Joey was a few metres from the three men, and didn't appear to be slowing. He covered the last two strides at a jog and launched himself at Damien, fists flailing recklessly. Damien, taken by surprise, could only back away, blocking Joey's swings when possible.

"Chill out!" Damien managed to say as he defended himself. "Just a joke!"

Samson, who had been trying to calm Joey down with words, then stepped in and grabbed the enraged man around the chest, dragging him backwards. Joey writhed for a moment more and then went limp, after which Samson let him slump to the floor. Tommy was laughing even harder now, hardly even able to breathe.

"What's his problem, man?" Damien asked, rubbing his cheek where it had been punched. "He's flipped!"

"He's had a bad day", Samson replied softly, wanting to diffuse the situation.

"We've all had a bad day, like. Doesn't mean we have to act like nutters!"

"Yes, well I am glad we have found you. Where are the others?"

"I dunno, man, it's just us two. We got knocked off the boat, all of us. Me and Tommy managed to grab on to a rock and then swam to the bank when we were rested up."

Samson was silent in thought for a moment, as Tommy's laughter gradually died down.

"That was a classic!" The teenager said, face flushed. "Wish we had that on camera!"

Damien winked back at Tommy, grinning and giving him a silent thumbs-up sign so as not to provoke Joey any further.

"Did you see anyone else in the water? Are they further along?"

Samson asked presently.

"Nah, not really. Well, we saw the gaffer. He was in the boat, all on his own. Didn't seem to recognise us."

Samson's forehead creased in concern. "Then we should keep going along the river. At least we know that there is someone else that way."

"Fair enough, Sams. Nothing better to do, anyway."

Tommy, Damien and Samson walked a short way onwards, and then turned back to wait for Joey, who was gradually picking himself up off the ground.

"Should have seen yourself, mate", Tommy said as the other man sidled indignantly towards them. "Never seen you take off that fast before!"

An hour later, Damien, Tommy, Joey and Samson had made very little progress through the dense jungle. As they continued on, the terrain had become less rocky and the ground softer. Rounding the trunk of a large tree, they were forced to halt as they reached an area of stinking, swampy water. Holding their noses, they glanced along the muddy area and saw that it stretched for some distance to their left, roughly at a right angle to the path of the river. They retreated a short distance back, away from the smell, to discuss their options.

"That smells rank, man." Damien said, grimacing.

"It is not very wide though. We should be able to cross it in a few minutes", Samson suggested.

"I dunno. Couldn't we walk round it?"

"We could try. But it is getting dark, and we do not know how far it stretches for. I do not mind, but I think we should get across as quickly as we can and then find a place near the river to spend the night."

Samson raised his eyes, looking at Joey and Tommy for their opinions. Joey, still sulking, shrugged his shoulders and looked away. Tommy considered his options for a moment, looking towards the swamp and back into the depths of the jungle with an expression of distaste.

"Yeah, okay. I agree with Sams", the teenager said with a sigh.

"Alright then, but we'll stink of swamp for a week after", Damien warned.

"Would have thought you'd be used to that, Damo", Tommy replied with a grin as he followed Samson back towards the swampy ground.

"Oy, you cheeky git!", Damien said, flicking the back of Tommy's ear.

The smell got worse as they proceeded into the swampier ground and their feet sank in up to their ankles and made a squelching sound as they withdrew them. Once they were about half way across, the mud started to get deeper, and after a few more steps, they were sinking in half way up their shins. The sticky mud made movement awkward, and the men found themselves stretching their arms out to balance as they gradually dragged their legs out of the morass. Tommy lost his balance and toppled over, covering his legs and chest with stinking mud. He picked himself up, cursing, as Damien chuckled and Joey smirked.

"Hold on", Samson said, halting and raising his arm. "I think we are sinking!"

"You what?" Damien replied, looking down at his own feet. Sure enough, he was very gradually sinking lower into the swamp.

"Oh shite, man, you're right. Come on, lads, it's not far. Let's get a move on!"

Damien then charged ahead as fast as he was able to in the pool of syrup-like mud. Panicked, the other men squelched their way after him, waving their arms this way and that as they struggled. It soon became clear that they were not going to reach the firmer ground that lay a few metres ahead of them. The mud was now above their knees, and struggling only seemed to make it worse.

"We must go back!" Samson suggested, trying to turn himself round.

"How?" Tommy replied, his voice tinged with fear. "I can't move!"

"Me neither, mate. Totally stuck", Damien added.

"What are we gonna do then? I'm still going down!"

"Stay calm, my friends", Samson said, trying to hide his own fear. "I saw it somewhere that you should lie flat when you are sinking."

"What, in this crap?" Tommy asked incredulously.

"Yes, I think so. It will stop you from sinking."

The men grimaced, cursing, and gradually laid themselves down in the putrid mud. Their heads and bodies sank in a few inches, but then remained stationary on top of the swamp.

"So, what now?" Tommy asked after a moment.

"I don't know. I am thinking", Samson replied.

"This is perfect!" Joey began, his voice cracking with exasperation. "I want to say thank you all, for my wonderful experience!"

"Yeah alright, Jo-Jo", Damien sighed. "We're all in the same mud, right? All having the same experience."

"Yes, and for you I have special thanks. You are the fool who made us all run in to this deep mud!"

Damien, momentarily lost for words, grabbed a handful of sticky mud and threw it towards Joey, scoring a hit on the man's neck. Joey, shocked, picked up his own handful and threw it back, screaming Portuguese obscenities. The two men continued to hurl mud at each other, both giving in to the frustration and hardship of the last few days and releasing their pent-up anger. Tommy found the situation too funny to intervene, and simply laughed at them. Samson, unable to move, did his best to calm the two men, but his words were ignored.

Suddenly, a deep, booming laughter came from the bank ahead of them, causing the fighting men to stop.

"What the..?" Damien began, sitting up slightly to peer in the direction of the laughter with his one eye that wasn't covered in mud.

"Alright, lads?" Said Gavin, who had just walked out of the tree line and was standing at the edge of the solid ground, chuckling at his friends' situation. "If you were gonna go mud-wrestling, you could have invited me!"

"Gav, mate!" Damien exclaimed. "Bit stuck here. Can you help us out, like?"

"Who's that? Damo?" Gavin asked, still chuckling. "Or the Creature from the Black Lagoon? Can't really tell. Sit tight then, lads, I'll see what I can do."

"Don't worry, skipper", Damien replied. "We're not going anywhere."

The four stranded men lay in silence for a few minutes as their heartbeats returned to normal. Presently, Gavin appeared again at the edge of the swamp, hefting a long, thick tree branch. He threw the branch out into the swamp, holding on to one end while the other landed close to Damien, who grabbed on to it with both hands. Sitting down at the edge of the swamp, Gavin strained and pulled the branch gradually, as if in a tug-of-war, inching Damien slowly out of the mud.

After a few minutes, Damien had been dragged free, and Gavin pulled the other three men out one by one. In silent agreement the men headed straight towards the river, a few minutes' walk away, to wash the foul mud off.

"Smelling nice, lads!" Gavin commented as they walked.

6

Gavin lay awake, sweating. In the pitch dark, all the sounds of the jungle seemed amplified, making them sound alarmingly close. It was a humid, oppressive night, and the mosquitoes were out in force, landing on his face and body and causing him to swat ineffectually at them. His head had been aching ever since he had laid down, a deep, throbbing ache in the back of his skull. Lying on his back had been impossible due to the wound on his head, and when he lay on his side, the hard, unyielding ground pressed his shoulder into his body.

It had started growing dark by the time Gavin had dragged his friends out of the swamp. After they had cleaned themselves up, there was barely enough light to see by, and the five of them had settled down near the river to eat the banana and mango which Gavin still had at the bottom of his rucksack. Their half-hearted conversation soon dried up, each man retreating into his own world, and judging by the snoring that erupted at various intervals, fell deep asleep.

Gavin was unable to sleep properly, though. Unsettling thoughts ran through his mind, mixing with the hum and twitter of the jungle, and he had drifted in and out of consciousness. When he did sleep, he was plagued by vivid and disturbing dreams, which often took place in darkness, causing him to be even more disorientated when he awoke.

At one point, after he had lain awake for what seemed like some time after a particularly intense dream, he could swear that he heard someone talking. The sound seemed close, but too far away to be his friends, unless they had walked off.

"Boys?" Gavin said, sitting upright. "Damo? Tommy? That you?"

There was silence for a moment, and then the voice started again, softer this time. It seemed to be English, but the words were muttered and incomprehensible, and were followed by a soft chuckle.

"Is anyone there?" Gavin called out again, but was once more met with silence. "Is that you, Damo, playing silly buggers? It's not funny, mate. Give it a rest, right?"

There was silence again, and Gavin moved on his hands and knees, feeling for his friends in the darkness, just able to make out their faces in the tiny amount of moonlight that filtered through the thick clouds. All four of the men were there, apparently fast asleep.

Gavin crouched there for what seemed like half an hour, but the voice did not speak again. Eventually, he lay back down again and returned to his fitful sleep.

Much later on, Gavin was once more plagued by a nightmare. In his dream, he had been in the middle of a stampede. The sound had begun softly, a rumbling from far away, but had gradually grown louder. As it grew closer, he had tried to sit up, but was rooted to the ground.

Suddenly, startled animals had come into view, at first just a few smaller deer and boars, but then a mass of animals of every sort, filling his view as they vaulted him, the sound of hooves and claws filling his ears.

He awoke with a start, looking around to find that it had started to grow light. It was another foggy morning, and the sounds of the jungle were deadened and muffled. He heard speaking again, this time in an unfamiliar language. Assuming he was still dreaming, he turned his head to look in the direction of the voice. Outlined against the mist was a group of three people, standing and watching him

Gavin lay there watching the strangers, waiting for the dream to change, but after a moment, he realised he was feeling cold. Although the mist lent his vision a dream-like quality, the coldness of the air and the hardness of the ground under his body were certainly real. With a start, he sprang from the floor into a crouch, his hands involuntarily making fists. His first thought was that the soldiers had finally tracked them down, but something about the stance and stature of their silhouettes made him think again. Tentatively, he called out.

"Alright? Who's there?"

His voice was deadened by the mist, and sounded almost like a whisper. The three strangers shared a few more words and then walked slowly towards Gavin, stopping a few metres in front of him. With relief, he saw they were certainly not soldiers, but his gaze still dropped warily to the weapons they were carrying.

The three were all men, and were all dressed very sparsely. The man standing slightly in front of the other two carried a worn machete, while the other two carried small bows, both with rough arrows notched, although they were not tensed, and were pointed away from him.

The man in front gestured towards Gavin and made some kind of comment, to which the other two men laughed. Gavin studied them more closely. The man with the machete was dressed only in a pair of dirty denim shorts. He was the tallest of the three, and very skinny, but his dark, wily eyes suggested a calculating mind.

The two taller men were also bare-chested, but wore more primitive loincloths made of what looked to be skins or furs. One of them carried a dead monkey, trussed together by its legs and slung over his shoulder. All three had tanned, Oriental features and faded, indistinct tattoos on their chests and shoulders. They seemed to be regarding Gavin with a mixture of confusion and amusement.

"Speak English?" Gavin asked hopefully.

His question was only greeted with blank stares, and he repeated himself more loudly. No recognition of his words registered in the men's' faces, and they began talking amongst themselves again, keeping wary eyes on Gavin. At a loss for what else to do, Gavin held his hands up in a placatory manner and turned to wake his companions up.

"What's going on, Gav?" Damien asked, looking momentarily shocked.
"I dunno, mate. They just turned up. At least they're not trying to kill us though."
"They speak any English?"
"Don't think so. At least, they don't understand me."
"That doesn't mean anything, mate", Damien replied. "A lot of English people don't understand you."
"You want to have a try then, Damo? Go ahead!"
Damien sidled towards the strangers, affecting a relaxed and friendly demeanour.
"Morning, fellas", he began. "How's tricks? Look, can you tell us where the nearest town is? Or just a telephone? You'd really be helping us out."
The three men backed off slightly, the leader raising his machete. They looked more confused than aggressive, but Damien took the hint and moved away, holding his palms towards them. Joey, who had been watching silently, now stood up and approached the strangers.
"Food? Do you have food?" He asked hopefully, miming the action of putting something in his mouth.
This provoked a positive reaction. The three men talked among themselves for a moment, and then looked back at Joey, seeming to have reached some sort of decision. The man with the machete waved his blade at the four of them and then gestured back in the direction they had come from. He and his friends then walked away, looking back at Gavin and his companions.
"We going with this lot, then?" Damien asked.
"Yeah, I reckon. Seems like they have food. Maybe even some transport or something." Gavin replied.
"Hold up then, lads", Damien called to the strangers as he set off after them. "Wait for us!"

The journey seemed to take somewhere between half an hour to an hour. In that time, the mist had cleared and the jungle had heated up. It was a dry, hazy heat, as opposed to the humid heat and rain of the past few days. Their newfound companions walked ahead, chattering to one another, laughing and occasionally casting a quizzical look back to check they were still being followed.
Presently, they came into an area where the jungle seemed to thin out somewhat, and evidence of civilisation could be seen in the trees and bamboo which had been cut down and laid in small piles. Ahead, they could make out the shape of a small hut, half nestling in the undergrowth and half poking out into the rough path they were following. As they drew closer, they could see that the hut's walls were made out of a bristly clay, and was roofed with branches of dry palm leaves. A child poked her head out of the hut as they walked by and watched them with

a look of wonder.

After a few minutes, more and more huts came into view, all of varying size and design but constructed of similar materials to the first one they had come across. They were led to a clear area where large, old logs formed a rough square and the embers of a fire smouldered in the centre. The man with the machete gestured towards the logs, and Gavin and his companions sat down, still unsure what to make of the tiny village they found themselves in. Saying a few words to his friends, the man walked off and entered one of the larger huts.

The other two men sat down opposite the new arrivals. One man grinned at them nervously while the other took out a small, crude knife and started to gut and skin the monkey he had been carrying.

"Christ, mate!" Damien exclaimed as the man pulled out the creature's intestines and threw them to the side. "Do you have to do that?"

"Leave him to it, Damo", Gavin said. "He might give us some."

"Oh fantastic", Damien replied, grimacing. "You'd eat that?"

"Bloody right I would! Hey, lads?" Gavin said, looking at Tommy, Joey and Samson, who all nodded solemnly, transfixed by the gory sight of their potential meal.

To take his mind off the unpleasantness of the butchered monkey, Damien decided to try communicating with the men again.

"Is there a phone here, fella?" He asked, standing up and addressing the grinning man. "Phone?"

Damien mimed holding a receiver to his ear and pressing buttons, making beeping noises as he pressed an invisible keypad. His friends sniggered at him, but the grinning man seemed none the wiser. Clearly disturbed by Damien's mining, he stood up and backed off a few steps before turning and disappearing inside a hut.

"Nice one, Damo. Think you got the message across there, mate", Gavin said, smirking. "I reckon he'll be back with a phone any moment now."

Damien shook his head, sighing, but then perked up when the man poked his head out of the hut, gesturing him over.

"How's that then, you sarky git?" Damien said, standing up. "Maybe he has got one!"

Hurrying over to the hut, Damien ducked inside and was silent for a moment. The other men glanced at each other, with a mixture of hope and fear, as if they were scared to believe that there could be a chance of communication with the outside world, but couldn't help imagining their salvation.

When Damien did reappear a moment later, their hearts sank as they saw he was only carrying a bundle of wood in his arms.

"No phone then?" Gavin asked half-heartedly.

Damien shook his head dejectedly.

"Plenty of bloody sticks, mind." He said, dumping his burden by the fire pit and slumping on a log.

The other man emerged from the hut carrying a wooden frame of some sort. Setting it down, he placed Damien's wood on the embers of the fire and blew on it until the flames caught. By this time, the monkey skinner had finished his gruesome task and set up the wooden frame, which now appeared to be some type of spit, over the fire, skewering the monkey on the central spike.

The companions watched with a kind of hypnotic fascination until they were interrupted by a high-pitched giggling from behind them. Looking round, they could see a group of three young children half-hidden behind a nearby hut, pointing at them and laughing. When they turned round, the children quickly disappeared fully behind the hut, although their giggling still gave them away.

Gavin, who had two young children of his own, grinned, glad of the diversion. Crouched, he crept quietly over to the hut until he was only just around the corner from the hidden children, and waited. After a moment, one of the children poked her head out again, and squealed when she saw Gavin crouched so close. She took off with the other two following her, and after they were about ten metres away they turned again, laughing so hard that they were practically bent double.

Chuckling himself, Gavin stood up, waving with his hands and making a kind of growling sound. The children jumped again, backing off slightly while whooping with laughter. This was short-lived, however, as one by one they became quiet and ran off, seemingly startled by something off to Gavin's left. Turning round, he saw that the man they had met earlier, who had carried the machete, was back, and was regarding Gavin with a look of disdain.

"Alright, mate?" He asked, determined not to let the other man make him feel foolish.

The man turned round, still giving Gavin a withering look, and waved him on, clearly expecting to be followed.

"Us too?" Damien asked him, standing up.

The man held his hand up towards Damien, shaking his head, and then waved Gavin on again.

"Just me, it looks like, lads", Gavin said warily.

"Alright, skipper. Just give us a holler if you need us."

Gavin nodded, following the man to the larger hut he had emerged from and ducking to enter as the man held back a hide curtain from the doorway.

It was dark inside, and the first thing that hit Gavin was the smell. It was a kind of damp, pungent smell, with undertones of smoke and sweat. Trying not to let his distaste show, he blinked, letting his eyes adjust to the dingy interior.

He could make out two men in the semi-darkness, and almost took a step back in shock when he saw the second man. Directly in front of him was a small, stooped man sitting on what appeared to be a pile of rugs. He wore various pieces of jewellery, and although his face was creased with wrinkles, his long hair remained a deep black. His sharp eyes regarded Gavin in a calculating way, reminiscent of the man who had ordered him inside. Gavin decided that this old man was probably the younger man's father.

But it was the man sitting to his right who startled him. Sitting on the bare floor, knees to his chest, arms wrapped around them, squatted a familiar face. The detached expression, silvery hair and single spectacle lens could only belong to Rudolph.

"Gaffer?" Gavin began, pausing for a moment to make sure his eyes weren't playing tricks on him. "That you?"

Rudolph gave a slight smile and inclined his head as if nodding politely. The other older man watched their reactions with interest and then spoke to Rudolph in his own language. Rudolph looked thoughtful for a moment, as if deciphering the foreign language, and then gave a slightly more positive nod and smile.

The old man regarded Gavin for a moment, the wily eyes making him feel slightly uncomfortable. Sitting back, the man started talking to Gavin, seemingly unaware that he would not be understood. When the man had finished, Gavin shrugged and shook his head, unsure how to react. The man paused for a moment, and then spoke to the man who Gavin guessed was his son. Nodding sharply, the son approached Gavin and pointed at the straps of the rucksack he was still wearing, and then gestured towards his father.

"Only a bit of fruit in here, mate", Gavin replied, grinning amiably.

The younger man was having none of this though, and repeated himself more loudly, eventually pulling the straps off Gavin's shoulders himself.

"Alright, steady on!" Gavin said, but thought better of struggling.

When the younger man had wrestled the rucksack from Gavin's back, he placed it down in front of his father and backed off again, watching Gavin suspiciously. The old man started rummaging through the pockets, pulling out a bruised and black banana before he eventually discovered the trophy, nestling at the bottom of the bag. Pulling it out, he gawped at it for a few minutes, turning it round in his hands.

"See, the thing is, um… Sir, is that's ours. It's really important, right?"

The old man held up his hand, still admiring the trophy, and then handed it to his son, who placed it on a rough table along with a number of other items.

"Seriously, mate, give us it back, can you?" Gavin said as he moved towards the table, arm outstretched.

The younger man reacted instantly, picking his machete up from the table behind him and holding it between himself and Gavin. His stance wasn't immediately threatening, but Gavin could tell by his expression that he would use the weapon if he had to.

"Take it easy, fella. You hang on to it for now, okay?" Gavin said, retreating a few steps and holding his hands up.

Sighing, Gavin shook his head, looking to Rudolph for some support, but the manager's expression was blank once more.

The old man started speaking again, this time addressing Rudolph, who turned with an expression of intense concentration. Once again, Rudolph nodded slowly deliberately. The old man turned once more to Gavin, studied him for a moment and then gestured towards the door. Unsure of what to do, Gavin stood there for a moment, but was quickly encouraged by the younger man and his machete that the best course of action was to leave.

With barely contained anger, Gavin stalked out of the hut, slamming the stick-woven door with an unsatisfactorily quiet crash. By the time he had reached the fireside, where Tommy, Damien, Samson and Joey were still gathered around the cooking monkey, his face had turned red with suppressed rage.

"Alright, mate?" Damien asked. "What's up?"

Gavin sat down heavily, shaking his head and avoiding eye contact. "Nothing. Just forget it, right?"

Damien and Tommy glanced at each other, deciding to keep quiet while Gavin was so clearly riled. And awkward silence descended on the group, and was thankfully ended by the monkey-skinner, who had been prodding the cooking delicacy with his knife, and with a grunt picked up the blackened stick holding the monkey and deposited it onto a small blanket of leaves he had placed on the ground.

Cutting off a leg, he wrapped it in one of the leaves and passed it to his friend, who tucked in enthusiastically. Cutting himself the other leg, the man was about to begin eating when he noticed that the four men opposite watching him with a mixture of longing and disgust. After sharing a few words with his friend, the man pointed at the butchered monkey with his knife, and then at the men opposite. All except Damien nodded enthusiastically. Prising four meagre chunks of flesh off the monkey's carcass, he wrapped them and passed one to each.

Gavin, Tommy, Samson and Joey looked at each other to see who would eat first. After a few seconds, Tommy shrugged and took a bite, chewing a few times and then nodding to his friends.

"It's alright, lads", he said, taking another bite.

Gavin and Joey needed no further prompting, and both started to devour their pieces. For a minute, the only sounds were the contented grunts of the men as they finished off the first meat they had eaten since the crash. Damien tried his best to ignore them.

"Not bad at all, eh?" Gavin said, licking his fingers. The food seemed to have improved his mood considerably.

"And it doesn't taste like chicken", Tommy replied.

"More like pork, I reckon. Hey, I wonder if we could get some of this imported back to England. It'd go down a treat with some mash and gravy."

"I was thinking monkey burgers."

"Monkey and kidney pie."

"Suckling monkey."

"Yeah, all right, fellas, I get the picture", Damien interrupted, sighing. "I'm off for a wander, then."

Shaking his head, Damien rose and looked about him. The meandering path along which they had entered the village continued on past the hut he had collected wood from. Wanting to take his mind off his own hunger, which had been made worse by watching his friends eat, he set off along the dusty track.

He was sure there must be something in the village that he could eat. He'd had nothing but fruit and a small amount of fish for days, and his stomach ached constantly. It was hard to admit it, but he had been seriously tempted to accept a piece of the roasted monkey. Perhaps if he went back and asked, it wouldn't be too late, he thought.

"Nah, the lads'd never let us live it down", he muttered to himself.

Damien had been walking with his head bowed, lost in thought, but was shocked out of his brooding by the sound of a gasp, not far off to his right. Following the sound, he saw a group of three women, sitting cross-legged under a canopy. All three were looking at him with a mixture of fear and fascination. Holding his hands up, he walked slowly towards them, not wanting to cause alarm. The women stood up, backing off as if they were about to run.

"It's alright, I'm not gonna hurt you", he said, stopping and standing still. "I was just after some food."

He began to make eating actions, and then rubbed his stomach, smiling with what he hoped was a friendly expression. Cautiously, the women moved slightly closer, coming out from under the shade of the canopy. Damien noticed that they all wore very striking jewellery. Their ears were distended with large golden earrings, and necklaces of coloured beads hung from their necks.

They talked among themselves for a moment, keeping a wary eye on Damien, and then one of them moved a few steps forward, studying him from head to toe. She was quite young, in her early twenties, Damien guessed, and although he wouldn't have called her beautiful, she had very pretty eyes, and he found himself grinning at her.

The young woman spoke to him, a short sentence that seemed to be some sort of question. Damien shrugged, shaking his head. He tried his eating mime again, and this time got a positive reaction. The woman nodded and turned away, keeping her curious eyes on him as she walked into the hut just next to the canopy they had been under.

A moment later, she returned with a small bunch of green bananas.

"Oh bloody hell, not bananas again", Damien moaned.

Damien shook his head gently at the woman, rubbing his stomach and making a pained expression. After a moment of confusion, the woman nodded and again and headed back into the hut. She was gone for longer this time, and Damien found himself smiling awkwardly back at the older women as they stared at him in silence, with disapproving expressions.

Thankfully, the younger woman came back again, carrying a coconut-sized muddy vegetable. As she got closer, he could see that it was some kind of root vegetable, something like a yam. Damien nodded excitedly, holding his hands out as the woman offered it to him. She stepped back once he had taken it, and regarded Damien again with her pretty eyes, this time smiling slightly at him.

"You're a diamond, sweetheart. Seriously, you've saved my life", Damien gushed, not caring that she wouldn't understand.

For a moment, they stood there and grinned at each other, but were soon interrupted by one of the other women, who began shouting in an angry way, pointing at Damien and then the younger woman. Still shouting, she strode over and grabbed the younger woman by the arm, dragging her back and making shooing motions towards Damien.

"All right, all right!" Damien said, backing off. "I'm going. Thanks for the yam thing, though, I owe you one!"

He winked at the younger woman and turned around, as if to head back to the fire, but his way was barred. The Chief's son stood in his way, machete unsheathed and anger in his eyes. He shouted a few words to the women behind, who replied irritably and scurried out of view. The man turned his angry eyes towards Damien, who was genuinely worried that the man would use his machete. Shouting, the man pointed back in the direction of the fire pit with his weapon.

"All right, mate. Chill out. I was only asking for a bit of food, right?" Damien said nervously, as he held his hands up and hurried away.

The man was still shouting at him and waving his machete when they reached the fire.

"What's going on?" Gavin said, standing up and getting between Damien and the angry man.

"He's a bloody lunatic." Damien replied, happy for Gavin to intervene.

The man carried on shouting, making stabbing motions towards Damien and then in the direction they had just come from. Then he held the machete up to his own neck and mimed drawing the blade across it. He shouted a final word and then stormed off into the Chief's hut.

"Looks like you've got a lifetime fan there, Damo. What've you been up to?" Gavin asked.

"Well, I was just looking for something to eat, you know?" Damien held up the muddy vegetable. "Watching you lot eat that monkey was making us hungry. Well there was a lass. She gave us this yam or whatever it is."

"Lass?"

"Yeah, well there was three of them really. This one was nice to us, though."

"Right, Damo. So you were chatting with this lass of yours when matey turned up, were you?"

"Well, we were just smiling, that's all. She gave us this yam, see?"

"Yes mate. Well I know I'm no Sherlock Holmes, but I'd say that our friend with the machete is gonna have something to say if he catches you chatting up his bird again."

Gavin reinforced his point by drawing his hand across his throat in the same way the angry man had done with his machete.

"His bird? Nah, she can't be." Damien protested, but he had to admit to himself that Gavin's reading of the situation made sense.

Sighing, he sat down by the fire, absently wondering how he was going to cook and eat his yam. Tommy shifted round on the logs until he was next to Damien.

"So, this lass, Damo", the boy said, nudging Damien conspiratorially.

"Yes, Tommy?" Damien sighed.

"Is she fit?"

Damien opened his mouth as if to agree with Tommy, but found that for some reason he felt protective of his meeting with the village girl.

"She's not your type." he replied.

As dusk began to shade the sky, the four men found themselves becoming impatient once again. Gavin had been brooding – sitting down for a moment and then getting up to pace up and down the path. Damien and Samson had tried to cook the yam, but after more than an hour of baking it in the fire with little success, Damien could wait no longer and ate it half raw. Joey had sat silently for some time, but then lay down behind one of the sitting logs to snooze in the shade.

Shortly after Damien's bust-up with the Chief's son, the man had emerged from the chief's hut, glaring at the group, and ducked into the next door hut to emerge a few minutes later with a selection of loin cloths, which he flung towards them, gesticulating that they should put them on. "I don't think he wants you walking about with your arse hanging out, Damo." Tommy commented, but the clothing was welcome nonetheless, as their own hastily made underwear had become little more than dirty posing pouches.

As they began to wonder whether they would be offered an evening meal, and even shelter to sleep in, a commotion started a short distance away, in the direction they had walked from to reach the village.

The Chief's son set off at a jog towards the shouting, and was quickly followed by the two men they had sat with earlier, as well as another who they had never met. All were carrying some form of weapon.

"Shall we go and check it out?" Tommy suggested.

"I'm up for it", Gavin agreed, striding off as Samson and Damien fell in behind him.

The path split off, with a narrower way going off to their left, and it was from here that the sounds were coming from. A moment later, the jungle opened out, and they came upon the river bank, and almost bumped into the group of men who had run from the village. They were talking heatedly with another two men who held bows that were notched with arrows and levelled at something across the river.

Not wanting to get involved in a seemingly hostile situation, Gavin held his arms out to stop the friends who followed him. The discussion seemed to come to a head, with the two bowmen making a final exclamation, aiming their weapons and firing. A second later, sounds came from the other side of the bank, and Gavin could have sworn that he heard someone shouting in English, and also that the voice was familiar.

"Hold on! Hold on, lads! Don't shoot!" Gavin exclaimed, moving into the group of men so that he could get a view across the river. The men looked angry, but allowed him past. Looking out over the river, he saw Marco, chest deep in the water, holding on to the dinghy by a rope, half-swimming, half-walking as he tried to drag the boat to the opposite bank.

"Marco! Hold up!" Gavin called.

Marco swung round, a look of surprise on his face. He peered at Gavin for a few seconds before he seemed to recognise his friend.

"Mate! Tell those bloody idiots to stop shooting at me, will you?" The big Australian shouted back.

Nodding, Gavin turned to the village men and tried reasoning with them

"He's a mate. One of us!" he said, tapping his own chest and then pointing towards Marco.

The machete man reacted angrily, pointing at the dinghy and then at the river bank in front of him.

"Yeah, alright. Give us a minute. No more arrows, okay?" Gavin pleaded, miming shooting a bow and shaking his head.

Turning back towards Marco, Gavin called out again.

"Come back to the bank here, Marco. They'll be alright."

"You sure?" Marco questioned.

"Yeah, mate. Trust me!"

Marco shrugged uncertainly, but began to move back towards the bank that his friends shared with the previously hostile strangers. After a few moments, he reached the bank, and hauled himself up, as one of the bowmen angrily took the dinghy rope from him.

"What happened then, Marco? Where have you been?" Gavin asked him after he had briefly greeted his friends.

"Well, I'm with Woody, Emil and Raph. We got split up from the rest of you guys when we went over in the dinghy. Raph hurt his arm real bad, and Emil rigged up some kind of splint for him. We figured we'd try to walk down the river, along the bank, and hopefully bump into you." Marco stopped to scratch the back of his neck, a pained expression on his face.

"The jungle became a bloody nightmare though, and we weren't getting very far. By that time Raph was in a bad way, and then he just fainted away. So we continued on for a bit, carrying Raph, and then about quarter of an hour ago we arrived here and saw the dinghy over on this side."

"The boat was here?" Gavin asked.

"Yeah, mate. You didn't leave it there?"

"Not me. First I've seen of it since we took that tumble."

"Well I dunno, then", Marco shrugged. "Anyway, when we saw it we figured you guys'd be around somewhere, and so I volunteered to swim across and get the boat, so we could float Raph across. I was doing alright until these lads started shouting at me and then firing those bloody arrows."

"I reckon they think it's their boat now." Damien suggested, looking warily at the village men.

"Well, you think you could get them to let us borrow it for five minutes? Raph's in a right old state."

"Well, I'm not in this bloke's good books right now, but Maybe Gav could have a go." Damien replied.

Gavin nodded, turning to the Chief's son, who seemed to have calmed down somewhat. Slowly, with much gesticulation and repetition, he explained that they had a wounded friend on the other bank, and needed to use the boat to get him across. The man considered this for a moment, and then nodded, pointing towards the boat and then drawing his blade and waving it in Damien's direction.

"So, if you don't come back with it, Marco, then Damo gets cut. No pressure, mate!" Gavin said with a grin.

Marco grinned back, and climbed back down into the water again, taking the dinghy rope and setting off once more for the far bank.

"Raph's broke his arm, then?" Damien asked after a moment.

"Looks like it, yeah", Gavin replied, wincing.

"That is very bad", Samson said, shaking his head. "There is not much we can do to help him, out here."

Gavin nodded grimly, unable to suggest a solution.

Shortly after Marco reached the opposite bank, two other figures emerged from the jungle, carrying the limp body of Raphaël between them.

"Alright, boys?" Damien called out, receiving tired waves in response.

Laying Raphaël in the boat, Emil and Woody also entered the river, and the three men swam back towards them, pushing the dinghy.

As they reached the bank, Samson held the dinghy steady while Gavin and Damien slowly lifted the unconscious Raphaël out, laying him down in a shady spot.

"He's pretty cold, isn't he? You sure he's alright?" Damien asked.

Emil checked Raphaël's pulse, nodding gravely.

"Yes, he is alive. But we will need something to help with the pain when he wakes up again."

"Right. Like what?"

"Do you know these men?" Emil motioned towards the villagers.

"Well, I wouldn't say they were mates, but yeah, we've spent most of the day with them."

"This is good. Will they have medical supplies? Or perhaps a first aid kit?"

"Doubt it, mate. We could try asking the Chief chappie though. Might be worth a shot."

"Okay. Which way do we go?"

With Samson's help, Emil lifted Raphaël up and hooked the man's arms around their shoulders. Trying to walk smoothly, they followed their friends back along the winding jungle path until they reached the fire pit area, where Joey was still happily snoozing.

As they were wondering where to put Raphaël, one of the villagers motioned towards the hut where wood was stored, and the unconscious man was carried inside and laid down in a clear spot on the dusty floor.

Woody and Marco, exhausted, lay against the log benches and stretched their weary limbs, but Emil was still focused on trying to help Raphaël.

"The people who are in charge. Where are they?" He asked Gavin, his hollow eyes giving away the tiredness that he was trying to fight.

Gavin sighed, shaking his head.

"I'll take you to him, mate, but you won't have much luck. Unless they're keeping it well hidden, there's no medicine or any stuff like that here."

With the Chief's son following close on their heels, Gavin and Emil pushed their way into the chief's hut, where they found that the old chief had lain down on his seat and was snoring loudly. From against the other wall, Rudolph watched them with a strangely empty expression.

"Is that..." Emil began, looking incredulously towards his manager.

"Yeah, but I don't reckon you'll get much out of him", Gavin replied. "Doesn't seem to recognise any of us."

"Boss?" Emil began, trying to draw a positive response from Rudolph. "Are you alright? Raphaël is hurt, we need something for pain."

Rudolph smiled back enigmatically, but seemed entirely unconcerned about Emil's news.

"He doesn't understand? Why does he just smile?" Emil asked, turning to Gavin.

"I dunno, mate", Gavin shrugged. "He's away with the fairies!"

The conversation had by now woken the Chief, who sat upright with a grumpy expression on his face. Gavin and Emil took it in turns to try to explain the situation to him, but although the man seemed to understand parts of what they were saying, he had no answer but to shake his head. As Gavin and Emil's gesticulation became more desperate, the chief's son grew more agitated, until he eventually drew his weapon and ordered the two men out of the hut.

The mood outside was not much better. The companions sat around glumly, avoiding each other's eyes as they realised how much harder their plight had become with the addition of an injured man.

"Any luck?" Marco asked, without much hope in his voice.

Gavin shook his head. "They've got no idea what we're on about. Don't reckon there's anything here to help Raph, anyway."

"We must move on, then", Samson suggested. "We need to find someone who can help him before he gets any worse."

"You must be mad, mate!" Marco cut in, raising his voice. "It took us most of the day to cover less than a mile in this bloody place. You just can't move at any speed when you're carrying a bloke between you, even if you're lucky and you find a clear bit of jungle!"

"I can make a stretcher for him. This will make it easier, I think." Samson replied, trying to keep his voice calm.

"Yeah, that's wonderful, Sams", Marco said sarcastically. "How about you make us a bloody helicopter, too?"

"Alright, big man, calm down!" Gavin scolded. "It's pretty much dark now anyway - no chance of going anywhere until tomorrow, whether we want to or not. Sams, you reckon you can make a stretcher then?"

Samson nodded. "The rags they gave us to wear - I think there are more. Maybe larger pieces."

"See what you can do then, okay? And the rest of us, let's get some rest. It's been a long day."

There were murmurs of agreement and the men broke up, a few heading to the still-smouldering embers of the fire to chat quietly, others to find a comfortable spot to lie down and snooze or think.

Gavin lay with his back against the wood store hut where Raphaël had been taken, and closed his eyes. It had been more than a long day. A disastrous day, more like it. That morning, the men had been in good spirits, having eaten fairly well for a few days. They had transport, they had a direction and most importantly, they were relatively healthy, mentally and physically. Over the course of the day, they had lost their transport, had one man incapacitated by injury, and another one seemed to have lost his mind.

Gavin was half tempted to sneak off and go it alone. He moved swiftly on his own, and wasn't slowed down by personality clashes or physical incapability. He could, maybe, find some help and then bring aid to his friends. He played with this though for a while, but then sighed, shaking his head. God knows what would happen to the lads if he weren't there. They were a good bunch but also completely useless in most regards. They'd be bound to get themselves lost or killed without him.

As he dozed off, he pictured himself running, crouched, commando-style through the jungle on his way to steal medical supplies from an imaginary enemy camp.

7

Damien was woken by the sound of clanging metal. Sitting up and looking up at the sky, he saw that dawn had broken at least two hours previously. The clanging sound came from the fire pit, where three of the villagers were stirring some kind of concoction over the fire in a beaten old metal cauldron. It was clearly not made locally, as it appeared to be manufactured out of a light metal, but judging by the blackened bottom and the dented rim, it had been in the village for a long time.

Stretching and moving over to the logs, he nodded towards the villagers, who seemed to be in good spirits as they helped the porridge-like goo out of the cauldron and into wooden bowls.

"Can you give us a bit?" Damien asked, pointing to the cauldron and making an eating motion.

The man across from Damien nodded, picking up a spare wooden bowl and filling it with the steaming food. Planting a rough spoon squarely in the centre of the thick goo, he passed it to Damien, grinning.

Warily, Damien sniffed the contents of the bowl. It had an earthy, sour smell, and he could not help but grimace. However, his stomach started to growl at the prospect of any type of food, and he resigned himself to eating it, whatever it may be. Forcing a smile, he pulled the spoon free and put it in his mouth.

The food was nothing like he had expected. It had a bitter, vegetable-like smell, and the texture was gritty. Trying not to gag, Damien glanced up at the man who had fed him, who was grinning proudly, obviously expecting some type of compliment. Damien forced himself to swallow, and then nodded at the man, making his best attempt at a satisfied expression.

The man seemed content, and went back to eating his own bowl of food. Damien looked down at his bowl with trepidation. He knew that he had to eat it, but the thought of filling his mouth with the disgusting goo again was making him feel ill. He waited until the three men were looking away and then held his nose, shoving a large spoonful of the food into his mouth and swallowing without chewing.

Over the next few minutes, he managed to finish the whole bowl without the villagers noticing his disgust, and then remembered his friends. Standing up, he walked around the area, prodding the other men.

"Breakfast's up, lads. Plenty for everyone!" He shouted, returning to the fire pit.

The first few men sidled tiredly over to the cauldron, studying the food suspiciously.

"What is it?" Joey asked, sneering.

"It's good stuff, Jo-Jo. A bit like rice pudding, but nicer", Damien encouraged. "I'll help you out a bowl, mate."

"I am very hungry", Joey said.

"No problem, pal", Damien replied, adding an extra few spoonfuls to an already full bowl. "Get stuck in!"

Joey sat down, watching his bowl hungrily, and eagerly tucked in. He had swallowed his first big mouthful and was in the process of refilling his spoon when his taste buds caught up. Freezing, he looked at Damien, eyes wide in shock. Gagging twice, he stood up and loped towards the tree line, holding his stomach.

"Is it that bad?" Marco asked, sniffing the remains of Joey's bowl.

"It's not great, Marco", Damien replied, chucking. "Give it a go, mate. It's edible, honest."

Marco took a small fingerful of the food and tasted it.

"Christ, it's rank, eh?"

"Well, I managed to get a bowl down us - holding my nose, mind."

"Give us a go", Tommy said, elbowing his way past Damien and taking the bowl from Marco.

The boy put a small spoonful in his mouth, watching the food warily. Slowly he began to chew, and then swallowed, shrugging.

"It's not that bad, you big Jessies", he said, refilling his spoon. "Not bad at all."

Damien and Marco exchanged glances, smirking, and were about to help more of the food out when they were interrupted by loud retching sounds coming from the direction in which Joey had run into the trees.

"Hey Joey", Damien shouted, cupping his hands. "You're up for seconds, right?"

"Lads! Lads, they're playing footy!" Tommy yelled, jogging back towards the fire pit area where his friends were gathered.

"Footy?" Marco repeated, sceptically. "We're in the middle of a bloody jungle!"

"Yeah I know, genius", Tommy replied, slowing down. "Come and take a butchers. Five minutes down the path here."

"This should be good!" Marco replied, standing up and sauntering towards Tommy.

In dribs and drabs, the other men stood up and followed. Although none of them believed Tommy, they were glad of something to distract from the bad atmosphere that had prevailed that morning. There had been much heated arguing, mainly concerning Raphaël, and whether they should stay in the village or head on. Gavin, who could usually be relied upon to keep the peace, was uncharacteristically quiet, preferring to sit and brood with a stormy expression on his face.

After a few minutes' walk, the men reached the end of the habitated area of the village, and Tommy turned down a small fork in the path. As they continued, they began to hear occasional shouting and laughter, interspersed with a thwacking sound. Tommy grinned back at his friends as he led them into a clearing, and held his arms out triumphantly, as if offering a rare delight.

In the clearing were a group of ten men, including the Chief's son and one of the monkey-eaters. They were clearly playing a team game, which at first sight reminded the men of a mixture of football, volleyball and hacky sack. A vine barrier, somewhat above waist height, was suspended between two tall sticks, and the villagers kicked a spherical wicker object to each other. They were so engrossed that they didn't notice the men watching them. After a few minutes watching, the companions deduced that the rules were indeed very similar to volleyball, with the ball being knocked over the barrier into the opponent's half and points scored if the opposing team was unable to return it without it touching the ground. Where it differed from volleyball was that the hands could not be used. The players seemed at liberty to use feet, knees, head, shoulders and chest to control and pass the ball.

The villagers were obviously practised at the game, as they kept the ball aloft with agility and were able to knock some very difficult shots into their opponents' half. After a skilful passage of play, the companions clapped, finally drawing the players' attention.

There was an awkward moment when neither group of men seemed to know what to do, with the villagers looking surprised and put off, while the companions worried that they may have disturbed something important. Damien broke the silence.

"Let's have a go, boys!" He grinned, nodding towards the ball.

The villagers exchanged a few words and then tossed Damien the ball, while the Chief's son crossed his arms and watched with a scornful expression. Damien threw the ball up and bounced it on his knee, letting it drop on to his foot, where he tried to flick it back up again. The ball only bounced a small way up before falling back to the hard earth.

"It's not very bouncy, lads", Damien commented, looking sheepishly back at his friends.

"Yeah, but you're a muppet, Damo." Tommy replied, joining Damien in the court. "Give us it."

Damien shrugged, passing the ball to Tommy along the ground. The boy let it roll onto his toes and then flicked it up. After a few desperate keep-me-ups, he lost control, and the ball rolled out of the court.

By now, the other companions had crowded round, eager to try the ball out themselves, with varying degrees of success. After a few minutes, the monkey-eater tapped Gavin on the shoulder, motioning to the net and then to Gavin and his friends.

"Do we want a game, boys?" Gavin asked, glancing around for support.

106

The men nodded, taking up positions on the court. The monkey-eater shook his head, amused, and held five fingers up to Gavin.

"Just five of us, okay?" Gavin said to his eager companions. "Joey, Samson, Marco, Damo. Us guys'll start, right? And we'll change over in a few minutes."

Five of the villagers left the court, squatting down at the edge to watch. Pointing his team into position, the monkey-eater threw the wicker ball up and punted it high over the net into the other half. Marco rushed forward and caught it on his knee, knocking it up slightly and trying to volley it back over the net. The ball swerved out of control, cannoning off his side of the net and out of play.

"Sorry, lads", Marco said sheepishly.

Gavin jogged over to retrieve the ball and then returned to his position, waiting for a nod from the other team's captain and then carefully kicking the ball. This time it sailed over the net, but arced so high that it gave the other team plenty of time to react. Controlling the ball, the nearest villager passed it across one of his team mates, who then flicked it skilfully back again, only just clearing the net. Damien, closest to the ball, dived in and tried to keep it up, but ended up sprawling on the dusty floor. A few chuckles came from the villagers, most notably from the Chief's son, who pointed at Damien and loudly shared a joke with his cronies.

This continued for some time, all of the companions trying their hand at the game without much success. Although they did show some improvement in controlling the ball, they were unable to win a point from the much more practised villagers. Eventually, the monkey-eater walked to the edge of the court, looked down at the ground, where he had been making a small mark after every point, and shook his head, shrugging at Gavin and waving his hands in a dismissive manner. The other villagers walked off the court to some rather half-hearted cheers from their friends.

Gavin wandered across to the edge of the court and knelt down to look at the scoring chart. A vertical line had been drawn, starting at the base of the pole that held up the net. On the villagers' side of the line, two rows of ten small marks had been drawn with a short, pointed stick. A longer mark crossed each row out and another longer mark was just below this. Gavin nodded, as if this confirmed what he had already worked out.

"Alright, lads, listen up", he said, standing and beckoning his friends towards him. "Looks like it was first to ten, best out of three games. We were bloody useless, but I reckon we just need a bit of practice, right?"

His friends avoided his gaze, clearly not as convinced of their potential skill as their captain was.

"Well, anyway, I'm going to arrange us a match for later. You all up for it?"

Again, his friends looked unconvinced, but eventually nodded.

"Nice one. Stay here a bit, okay?" Gavin said, grinning for the first time that day. "I'm gonna go and work something out with that smarmy little git over there."

Returning to the scoreboard, Gavin beckoned to the Chief's son until he grudgingly stood up and sauntered over.

Gavin waited until he had the man's full attention and then wiped out the scoring marks next to the court.

"We want another game. You and your lads against us", he said, pointing at himself and his friends, then at the man and the other villagers, and finally at the court.

The man nodded, laughing derisively.

"Right. If we win it, we want our trophy back."

Pausing to think for a moment, Gavin pointed at himself and then made three rows of ten marks with the short stick, crossing out each row as he finished them. He then drew a crude picture of the trophy. The Machete Man studied Gavin's drawings for a while and then nodded slowly, scratching his head in thought. After a moment, he knelt down next to Gavin, wiped out the drawings and made some of his own. This time, the three rows of marks were drawn next to the other side of the court, the drawing stick resting next to the marks as he looked questioningly at Gavin.

"What do you get if you win?" Gavin said as he deciphered the man's question.

For a moment, Gavin knelt silently in thought as the man waited for his answer. Reluctantly, Gavin leant forward and drew a crude picture of a man. The Chief's son looked confused, so Gavin dramatically raised his finger and pointed to Damien. With a gradually growing grin, the Chief's son stood up, beckoning Gavin to his feet. Taking Gavin's arm in his hand, he drew a long scratch with the drawing stick on Gavin's forearm. He then handed Gavin the stick and offered his own arm.

"You want to shake on it, right?" Gavin said, taking the stick and making his own mark on the man's arm.

The man then pointed at the sun, which was almost directly above them in the sky. He moved his arm slowly round until it pointed about half way between the sun and the horizon.

"Mid afternoon", Gavin said, nodding. "Gotcha. We'll be here."

Looking cocky, the Chief's son turned and strutted back to the other villagers, getting a laugh from them as he explained what had just been agreed.

"What was with you pointing at us?" Damien asked suspiciously as he wandered over to look at the drawings.

"Don't worry about it, Damo." Gavin replied.

"Just tell us you haven't bet us on a game, Gav." Damien looked ominously at the picture of the man.

"Relax, mate, I won't let him do anything to you. Anyway, we're gonna win the game, right?"

The next few hours were spent practicing the awkward ball game, and by the time the villagers started making their way down to the court, Gavin had already resigned himself to a loss, and was wondering how he would be able to protect Damien from the Chief's son.

It seemed as if most of the village had made their way down to witness the companions' humiliation, as the logs and rocks around the court were gradually filled with chattering people and more gathered round to stand and watch.

With a wave from Gavin, the men formed into a group to discuss their game plan.

"We're all hopeless at this game", Gavin began, perhaps a little too honestly. "But five of us'll have to try. Damo, Joey. You two are probably the best of us, not that that's much of a compliment. Woody, you've got a good serve, so you're in. I'm the captain, of course. After that it's either Tommy or Emil."

"I'm up for it, Gav", Tommy immediately replied. "Give us a go, yeah? I reckon I've got the hang of it."

Gavin glanced at Emil questioningly.

"It is fine. Let Tommy play", the Dutchman said. "Someone must check on Raphaël. I will see him and then come back later. Good luck."

"Nice one, Emil", said Gavin. "Right, so everyone knows the plan? Stay in the formation we just worked out. One man in each corner, one man in the middle. Joey, Tommy – left and right attack. Me and Woody'll stick at the back. Damo, you go in the middle there. Always call for the ball if it's yours. Communicate! If you're in a good position, let us know. If you don't have a clear shot then just knock the ball up for someone else. Alright?"

The other four men nodded excitedly.

"And the main thing – concentrate!" Gavin tapped his head. "We can't afford to lose this one!"

By now, the opposing team had gathered on the other side of the court. The Chief's son was standing in the middle, glowering at Gavin and his men. He had covered himself in some oily sort of liquid, so that his body glistened. Four other men stood around him, and the monkey-eater who they had played against before stood just outside the court beside the scoring area, apparently there to act as a sort of referee.

Looking at the gathered spectators, the companions noticed that the Chief himself had come down to watch the match, and was sitting on a pile of skins on top of the most prominent rock, Rudolph to his left and the trophy in front of him. The other spectators seemed to be split according to gender. The main bulk of them were men, sitting on logs or standing around, but a small group of women were also seated at the far end. Peering at the group, Damien saw that the village girl with the pretty eyes was indeed one of them, and that she seemed to be watching him. He gave her a friendly grin and was sure that she smiled briefly back at him. For a second, she held his gaze, but then she glanced nervously at the Chief's son and cast her eyes downwards.

After a moment, the spectators quietened down, and they noticed that the referee was holding the ball high in the air above his head, and glancing alternately at the Chief's son and Gavin. The two captains made their way over to the corner of the net and watched as the man spoke to them. The Chief's son seemed uninterested, and Gavin could not understand a word, but the man continued to speak for a short while and then lowered his arms.

Placing the ball on the ground in front of him, he picked up the short scoring stick and turned away, doing something with his hands. When he turned back, he held his hands out in fists, obviously expecting the captains to choose which hand contained the stick. Without hesitation, the Chief's son reached out and tapped the man's left hand. The referee glanced at Gavin with an almost apologetic look, and opened his hand to reveal the stick in his left hand.

"Looking forward to a fair game then, ref?" Gavin said sarcastically, sure that the two villagers had fixed the choice.

The referee ignored Gavin, picking up the ball and handing it to the Chief's son, who strutted back to the edge of his side of the court and got ready to serve.

"Alright, lads, good luck. And remember – concentrate!" Gavin said, taking up his position.

Now that both teams were ready, the chief's son barked out some orders to his men and kicked the ball into play. It was a low shot, just clearing the net and dipping nastily. Damien was first to react and moved forward, kicking the ball back up and over with the side of his foot. Some brief cheers of appreciation came from his team mates. One of the villagers collected the ball easily, controlling it on his chest and then flicking it up with his knee. Rushing towards the net, the Chief's son swivelled on one foot and volleyed the ball. He struck it with such power that, had it been left to travel, it would have easily gone out of play. But unfortunately, it was headed straight for Damien, who was still close to his side of the net, and it struck him squarely in the face before dropping to the ground in front of his feet. The Chief's son put his hands in the air and shouted in triumph.

"Twat!" Gavin yelled at the man as he ran over to check on Damien, who was crouched with his hands over his face. "You alright, Damo?"

Damien took his hands away, looking in surprise at the blood that came from his nose.

"Yeah, man", Damien replied, looking more angry than hurt. "Just a bit of blood. Nothing broken."

"You sure you wanna carry on? We could bring Marco on."

"Naa, I wanna play. It's nothing. Let's go!"

Damien stood up bravely, wiping away blood from under his nose and spitting out the blood that had trickled into his mouth, all the time watching the Chief's son with a defiant expression.

"Okay, mate. But watch that one. If he does it again, duck!"

Damien nodded grimly as Gavin picked up the ball and handed it to Woody, who was standing ready to serve. Taking a few seconds to pick his spot, Woody threw the ball up and kicked it to the other team. His shot was good, but the villagers controlled it, passing it twice between their team and then knocking it low over the net. Joey scrambled forward and managed to keep the ball in play, passing it left to Tommy. The boy put his arms out to balance and then swung, contacting with his shin and sending the ball back over the net at a wild angle. The villagers stood still, watching as the ball arced out of play and landed among the dry leaves that had been swept into piles outside the court.

"Sorry", Tommy said dejectedly.

"Forget it, Tommy", Gavin said, hiding his disappointment. "Keep your concentration up, okay? And if you're off balance, just play the simple pass."

The rest of the first game continued in similar fashion, with the companions failing to score a single point. Scattered laughter had begun to come from the crowd as Gavin and his team dropped further behind. As the referee held his arms up to signify a break, the two teams gathered round to talk.

"Ten-nil", Woody said, shaking his head disconsolately.

"We look like a right bunch of donkeys", Damien added.

"Right, lads", Gavin sighed. "If we carry on playing like that we're gonna get thumped again. We've got to stop panicking and playing the first shot we get. We've played this game before in the training grounds. Well, it's a different ball and that, but it's the same idea. Control it, pass it around. Play the easy balls and wait til you've got a good shot lined up. We lose this one then it's two games to them, and we're out, so no more fannying about."

The companions nodded gravely as the referee barked an order and the opposition wandered back into formation for the second game.

"And use your heads!" Gavin added as his team moved into position. "These lads hardly ever do that. Lift a ball up near the front for someone to nod over the net. That kind of shot'll catch them out, I reckon."

Pausing until they were ready, the referee threw the ball to Woody and nodded for him to start. The companions were silent in concentration as they watched Woody take a deep breath, ready himself and serve. The ball looped dangerously. It was not a massively powerful shot, but it seemed to swerve unnaturally over the net. Caught off-guard, the nearest villager stretched to reach the ball and knocked it high into the air, slipping as he did so.

"Mine!" Shouted Gavin as the ball came down on his side of the court.

Taking the pace off the ball with his thigh, he lifted it up again with his other foot, sending it drifting towards Damien, who also controlled the ball on his thigh.

"Joey! Far post!" Damien yelled as he side-footed the ball forwards and outwards.

Joey responded instantly, moving ahead to meet the ball as it came in at head height close to the net. Bending his arms, he headed the ball gently, just clearing the net and surprising the villagers as it dropped like a stone to the floor.

The companions mobbed Joey, slapping his shoulder or rubbing his hair in joy.

"Played, Joey", Damien grinned. "Nice header!"

Joey paused for a moment to check that Damien was being sincere.

"It was a good pass", he conceded, grinning back.

"Heads, up, lads!" Came a bellowing shout from the spectators.

Snapping their heads round, they saw Marco standing up, gesticulating wildly towards the opposition half. Following his arm, the saw that the villagers had wasted no time getting into formation, and the Chief's son was pulling his leg back to serve.

The companions scrambled towards their positions as the ball was launched into their half. The serve was a strong one, heading for the right-hand rear corner of the court. Stretching his leg, Woody was just able to keep the ball in play, knocking it practically vertically upwards as he himself rolled out of the court. Gavin rushed towards the falling ball, bending back and kicking it high over his head and towards the opposition half behind him. With plenty of time to prepare themselves, the villagers changed formation, the Chief's son yelling orders as he moved forward.

The ball finally dropped, was controlled and then lifted forward. Another villager passed it across the court, where the Chief's son once again volleyed it with power.

Caught off-guard and flummoxed by the villagers' quickly-taken serve and his team's desperate defending, Damien had little time to react as the ball rushed towards him once more, but his experience in the last game had lent him some nervous speed. Jerking his head to the side, he heard the whoosh of the ball as it narrowly missed his face and flew out of play.

"Come on then!" Damien yelled, losing his cool and moving up to the net, glaring at his attacker. "Have a go if you like!"

The Chief's son also advanced, scowling, until the two were standing chest to chest at the net, eyes boring into each other. The referee immediately rushed over, grabbing both men by the shoulder and trying to separate them.

"Leave it, Damo", Gavin said, jogging over to the net to help. "Just ignore him!"

"He's winding us up, man", Damien replied, eyes fixed on his enemy. "Asking for it."

"Wouldn't be the first time, would it?" Gavin put his arm around Damien's chest and pulled him away. "Let the ball do the talking, eh?"

Gradually, eyes still locked on the Chief's son, Damien let himself be pulled away from the confrontation. As he turned away, he winked cheekily, grinning at the man.

The companions' two point lead seemed to rattle the villagers, who proceeded to lose two more points due to mis-kicks and another to a close header, similar to Joey's first point. This second scoring header enraged the Chief's son, who stormed up to the net, shouting and gesticulating wildly towards the referee before he could mark down a point for Gavin's team. The referee seemed nervous, clearly anxious not to anger his superior, but not wishing to punish a tactic that he considered perfectly legal.

After a lengthy rant, the Chief's son stood in front of the referee, arms folded, eyes angry and expectant. The referee seemed to shrink from him, and approached Gavin apologetically, gesturing towards his head and the ground near the net, and then crossing his arms in a gesture of forbiddance. Gavin's mouth fell open in outrage, his face turning a deeper crimson colour.

"You're joking, right, ref?" He shouted, holding his arms out in disbelief. "You can't change the rules because that little tosser tells you to!"

The referee shrank further, caught between the Chief's son's threatening demands and Gavin's hulking crimson anger. Smiling in what he hoped was a placatory manner, he shrugged at Gavin and backed away.

"No way!" Gavin yelled, striding over to the side of the court, marking down his point on the scoreboard and standing directly in front of the Chief's son, arms folded. The Chief's son took a step back, hesitating for a moment. Other than Marco, Gavin was the largest man he had ever seen, and Gavin's angry red face coupled with his shock of orange hair were alien and disconcerting.

The chief's son stepped back, as if admitting defeat, but then barked out orders to various people in the crowd of spectators. At his command, a number of men moved out of the crowd to surround Gavin, a few of them carrying heavy sticks or bows. Gavin's friends reacted, springing forward to stand near their captain, and the two groups faced off against each other, their shouts of warning clear to one another even through the language barrier.

Just as it seemed that the situation would come to blows, a new voice rang out from the crowd. This had an immediate effect on the villagers, who stopped arguing and turned towards the voice. The Chief had managed to raise himself from his seat of skins, and was watching his son with deeply furrowed brows. At an order from him, the group of village men backed away from the court and returned to the crowd. With another order, the Chief's son prowled indignantly towards his father and stood with his head bowed.

There was then a heated exchange between the two, with the son seeming to plead and the Chief holding his hands up and replying firmly. After a moment, the Chief's son turned and came back to the court, practically shaking with anger.

Avoiding his superior's eyes, the referee turned to Gavin and motioned towards his head and the scoreboard, nodding. Gavin nodded back, calming down as he returned to his half of the court to continue the game.

The confrontation seemed to galvanise the villagers, and they came back into the game with much more concentration than they had shown so far. After an intense fifteen minutes, the score sat at eight all, and the momentum seemed to be with the villagers.

Woody was next to serve, and he paused in concentration, knowing that the next point would be the most important so far. Closing his eyes and imagining the shot he was about to play, he drew his leg back and served. It was another great delivery, just clearing the net and then swerving down and to the left. The nearest villager scrambled to meet the ball and managed to lift it for his team-mate to control. With a deft touch of the outside of his foot, the villager eased the ball over, his subtle kick falling dangerously close to the companions' side of the net. In desperation, Joey lunged forward, trying to keep the ball up, but it was too late.

As the villagers celebrated their point, a voice spoke up from behind the companions' end of the court.

"Push up!" The voice suggested in a calm but firm manner.

Turning in confusion, the men saw that Rudolph had risen from his place next to the chief and had wandered over, unnoticed, to the edge of the court. Aside from his unkempt appearance, tattered pieces of clothing and single-lensed spectacles, he looked normal, his far-off gaze replaced by his usual collected and focussed expression.

"Gaffer?" Said Woody, who was closest to his manager. "You alright?"

"Yes, why would I not be?" Rudolph replied, seemingly oblivious to the fact that he had until a few minutes ago been apparently lost to the world.

"Good to have you back, boss!" Damien grinned, slapping Rudolph on the back.

"Back?"

"Yeah, man. You've been.... Well, never mind. How's about helping us out with this game, then? My life literally depends on it!"

"Yes of course. That is what I'm here for."

"Nice one!" Gavin interrupted. "Hang on a bit, I need to get us some time."

Gavin jogged over to the referee, who along with the village team was looking impatient. After a brief exchange of gestures, he returned to his team mates, grinning widely.

"Right, lads. We've only got a few minutes, so listen up and pay attention to the gaffer", he said, nodding to Rudolph to take over.

Rudolph smiled thinly, making eye contact with each of his players to check that they were listening.

"You are playing too far back", Rudolph began, pointing to the court. "They play balls just over the net and there is no-one there to collect them. You must move forward when they have the ball. Joey and Tommy – stay right next to the net. Woody and Damien will play off them, slightly further back and more central. Gavin, you will play sweeper. Just stay at the back and watch for high balls."

Rudolph paused, waiting for his team to nod their understanding.

"When we have the ball, we must spread out.", Rudolph continued. "Joey and Tommy will be at the net, ready to head it over or lob the other team of they are too close to the net. Damien, you will dictate the play. The ball should normally be played to you when we have control of it. Pass to Joey or Tommy if they have a clear shot. If the other team are marking the two of you, Woody or Gavin should come forward and surprise them."

The team nodded once more.

"Anything else, gaffer?" Gavin asked.

"Yes. Many things. But the referee is now waving for you to start. You must win these next two points and then we will talk properly before the final game."

Slapping each other's hands, the team returned to their new starting positions. On the other side of the court, the Chief's son prepared himself and then kicked the ball. It was a high, long shot, obviously intended to catch the other team out because they only had one man back, but Gavin still had plenty of time to reach the ball and caught it on his chest, controlling it once on his knee before knocking it forward to midfield. Damien caught the ball on his thigh and then flicked it over his head, turning so that he was facing the net. At a shout from Tommy, he lifted it forward and to his right, where the boy took it on his head, skilfully playing it over both the net and the head of the villager who stood in his way. Despite a desperate scramble from the opposition, the ball fell to earth, and the companions cheered wildly, rushing forward to congratulate the ecstatic Tommy, as Damien jumped on his back, almost forcing him to his knees.

Marking their point down, the referee couldn't resist a smile, which was quickly wiped away at a stern glance from the Chief's son. Retrieving the ball, he walked over to the celebrating companions and pressed it into Woody's hands.

"Alright, lads, that's enough", Gavin said, moving to his position near the back of the court. "One more point. Stay cool, stay focussed. Woody, make it a good one, mate."

Woody nodded gravely, his handsome face set in a resolute expression. He breathed evenly, studying his opponent's formation for a weak spot. Taking two long steps backward, he tapped his foot on the ground for luck and then sprang forward, kicking the ball as he reached the edge of the court. The ball curled viciously, almost going wide of the right hand net post before whizzing inwards. The nearest villager, fooled by the ball's movement, was caught off balance, throwing his foot high to try and parry it back over the net. The weak return slammed into the top part of the net, and the men watched with their hearts in their mouths as the ball threatened to trickle over on to their side of the court. Fortunately, it lost momentum and dropped to the ground on the villagers' side.

As the referee held his arms up to the side, a finger of each hand raised to show that the match now stood at one game all, the companions whooped with joy, gathering into a group to congratulate each other. On the other side of the court, the Chief's son advanced on the villager whose shot had lost that game, shouting. The villager backed away, holding his hands out in earnest. Ignoring the man's submission, the Chief's son pushed him with both hands, knocking him to the ground, where he stayed, shaking his head in defeat.

The companions headed over to their area beside the court to join Rudolph, who had been drawing tactical diagrams in the dusty earth. On the other side, the Chief's son continued to harangue his team, clearly outraged that outsiders who were new to their sport had taken them to a deciding game.

"Got some ideas then, Gaffer?" Damien asked, standing over Rudolph's plans and trying to make sense of them.

"Yes, I think so", Rudolph replied, smiling his thin smile as he finished off the drawings. "This is not a complex game. It is all about how you are placed when you are in control of the ball and when you are not."

By now, the whole team had squatted down by Rudolph and his drawings, and watched intently as he explained his tactics to them. By the time the referee came over to beckon them back to play, they were as well drilled as they could be in such a short time, and they approached the court feeling focussed and confident.

The early stages of the deciding game didn't go according to the companions' plans, though. The village team came back to the game with a real fire to their play, obviously chastened by the Chief's son's criticism. They took the first three points in slick style, passing the ball about in their half of the court and playing punishing shots when they had opportunities. Damien and Joey stepped up in response, raising their games and scoring some sublime points between them. The balance of the game went back and forth, both sides fighting with everything they had.

Eventually the score stood at nine-seven to the villagers, and the atmosphere was thick with tension. Even the crowd's reaction to the play had changed. Where before they had cheered and laughed, they now gasped and whispered.

There was a collective holding of breath as the Chief's son stepped up to serve what could be the final ball of the game. His kick was high, and seemed to be going out of play, but it dipped rapidly, giving Gavin little time to position himself. Seeing that the ball was going to land in, he threw himself forward, managing to kick the ball up before he slid to the ground. Gavin's wild shot span high, heading out of the court on the right hand side. The crowd groaned, thinking that the game was over, but Damien started running full pelt to intercept the ball before it fell. Swivelling, he played a beautiful cross-court volley, surprising the villagers so much that they were hardly able to react to it. The ball looped and dived, throwing up a puff of dust as it landed in.

"Don't think I've ever seen you run so fast, Damo", Tommy commented, eyes wide in admiration.

Damien, now so focussed that he was beyond joking, just nodded back with an intense and serious expression on his face.

"Come on, lads! Let's do this!" He urged, looking each of his team mates in the eye for a few seconds and then stooping to pick up the ball and press it into Woody's hands.

Woody served once more, stepping back from the line and bursting forward to kick the ball. This time he blasted it down the middle, clearing the net by an inch and causing the central villager to duck instinctively. The Chief's son, covering from the back, rushed up and headed the ball back over the net, moving forward to block any return. Damien intercepted the shot, bringing it down and keeping it up while he waited for an opportunity. At a shout from Joey, he passed the ball left at waist height. Reaching his arms out for balance, Joey swung, his leg ending up horizontal when he connected with the ball. It was a deceptive shot, coming off the outside of his foot and arcing high over the villagers' heads. Stranded near the net, the Chief's son raced back, trying to reach the ball as it fell to the ground at the back of the court. He lunged, but was only able to touch the ball with his toes, knocking it along the ground towards the crowd.

As the companions whooped with joy, the Chief's son punched the ground, wanting to blame someone, but knowing that the point was his fault for straying out of position. After a moment, the referee retrieved the ball and offered it to the Chief's son, holding out his hand to help the man up. The Chief's son waved him away angrily, standing up and snatching the ball as he stomped to the edge of the court and made ready to serve.

"Heads up!" Shouted Gavin, who was still celebrating the previous point with his team mates.

The companions scrambled back to their positions, expecting the Chief's son to serve early and catch them out. As they reached their places, though, the man left his serving position and froze, staring at each of the companions with contempt. His eyes eventually settled on Damien's, and he raised his hand to point threateningly, an ugly sneer contorting his face. Damien smiled back at him, unblinking, and then raised his hand to his mouth to blow a kiss at the man.

The other companions stood taut, their bodies charged with adrenalin at the prospect of the final point. Although they had all been in far more important games, somehow this meant as much to them as a cup final. Although they would win no money and no-one in the outside world would ever be likely to hear about it, they needed this win. Their hardships and helplessness had begun to wear them down, causing friction and despair, but this game seemed to have reignited their common bond of sportsmanship. Rudolph also stood by the side of the court, hands clasped together and pumping in expectancy.

Closing his eyes and taking a deep breath, the Chief's son stepped up, dropped the ball and kicked it. His shot was fierce, swerving and dropping over the net. Woody got a foot to it, taking some of the pace off it and lifting it to head height. Damien reacted first, heading the ball just over the net in the hope of catching the villagers out. They were wise to this kind of shot by now though, and one of them darted forward to keep the ball up with his toes. The villagers now passed it around effortlessly between them, waiting for their opportunity.

"Movement!" Gavin yelled, noticing that his team were starting to ball-watch.

It seemed that the Chief's son had also noticed this, because from out of nowhere, he suddenly lobbed the ball directly over Joey's head, rolling it to make it drop early. Joey, caught by surprise, reacted as best he could, spinning and managing to get a knee to it, but the ball was still out of control, moving away from Joey and dropping fast. In desperation, Joey threw himself towards the ball, leg outstretched. He made contact, knocking the ball back up again, but it was a poor pass, spinning towards the opposite side of the court at chest height.

The ball seemed to move in slow motion as they realised that the ball was heading out and that no-one was in a good position to stop it. Tommy was nearest, but had his back to the net, and with the ball so high in the air, seemed to have no chance of playing it. With his eyes practically bulging out of his head with adrenalin, though, he leaped as the ball came level with him, swinging his left leg up and connecting with it above his head and then falling to the ground, shoulder first. The overhead strike was sweet, whizzing over the net and speeding towards the back corner of the villager's side. Two of them flailed at the ball as it passed them, but Tommy's kick was so unexpected that they had no time to react properly, and the ball came down with a soft thwack and a small puff of dust.

The companions stood silent for a moment, unable to believe that they had won, but as the referee raised his arm in their direction they started to cheer wildly, looking at each other with shocked and ecstatic expressions. The Chief's son didn't stay to watch their celebration. With a disdainful look at his team, he strode off in the direction of the village, shouldering his way past the spectators. The other village players were more sporting, coming forward with surprised smiles and slapping their opponents on the back.

In the middle of the jubilation, Gavin sat down. Sighing in disbelief, he shook his head.

"Unbelievable", he said quietly to himself. "Unbelievable..."

As the sunset gave way to a calm, cool night, the companions were gathered round the fire pit. More logs had been dragged around the fire so that some of the villagers could join them – all of the team they had played against earlier (minus the Chief's son) and a few of the older men – and they seemed in good spirits, chatting and laughing with each other and nodding or smiling at their guests in a friendly way. Samson, who had been looking after the injured Raphaël, had now emerged from the hut, reporting that his charge had slipped into a peaceful sleep.

For the first time in days, they felt like a team again. Their niggles and feuds were forgotten as they sat and chatted happily, reliving their unlikely victory and embellishing the slower parts of it with their own exaggerations. They had been given a small meal of some type of over-cooked meat and fire-baked plantains, and for once their bellies felt full.

There was a commotion among the villagers as one of the older men fetched a battered old cauldron from a nearby hut. Two of the villagers moved aside for him, grinning widely, as the older man placed the cauldron next to the fire. Seeming very pleased with himself, he produced a wooden bowl and plunged it into the cauldron, taking it out brimming with a murky liquid. He grinned conspiratorially at his fellows and then raised the bowl to his lips, slowly drinking it dry. After finishing, he wiped his mouth on his arm and refilled the bowl, passing it to the man on his left.

One by one, the villagers took their turn to drink, the older man refilling the bowl each time. When they had all drunk, the man filled it once more and offered it in the direction of the companions. They glanced about at one another for a moment, but then Damien nodded, accepting the bowl with a wink.

"Alright, lads, if you insist", Damien said, sniffing the bowl.

It had a musty, coconutty smell, and was definitely alcoholic. Shrugging, he lifted the bowl and drained it.

"Not bad. Any more for the rest of us?" Damien asked, gesturing towards his friends and handing the bowl back.

The old man chuckled, nodding encouragingly as he refilled the bowl. Gavin, Emil and

Marco immediately accepted, while Woody, Samson and Rudolph took some persuading. Joey, though, just shook his head and pushed the bowl away.

"It smells bad. I do not want it", he said, puckering up his face.

"It's pretty good, you know, mate", Woody encouraged. "Give it a try."

"What is the point? I do not like to drink."

"Come on, Joey, loosen up", said Damien, who was starting to feel warm and mellow from the drink. "Don't be such a lightweight!"

"I am not 'lightweight'!" Joey snapped back. "I can drink if I want, but I do not want."

"Yeah, course you could", Damien goaded him sarcastically.

For a moment, Joey looked as if he was going to lose his temper, but then he stood up, taking the full bowl of drink that was being offered to him.

"I will show you 'lightweight'", he said, lifting the bowl and downing the liquid.

The other men clapped and cheered, glad to see Joey joining in with the group. But he was not finished.

"Another", he demanded, handing the bowl back to the old man demandingly.

The man shrugged, grinning at the villager next to him, as he refilled the bowl and handed it back. Joey took the bowl and once more drained it.

"Is this 'lightweight'? Joey demanded.

"No, Joey. You're the man, mate", Damien grinned, giving a small bow.

Joey paused for a moment, considering Damien's words, and then sat down again, satisfied he was not being mocked. The villagers seemed to find Joey's display of drinking bravado hilarious, and were chuckling among themselves and nodding approvingly at Joey. Looking pleased with himself, Joey stood up, puffing his chest out slightly.

"I will be back soon. Toilet", he said as he walked away towards the nearest part of the jungle.

The conversation became louder and more raucous as the drink started to affect the companions, warming and relaxing them. It was Gavin who first noticed that the warming feeling in his belly was gradually becoming more and more unusual. His stomach felt light and floaty, as if it were pulling him upwards, and he felt the urge to take deep breaths. Looking upwards, he saw tiny pinpricks of light dancing in the sky.

"Fireflies?" He said, nudging the old villager next to him and pointing at the lights.

The old man just nodded, grinning broadly. Looking back down, Gavin noticed that the hot embers of the fire were glowing strangely, subtly shifting their colours from red to black in an almost rhythmic way.

"You seeing this too?" He asked, pointing and turning to the old man again.

"No, just you, mate. You're a nutter", the man replied.

Gavin chuckled, looking back at the fire. It was a moment before it hit him that not only had the old villager spoken to him in English, but that he also had a broad Scouse accent.

"Say again, mate?" Gavin asked, turning to the old man in shock.

The man just stared back, grinning, and Gavin noticed that the whites of his eyes and his teeth had taken on a subtle, luminous glow. Taking a deep breath, Gavin turned to Damien, who was sitting the other side of him.

"Hey, Damo", Gavin said, slapping his friend lightly on the shoulder. "Reckon there was something in that drink."

Damien started, as if shocked out of a private contemplation. Blinking, he slowly focussed on Gavin.

"Something..."

"In the drink, yeah", Gavin prompted.

Damien pondered for a moment, as if translating Gavin's words.

"You're right, man. Slipped us a mickey", he said vaguely, with an expression that looked half worried and half amused.

"What did you put in that?" Gavin said, turning back to the old villager.

The villager just carried on grinning, and Gavin noticed that the lines on his face had become deeper, lending his face an almost mask-like appearance. Looking away, he turned to one of the other villagers. With a kind of primal fear, he realised that all of the villagers at the fire were staring at him, each with an unnaturally large grin and softly glowing eyes.

"Damo. You coming for a quick walk?" Gavin said, turning away from the disconcerting gaze of the villagers.

"Yeah, right. With you", Damien replied, standing up and sucking air through his pursed lips.

Damien and Gavin walked a short distance away from the others. They were consciously avoiding looking at other's faces, as when they did so the other man's face seemed strange and alien. Although they knew that their visual hallucinations and distortions should be disturbing to them, they could not help but feel light-hearted and careless, as if the whole situation was absurd and disconnected from their real lives. They realised that they had been standing side by side, grinning and watching the sky for a number of minutes.

"Should we be worried about this, Damo?" Gavin asked after a moment.

"I dunno, man", Damien replied, still grinning vacuously. "Not much we can do about it really."

"Ride it out, then?"

"Looks like it."

"Is the moon normally that big, Damo?" Gavin asked after a moment.

Damien was silent for some time, as if he was ignoring the question, but then answered quietly.

"I don't remember, mate. Looks amazing though, eh?"

"Yeah, right. Don't think I've ever looked at it proper before."

The two men gazed up in silence for a few minutes, but were interrupted by raucous laughter from behind them. Looking back, they saw their friends gathered around the fire, silhouettes outlined in the orange glow of the flames.

"You reckon they'll be alright?" Damien asked.

"Hope so", Gavin replied, unable to take the situation seriously. "They all had it, right?"

"Yeah. Even the gaffer."

"Might loosen him up a bit. How about Tommy?"

"He'll be fine. The kid's rock hard. Stronger than a lot of the older lads."

The thought came to them both at the same time, and they turned to each other in shock.

"Joey!"

In their altered states, it was difficult for them to work out how long Joey had been gone, but he was certainly not with the other men by the fire. He had wandered off into the jungle alone before the villagers' brew had taken hold of them, and had drunk twice as much as any of the others.

"Which way did he go?" Damien asked, disorientated.

"Over there, I think", Gavin replied after getting his bearings.

They set off at a fast walk, blinking as they tried to see their way in the semi-darkness. The jungle was sparse close to the village, but as they passed the tree line it seemed to envelop them. They were suddenly cut off from the sounds of their friends and the light of the fire, the moonlit jungle taking over with its strange animal sounds and shifting foliage. The rustling of the leaves seemed to make a slithering sound, as if they were surrounded by snakes.

"This is spooky, man", Damien commented.

"Let's just find Joey and get back, right?" Gavin replied, refusing to get rattled.

They took it in turns to call Joey's name, moving a short way apart from each other and slowly advancing through the jungle.

For what seemed like many minutes they searched, sometimes

changing direction to check a previously unexplored part of the surrounding area. Without realising it, they found themselves stooping into a crouch and walking almost soundlessly as if to avoid waking the sleeping jungle.

"Gav! Gav!" Damien hissed in a harsh whisper.

"Where are you?" Gavin replied in the same tone.

"Over here!" Damien whispered more loudly.

"Why are we speaking like this?" Gavin hissed as he reached his friend.

"Like what?"

"Whispering."

Damien paused to think for a moment.

"I dunno mate!" He said finally, grinning at Gavin.

The two of them started laughing, quietly at first, but then rising in volume until they were practically crying with laughter. It took them some time to recover from their uncontrollable amusement.

"Okay, stop looking at us now", Damien said, trying to avoid Gavin's eyes. "You'll set us off again."

"I never started you off before, mate!" Gavin replied, forcing himself to stop laughing. "Anyway, what did you want?"

"Want?"

"You were calling my name."

"Oh yeah, right. Check it out", Damien said, pointing ahead through a gap in the undergrowth.

In a small, moonlit clearing stood Joey. He was motionless, staring at a point on the ground a few feet in front of himself, loincloth round his ankles.

"Joey", Damien said, choking back a laugh. "You alright, man?"

"Is he…?" Gavin began, moving out of the undergrowth into the clearing.

"It is moving", Joey suddenly spoke, eyes still cast down.

"What's that, mate?" Gavin asked, patting Joey lightly on the shoulder.

"The head", Joey answered with a kind of horrified fascination. "It is moving."

Slowly, he brought his arm out to point at the ground before him. It was a moment before Damien and Gavin realised what it was that Joey was looking at. Coming into the clearing, Joey had obviously removed his loincloth to squat down and relieve himself. On finishing, he had turned round and become morbidly fascinated by his creation.

"What are you doing, Joey?" Gavin said, wrinkling his nose. "Disgusting!"

"It was moving its head up and down", Joey repeated. "Like… Like an alien."

"Christ's sake, man", Damien said, taking a step back.

"Damo, do us a favour, will you?" Gavin asked. "Pull his pants back up."

"Why do I have to do it?"

"Just do it, mate, okay?"

"You owe us one", Damien said, shaking his head as he bent down and hoisted Joey's loin cloth up at arm's length.

"Alright then, Joey. Come with us now, okay?" Gavin coaxed, putting his arm around Joey's shoulders and steering him towards the distant sounds of merriment from the village.

After momentary resistance, Joey let himself be guided out of the clearing and through the undergrowth in the direction of the fire.

"It must have been inside me…", Joey began, frowning deeply.

"Hey, Joey", Damien interrupted, trying to change the subject. "How about the game today? You played a blinder!"

"The game?" Joey answered, looking up.

"Yeah, you remember", Gavin prompted, "We won. Got the cup back."

"I remember", Joey said after a moment's though. "It was a long time ago."

"Well, only a couple of hours, man", Damien replied, confused. "But yeah, couldn't have done it without you."

"Yes. I was playing very good", Joey nodded.

"That's more like our Joey", Damien grinned.

"You were playing good, too."

"Nice of you to say it, man. We made some team, eh?"

The three men had by now reached the edge of the jungle and were making their way along the dusty path, back towards the light of the fire. Suddenly, Joey stopped, staring at Damien with an earnest expression.

"What's up?" Damien asked, stopping to face Joey.

For a minute or two, Joey seemed to struggle with his thoughts, but then his words almost blurted out.

"I am sorry we are always fighting. I do not hate you"

"Yeah, me too, pal." Damien replied, grinning. "Sorry I'm always winding you up, like."

"It is good. You are a funny man", Joey said, grasping Damien by both shoulders, his expression becoming even more earnest. "I like you. I like you. You know?"

Damien was now becoming slightly uncomfortable with the man's intensity, but didn't want to risk letting Joey slip back into the morbid mood in which they had discovered him.

"Yeah, I know", he replied, slapping Joey's shoulder in a comradely manner. "You're a good lad."

Damien hoped that this would be the end of Joey's unusual outpouring of emotion, but if anything the man's eyes became wider and his grip firmer. Damien was about to pull away from Joey's grasp when he noticed how pale the man's skin was, and that it was covered in a sheen of sweat even in the cool evening air.

Joey was standing with his back towards the fire pit, holding onto Damien's shoulders as he stared into his face. His recent outpourings were forgotten as Damien's face transformed before Joey's eyes. It began in Damien's pupils, a tiny flickering reflection of the fire at his back. This spark evolved and grew until his eyes were taken over by a pulsing, rotating wheel. From there, the pattern grew, spreading across his cheeks and lips until his entire face was filled. Joey gawped in wonder. Damien's face looked old, wise and beautiful amid the overlay of patterns as they shifted and swam. One moment he had tessellating shapes emanating from his flickering eyes, the next he had identical, tiny rainbow lizards spiralling outwards in perfect unison. The patterns grew more intense and scintillating, quickly blocking out all of Damien's features. By now, Joey had forgotten where he was and who he was with. The patterns were the only thing he was conscious of, and with a comforting jolt, they snapped out of the silhouette of Damien's head until they completely filled his vision.

With a small, awestruck gasp, Joey went limp and fell to the floor in a faint.

8

Gavin awoke to a hot, sticky morning. The sun seemed to burn the back of his eyes, and he flinched away from its brightness. With eyes half-open, he swiftly got his bearings and ran to the shade of the wood-hut. As he slumped against the side of the hut, his head started to throb with pain. Closing his eyes and rubbing his temples, he tried to breathe evenly and deeply. His cramped and rumbling stomach and his parched throat told him that he had not eaten or drunk anything for some time. Crouching there, waiting for his headache to subside, he tried to piece together what had happened the night before.

He clearly remembered winning the game and the celebrations that followed, including the team being given some type of drugged drink. His memories after that became somewhat hazy, as if he couldn't distinguish actual events from dreamed ones.

A vivid flash of himself and Damien caring for Joey came back. Joey had fainted and had been carried into the wood-hut where Damien had made him drink a large quantity of water. Puzzled and distressed, Joey had ordered them to leave him alone in the hut so that he could sleep.

Outside the hut, most of their friends had left the fire pit area. Brushing aside their concern, a surprisingly lucid Tommy had assured them that he was fine and didn't need looking after, but that the others were acting "like plonkers" and had left to go to the river.

Walking down the twisty path towards the river, they had been overcome once again by the sense that the jungle was a living being, and sneaked in silence so as not to invoke its wrath. It had soon became apparent, though, that their silence was pointless, as a loud singing came from the jungle ahead. Reaching the clearing by the riverbank, they found the source of the noise. Samson was standing up straight, head raised to the sky, arms spread out wide, singing some kind of song at the top of his voice.

Leaving Samson to his rapture, they had continued to the bank and almost tripped over Woody, who was lying face-down on the bank with his head over the river, watching his reflection in the moonlight. "Beautiful!" He had repeated over and over again.

Looking out over the river, they had seen Marco and Emil, up to their waists in the gently-flowing water, splashing each other and giggling. Realising that Rudolph was still missing, they had asked their nearby friends if they had seen him, eventually getting a reaction from Emil, who had pointed vaguely into the trees behind where they were standing.

Pushing their way into the jungle, they had spent some time searching the surrounding area, eventually hearing Rudolph's voice as he chatted away. Following the sound of the voice, Gavin and Damien had come upon their manager with his arms wrapped around the trunk of a great tree, a besotted smile on his face. Noticing his players approaching, Rudolph had retreated guiltily, moving away from the object of his desire. Asked what he was doing he had replied rather sheepishly, "Well, she is very pretty, no?"

Gavin laughed at this memory, and opened his eyes to the harsh light of day. His head was still throbbing, but not with the same intensity as it had been. He saw the sleeping bodies of his friends dotted about the area, some of them beginning to stir. At the fire pit, two of the villagers sat stirring the battered cauldron. Wandering towards them, Gavin nodded blearily at the men, leaning to peer into the pot. It was the same stodgy, foul-tasting mush that they had eaten yesterday, he realised with a grimace. Noticing him watching, one of the villagers motioned towards the cauldron, offering him some of the food.

Before Gavin was forced to decide between his stomach or his taste buds, a commotion began in the village nearby. The sound of a woman screaming and two men shouting began, and seemed to be drawing closer. The two villagers stood up, looking concerned, and started walking towards the disturbance. After a moment, Damien came into sight, rapidly backing down the path towards them. He was followed by the Chief's son, who was shouting in a hoarse voice, machete raised as if to strike. Damien jumped backwards as the blade swung towards him, narrowly missing his stomach. As the Chief's son raised his arm again, a woman came into view. She was wailing, hands held towards the Chief's son in an imploring manner.

As Gavin and the two villagers jogged toward the angry group, they saw that it was the girl with the pretty eyes who was pleading with the Chief's son. Inwardly cursing Damien's stupidity for getting mixed up with the woman again, he called out as he approached.

"Damo, get over here behind me. And keep your gob shut."

"But he's gone crazy, Gav", Damien replied, torn between his wish to seek safety with his friend and his impulse to protect the woman. "I was only grabbing a drink of water off her!"

As Gavin approached, the Chief's son swung round, holding his weapon out defensively. The men stayed still, locked in a wary standoff as the woman began pleading again in a more controlled voice. In a flash of inspiration, Damien gradually lowered himself to his knees, holding his hands up in surrender. The Chief's son watched him suspiciously.

"I'm sorry, mate", Damien said to the angry man who still held his machete threateningly high. "I promise I'll not chat to her again."

Damien put on his most sincere expression, bending over submissively in the hope that the man would calm down. The Chief's son seemed to relax for a moment, as if he was satisfied, but then his face changed to one of sudden rage. Grunting, he raised his machete to strike Damien as he lay prostrate on the ground. Gavin instinctively leaped forward, but he knew he was too far away to be able to stop the blow. However, the man's machete arm stopped just as it was about to fall, and Gavin saw that the woman, who was closest to him, had grabbed the Chief's son by the wrist. Turning round in blind rage, the man swung with his other arm and slapped the woman hard around the face, knocking her to the ground. Without stopping to think, Gavin formed his hand into a fist, and he struck the Chief's son squarely on the cheek, sending him reeling backwards and on to the dusty floor.

The two villagers glanced at Gavin in horror, moving forward to help their superior to his feet. The Chief's son shook them off as they tried to take him by the arms, and picked himself up off the ground. He took two steps towards Gavin, hate burning in his eyes, but found that he could barely remain upright due to the heavy blow he had received. Staggering back a step, he tried to throw his machete, but it landed harmlessly near Gavin's feet. The man began yelling once more, pointing to the opposite end of the village. By now his voice was raw and cracked with rage and strain, and Gavin had the sinking feeling that they would soon have to leave their temporary home. After a few more yells of rage, the Chief's son turned around and walked away, supported by one of the villagers. The remaining man moved warily towards Gavin to confirm their fate. He pointed vertically up in the sky and then towards the other side of the village. Assuming Gavin would not understand his meaning, the man began his gesticulation again.

"It's alright, mate, don't trouble yourself. I get the message", Gavin sighed, patting the man on the shoulder. "You want us to get the hell out of town by midday."

The air became hotter and dryer as the morning progressed. After their run-in with the Chief's son, Gavin and Damien had set about rousing their friends from their deep and sedated sleep. The other men woke, grumbling, but despite Gavin's annoyance with Damien for causing this trouble, the man seemed so downcast after the fight that he decided it was better not to add to his woes by telling the others what had happened. Instead, he simply told them that the Chief had demanded they leave now, as they had outstayed their welcome.

The men looked distinctly the worse for wear after their night of revelry, and with expressions ranging from disgust to grim acceptance, they helped themselves to the foul breakfast mush which the two villagers had left in the cauldron. With great care, Raphaël was placed on the stretcher that Samson had constructed, and was carried outside into the shade of the wood-hut. The companions tried not to look too alarmed at Raphaël's condition. His eyes, which opened and closed in confusion, had a sickly yellow tinge to them, and he was covered in a sheen of clammy sweat. His breathing was ragged and pained, and he gnashed his teeth constantly.

"We should not be moving him", Emil said, shaking his head.

"But we cannot stay here for ever", Samson replied with a sigh. "He needs some medicine. To help with his fever."

"Sams is right", Gavin agreed, folding his arms and looking around at his friends. "We need out of this jungle soon, or we're all gonna go crazy."

The men nodded and mumbled their agreement.

"Where are we gonna go then, Gav?" Woody asked. "You know, we could be walking in circles."

"How about the boat?" Tommy suggested.

"Gone", Damien said dejectedly.

"What's that, Damo?" Gavin prompted.

"I went down there this morning. The boat was gone and there were a couple of lads there with sticks, shooed me off."

"Bollocks!" Gavin swore, hunching his shoulders in despair.

"We should keep heading south", Emil said after a moment.

"What do you mean, mate?" Marco asked.

"The river was flowing south. I watched the sun rise and set. We can continue south even though we are no longer on the river."

"Not bad, Emil", Gavin said after a moment's consideration. "It's the best plan we've got. You reckon you can keep us going in the right direction?"

"I think so." Emil replied with a slightly pained expression.

"Alright, sorted", Gavin said, checking the sun and then shouldering his rucksack which contained the trophy. "We'd best get a move on then, lads. This way, right, Emil?"

"Through the village first. Past the ball game court. And then we will need to change our direction slightly."

"Sams, are you and Marco okay carrying Raph for a bit? We can swap round when you get tired."

The two men nodded, picking up their injured friend gently and moving off along the path through the village. As the group made their way along the dusty track, they glanced around at the eerily quiet huts along the way. Here and there a door moved shut as if the hut's occupant had been watching but did not want to be noticed. Damien looked up expectantly as he passed the communal area where he had first seen the village girl, but it was now deserted, and he eventually gave up, his head drooping sadly.

After a few minutes, they reached the end of the village and the path narrowed as it began to be reclaimed by the jungle. As they passed the turning towards the ball game court, they heard a sharp hissing sound from a nearby tree. Starting in surprise, the men backed away, trying to locate the source of the sound. The hissing came once more, and this time they looked upward into the lower branches of the tree. With his legs dangling beneath him, the referee sat on a thick branch, grinning. He raised his hand in greeting and then dropped from the tree, landing lightly on the path opposite the companions. On his shoulder he carried a small bag woven from long, dried leaves, which he removed and handed to Gavin. Moving over to Damien, the man presented him with a yam, chuckling slightly as he handed it over.

"Thanks mate", Damien said, forcing a grin.

Nodding, the man moved back a few steps and waited until he had everyone's full attention. Looking upwards, he pointed towards the sun, which was visible through the thin canopy. Pausing for a moment, he then moved his arm in a slow arc, clearly tracing the route of the sun as it moved from east to west. Waiting for the men to nod their understanding, he gestured towards the group and then pointed his arm into the jungle, holding his pose while the men gathered round to see exactly which direction he was suggesting.

"This making sense to you, Emil?" Gavin asked.

"I think he is saying we should go roughly east-south-east", Emil said, pointing off in the same direction as the referee.

Seeing Emil's gesture, the referee nodded vigorously and then backed away, giving the men a final grin before he turned and disappeared behind one of the trees along the path back to the village.

"I will lead, okay?" Emil said, moving off in the direction indicated by the villager.

The men nodded their agreement, falling into step behind the Dutchman as he weaved his way between the trees and bushes of the jungle.

"What's in the bag, Gav?" Tommy asked, looking hopeful.

"Looks like some sort of dried meat", Gavin replied, rooting around in the makeshift bag that he had been given. "A bit like jerky. Smells pretty bad."

"It's probably more monkey", Tommy said with a chuckle. "Give us a bit to try, then."

"Not now, eh, Tommy?" Gavin shook his head. "We've got to ration the stuff. Didn't you just have breakfast, anyway?"

"Still hungry though, Gav."

"Ask Damo for some of his yam then, eh?"

"I'm not eating raw yam when there's monkey jerky to be had!"

"Sorry, mate. Later", Gavin grinned, stowing the little bag of dried meat in his rucksack with the trophy.

Damien had dropped back to the rear of the group, and was examining his gift from the villager. The other men hadn't seen that he had been handed another small object as well as the yam. Looking ahead to check that he wasn't being watched, he gripped the yam under his arm so that he could examine the object. It was a small piece of leather containing something hard, and was held closed by a sinuous drawstring. Loosening the drawstring slightly, he emptied the contents into his palm. There were two wooden objects, both about the size of his thumb. Bringing them up to his face to examine them, he realised that they were simple carvings. One of them was slightly larger and was carved in the shape of a nearly naked man with a beard, while the other was shaped like a woman with large eyes and an ear-to-ear grin. Smiling back at the sculpture, he looked more closely at the first one and realised that it was meant to resemble himself, while the other one represented the village girl he had taken a shine to.

A warm feeling spread through his stomach, banishing his depression. The village girl had liked him too, he decided, and had obviously spent some time thinking about him, otherwise she wouldn't have taken the trouble to make him a present and have it smuggled out to him. He was struck by the wild impulse to make something himself, and to find a way to give it to the girl, but soon realised that this would only cause more trouble for her.

Wrapping the tiny sculptures up in the leather, he stashed them in his loincloth, feeling slightly ridiculous. He had only seen the girl twice, for a matter of minutes. Neither spoke a language the other understood and they lived completely opposite lives. She was no beauty in the conventional sense, but she had something about her that Damien found very sweet. He began to laugh out loud to himself as he realised what a teenager he was being.

"Crazy. I must be bloody crazy", he said between belly laughs as his friends looked back at him questioningly.

Their shared glances confirmed that they agreed entirely.

Gavin plodded on, placing one foot in front of the other in a kind of trance. It had been three days since they had been forced to leave the village, and they had seen no signs of civilisation. The group had become sullen and touchy as they all started to entertain the thought that they had been sent off in a pointless direction. The last of the jerky had been finished the night before, and although the men had found a number of banana trees, their fruit had all fallen and rotted in the interminable drizzle. The rain had started the evening after they set off from the village, and had continued until late the previous night, sometimes falling in heavy sheets, but mostly seeping down with a depressing constancy. The nights had been cold and the days wet and tiring, and the conversation had dried up, taking with it any real hope of rescue.

The only positive thing was Raphaël's improvement. His fever had all disappeared and, although his wrist still gave him pain, he had been able to walk without help for most of the previous day.

"How much further are we gonna go before we admit that we're lost in the middle of nowhere?" Marco scowled.

Gavin realised that these were the first words any of them had uttered since the group had set off that morning. Seconds passed in awkward silence as each man hoped that someone else would have some words of encouragement.

"We cannot stop here", Emil replied eventually. "We will never be found."

"Great, mate, but how do we know we're not walking around in circles?"

"I have been keeping an eye on the sun's position", Emil said with more confidence than he actually felt.

"Don't give me that crap, Emil. We haven't seen the bloody sun for three days."

"It is true", Emil conceded with a sigh. "But the clouds are brighter in some places. It is possible to estimate where the sun is."

"Oh please, mate. Do you think I'm a bloody moron? That could be anything. Maybe the cloud's just a bit thinner there."

"Drop it, Marco, eh?" Gavin interrupted. "The man's doing the best he can."

"I'm sure he is, mate, but that's not a lot of bloody good, is it?"

"It's not like we've got a lot of other options, Marco. Unless you've got a suggestion?"

"Well I don't know why we left he village in the first place."

"That's what I was thinking", Woody chimed in. "You know, we had food and shelter there."

"There was more chance of someone finding us there also." Rudolph added.

"Alright, calm down, lads", Gavin said, exasperated. "It's not like we had a lot of choice."

"Why not, Gav?" Marco asked irritably. "Why didn't you have had a word with the chief or something? Or that bloke who gave us the jerky."

"You should have asked him for more food", Joey announced, looking accusingly at Gavin. "I am very hungry."

"Why's it always up to me?" Gavin snapped, his temper finally getting the better of him. "You're not my kids! Can't you help yourselves once in a while?"

Gavin looked back and forth between his friends' faces. They had all stopped walking, shocked by his outburst.

"Maybe I'm hungry too, eh? Maybe I'd like some food and a good night's kip. But no, all I get is moan, moan, moan." Gavin paused to scan his friends' faces again, but none of them answered. "Well, bollocks to you! Look after yourselves!"

Shaking his head in frustration, Gavin turned on his heel and stormed ahead, breathing deeply with suppressed rage. The other companions stood and watched, wanting to call him back and apologise, but too deep into their own depression and hopelessness to make the effort.

Gavin soon regretted his fit of temper, but his patience had worn so thin over the last few days that he felt like he had to get away for while. He would go back and join them soon. Maybe make a joke about his outburst to break the ice. For now, he just wanted to be on his own, and to walk at his own speed without people slowing him down.

Gavin strode on, head down, so caught up in his frustrations that he didn't notice the man with the gun until he was almost beside him. His first instinct was to run, but his common sense told him that the man would shoot him down before he could reach cover. Dropping into a fighting crouch, he looked the man up and down.

He certainly didn't seem like a soldier. He stood roughly five feet tall and was dressed in short, baggy trousers and wore dirty leather sandals. A thick, woven tunic was secured around his torso by a piece of rope. On his head sat a wide-brimmed coolie hat that dripped with rain. His gun was also less threatening than it had seemed at first. It was an ancient, bolt-action rifle with a wooden stock that was worn and chipped with age. Gavin relaxed as he noticed that the man seemed at least as surprised and scared as himself.

The man's first reaction was also to run. He had left his home that morning on the pretence of going hunting, but really to smoke and indulge in idle thought without being chastised by his wife. He had been wandering for half an hour, walking a route he often took, when he heard a crashing sound. His first reaction was that it must be a large, enraged boar, and he had readied his rifle to defend himself, but what came striding through the thick undergrowth was more unexpected than any jungle animal.

It was a man, although at first sight it appeared to be some sort of demon. Seemingly naked except for a bright red shirt, the man was also red. His hair and beard, spiked with the wet, was an unearthly shade of orange, and his sunburned face surrounded green eyes that seemed to be standing out on stalks of anger.

Gavin stared back at the small man, unsure of what to do. He seemed on the verge of bolting, but then his face changed to one of revelation as he looked at Gavin's shirt. For a moment he hesitated, but his smile gradually broadened as he held out a finger to point at Gavin.

"Manchester United!" The man declared triumphantly.

The other companions, a good three hundred metres behind, heard Gavin's scream of anguish and came running.

The small man chattered constantly as they walked, turning now and then to grin encouragingly at his new friends. He had uttered no more words in English since his first words to Gavin, although the companions had picked up from his gesticulation and repetition that his name was Kwei and that they were being brought to his home.

The men were in a jubilant mood, partly because of the immediate prospect of food and shelter, but also because Kwei was the first civilised man they had met who had not tried to kill them, and that meant that they had a link to the outside word, and rescue.

Kwei grew more exuberant as they emerged on to a rough track, pointing ahead and grinning broadly. A moment later, a makeshift shack came into view. The walls and windows were made of variously shaped and coloured materials that appeared to have been scavenged from other buildings. A small metal chimney protruding from the corrugated iron roof coughed puffs of smoke into the still air. The men peered around, looking for other buildings, but this appeared to be the only dwelling in the area.

Reaching the shack, Kwei pushed open the woodwormy door and stepped in, waving the companions inside enthusiastically. The interior was as ramshackle as outside, filled with odd bits of furniture and various other junk. Three other people stood at the far end of the room, staring back at the men suspiciously. In the middle was a middle-aged woman, presumably Kwei's wife. She was at least six inches taller than her husband, and extremely fat. Her two daughters clearly took after their mother more than their father. The older girl was already taller than him, while the other was about the same height, and both of them were a lot more bulky.

Kwei started to speak animatedly to his wife, pointing at the companions and gesturing in the direction they had walked. The woman replied irritably, waving her husband away, but Kwei moved forward as he replied in his mollifying voice, hands clasped in an almost begging manner. After sighing and shaking her head for a moment, she finally nodded curtly and turned towards the simple cooking stove behind her, on which two pots steamed.

Kwei turned to the companions happily, pointing them towards a table as he chattered away. There were only four chairs to sit on, but he scurried out of the house for a moment and returned with a number of small metal barrels, which he placed around the table for the rest of the companions to sit on. Behind him, his daughters stared in fascinated disgust at the dirty, bearded men who had been invited into their house. With an exaggerated clatter of crockery, Kwei's wife pulled an assortment of plates and bowls out from under her stove, sighing and mumbling constantly. Brandishing a ladle, she slopped food from both her two pots on to each plate, screaming for Kwei to collect them. The small man scurried over, grabbing two plates and placing them onto the table in front of the companions, giving a small bow before he hurried back for more.

Tommy and Joey, grabbing the first two plates, poked about in the food. It was rice with some sort of overcooked meat in a light brown sauce. It smelt bland and unappetising, but they grabbed a spoon from a tin in the middle of the table and tucked in happily, nodding their appreciation. As more bowls and plates arrived, the rest of the companions began eating, all silently focussed on their food after so many days without anything proper to eat. Damien considered trying to ask for a bowl with just rice in it, but one look at the unfriendly expression on Kwei's wife's face dissuaded him, and he shovelled the largest pieces of meat on to Tommy's plate before hungrily devouring the rest of the portion.

As the first plates were finished off, Kwei picked them up and returned them to his wife, motioning for her to refill them. This seemed to push the irritated woman over the edge, and she started yelling at her husband, snatching the plates off him and shooing him away. Kwei returned to the companions with a shrug of apology.

"It's okay, mate. Not to worry. This was fine." Gavin said, patting Kwei on the shoulder and smiling gratefully at the woman.

Kwei seemed pleased, and crossed to the far corner of the room, beckoning towards Gavin. Patting his stomach contentedly, Gavin sauntered over to the man. Kwei was pointing excitedly towards a dog-eared poster that hung in the corner of the wall above a shrine containing a small brass Buddha and a wooden joss stick holder. As Gavin approached, Kwei pointed to the poster again and then at Gavin's shirt.

From a distance it was hard to tell what the poster depicted due to the fact that the light was bad in the room and the poster had discoloured with age. But as Gavin peered at it, he realised with a sigh exactly what it was. The poster, pulled from the inside of a magazine, showed the Manchester United team assembled after their treble-winning season. Their grinning faces seemed to leer out of the page at Gavin as they kneeled or stood in front of the three trophies. Kwei waited for recognition, and Gavin was tempted to just smile and let the matter lie, but something stopped him.

"We're Liverpool", Gavin said, grabbing his shirt and showing it to Kwei. "Not Man United!"

"Man United!" Kwei nodded, over the moon with joy. "Goal!"

"Christ's sake, mate", Gavin replied, wiping sweat from his forehead. "Liverpool. Liverpool!"

Kwei appeared not to understand, and was glancing between Gavin and the poster, seemingly very pleased with himself.

"Okay, hang on a moment"

Picking up his rucksack, Gavin pulled the gleaming trophy from inside.

"See here? Liverpool!" He said, pointing to the words engraved on the silver plaque at the bottom of the trophy.

Kwei studied the trophy, fascinated, and then looked back at the poster, clearly comparing Gavin's trophy with the ones pictured. After a moment, he shrugged, looking confused. As Gavin returned the cup to his rucksack, he noticed that Kwei's wife had moved over to take a look, clearly attracted by the trophy.

Emil, joining the small group in the corner, changed the subject.

"Is there a telephone?" The Dutchman asked, miming picking up a receiver.

Kwei shook his head, shrugging.

"A map?"

This second suggestion took more imagination on Emil's behalf to mime, but eventually he pretended to fold out a large piece of paper, follow a path on it with his finger and then fold the paper up and set off walking.

Kwei scratched his stubble for a minute and then grinned, nodding and rifling through a small pile of magazines. Eventually, he returned and presented Emil with a black and white printed magazine that featured an occasional photo. The entire publication was printed in an Oriental script that Emil had never seen before. Turning a few pages, Kwei pointed to a half-page map, holding his finger over a location in the jungle as he pointed at the ground with his other hand.

Emil studied the map for a few minutes as the other men gathered round, their interest piqued by the prospect of finding a way out of the jungle.

"It is good and bad", Emil said calmly. "I can see that there is a road nearby that leads to a town or city, but I cannot understand the name of the town. Also, it looks as if it is far away. Perhaps a hundred miles, perhaps more. The map does not look very accurate."

"Maybe ask matey if he knows how far it is", Woody suggested.

"Here", Emil said, pointing to the town as he showed the map to Kwei. "This town."

Kwei nodded, saying a word that meant nothing to Emil.

"Can we walk?" Emil made a stylised walking motion, tracing a route between Kwei's location and the town.

Kwei shook his head gravely, looking at the men as if they were crazy.

The door swung open as Marco, who had left the table to go outside after finishing his food, returned.

"There's no-one else around here, from what I can see", the Australian said, closing the door behind him. "This is the only place for miles."

"Are there any vehicles, Marco?" Gavin asked.

"Yeah, there was a beat up old combi. Heap of junk though."

"It might have to do", Gavin replied, nodding. "Show us where it is."

The men trooped outside, Kwei following them with a confused expression on his face. Marco led them round to the other side of the shack, towards a small shed made of corrugated iron. Inside nestled a neglected camper van with most of its roof sheared off. The vehicle had once been beige, but more of its body was now covered in dirt and rust than the original paintwork.

"Does it work?" Marco asked Kwei, miming turning a steering wheel. Kwei shrugged, raising a finger and then scurrying back into the shack. Meanwhile, Marco opened the bonnet to look inside.

"Engine's not too bad, by the looks of it", the Australian said after a moment.

"Reckon it'll run?" Gavin asked.

"I wouldn't bet on it, mate."

Kwei returned brandishing a battered jerry can and a key, which he handed to Marco. Prising the fuel cap off, he tipped some of the petrol from the can into the tank and sat in the driver's seat, placing the key in the ignition and turning it as his friends looked on in anticipation. The engine was silent as Marco tried a number of times to start it.

"Battery's dead, probably", Marco said with a sigh.

"Anything we can do?" Gavin asked.

"Well, there's no electric here so we can't charge it. We could try bump-starting it."

"Okay Marco. Just tell us what to do."

"Everyone get behind it and push it out of the shed first."

One at a time, the men filed past the old vehicle into the cramped space at the back of the shed. After a count of three from Marco, they leaned forward and shoved. The van refused to budge an inch.

"Okay, hold on lads", Marco said, grinning and shaking his head. "Hand brake. Sorry!"

Ignoring the curses of his friends, Marco squeezed out of the shed and released the handbrake.

"Give it a shove!" He shouted, moving the gear stick into neutral.

As the companions pushed, the van started to move almost immediately, creaking and grinding as it gradually emerged from the shed.

"All right, keep it going!" Marco yelled back at his friends. "Give it some speed!"

Marco turned the steering wheel, pointing the vehicle towards the rough path, which ran slightly downhill. After a moment, the speed had built up and Marco forced the old van into gear, letting off the clutch. The engine complained bitterly, spluttering and making the van judder and slow.

"Keep pushing, lads!" Marco shouted desperately. "Don't let it stop!"

At the back of the van, the men were sweating with the exertion, trying their best to force the old vehicle forward. The engine gave a cough, expelling some black smoke from the exhaust, and then burst into life. Marco, who had put the van in second gear and had his foot on the accelerator, was looking back at his friends when the engine started working, and had to swerve to avoid a tree as the vehicle picked up speed. Marco battled to regain control of the van, attempting to steer it onto the track, which looked barely wide enough for the vehicle to drive along.

As Marco and the van became obscured by the trees lining the track, the companions heard his desperate yell; "No brakes!"

For some time the men stood watching the track as the sound of the van got further away.

"Think he'll be okay?" Woody asked nervously.

"We will hear him if he crashes", Samson replied encouragingly.

"Perhaps he will continue on his own, and bring help", Rudolph suggested.

"The main road is that way", Emil said, pointing the opposite way up the track. "It soon comes to an end in this direction, I think."

The men exchanged glances, some of them wincing. Silence fell again as they listened for the sound of a crash. Just as Gavin was about to suggest that they set off after Marco on foot, the van's engine sound returned. The men cheered in joy as it grew gradually louder, and a minute later Marco appeared, waving as he drove back up the track towards his friends. Stopping a few metres away, he stood up and bowed, grinning from ear to ear.

"You alright with no brakes then?" Gavin asked when the cheering had died down.

"Yeah, just stick it in neutral and use the hand brake, mate", Marco replied, climbing down from the idling van. "And don't stop the engine if you can help it."

"We are just going to take his van?" Samson said, speaking quietly to Gavin.

"No other choice really, Sams", Gavin replied. "We need to get to that main road."

"It seems like we are stealing from a man who helped us. He is a poor man"

"Yeah alright, mate. I'll have a word with him."

Kwei now looked slightly out of his depth as Gavin strolled over to him and put his arm round the small man's shoulders.

"Kwei, old mate. It's about your van", Gavin began, pointing towards the vehicle and waiting for the man to nod. "We really need it. Can we take it with us?"

Gavin mimed driving, pointing off up the track in the direction Emil wanted them to go. Kwei looked troubled, as if caught between the wish to be generous to his new friends and his need of a vehicle. He mumbled to himself for a few minutes before coming to a decision. Grasping Gavin's shirt with one hand, he pointed at the vehicle with the other, looking up at Gavin questioningly.

"You want my shirt eh? It's a special one, though." Gavin considered the offer for a moment, eventually shaking his head as he pulled the shirt over his head and handed it to Kwei. "Here you go, mate. Look after it, right? I don't wanna see it on Ebay next week."

Kwei grinned, removing his tunic and pulling on the dirty red shirt. It was far too big for the man, reaching almost to his knees and covering his hands, but he looked very pleased with his new acquisition.

"Okay, sorted", Gavin said, turning to his friends. "Let's get going, eh? I'll grab that petrol can."

The men piled in to the roofless back of the van, with Marco jumping into the driver's seat and revving the engine. As Gavin returned carrying the jerry can, he saw Kwei's wife heading towards the van, face like thunder. She raised her arm as she came level with Marco, a huge metal serving spoon in her hand. Gavin opened his mouth to warn his friend, but it was too late.

The woman struck Marco over the head with her spoon, producing a dull ringing sound as she drew her arm back to strike him again. Her arm descended four more times before Marco was able to get out of the van and raise his arms to defend himself. Having removed Marco from the vehicle, the woman turned her attentions to Kwei, screaming at him and gesturing towards the van. Kwei replied calmly, approaching his wife with hands clasped, but she raised her arm again, menacing her husband with the spoon. Kwei pleaded softly for a moment before his shoulders sagged and he sighed in resignation. Taking a few steps towards Gavin, he pointed towards the van and shook his head, bowing in apology. Seeing Gavin's frustration, he made to take the shirt off.

"No, no, no, mate!" Gavin said, grasping Kwei's shoulder in earnest. "Keep the shirt. We have to take the van, see? We need to get out of here."

Kwei shrugged, gestured towards his wife and hung his head. Deciding that Kwei had given up, Gavin turned instead to the woman. She still held her spoon up threateningly, watching Gavin and his friends closely. Gavin took a step towards her and held his hands together as if in prayer, bowing his head to her height and looking at her pleadingly. A moment later, the woman reached her free hand out to point at Gavin's rucksack, barking an order.

"The bag? You want the bag?" Gavin said hopefully. "No problem, it's yours!"

Gavin fished the trophy out of the bag, pulled the drawstring and tossed the empty bag towards Kwei's wife, but her expression was still as cold as steel. Giving him a withering look, she shook her head and pointed at the trophy in Gavin's hand.

"What? No, you've gotta be kidding", he said, holding his prize up longingly.

Marco came to stand beside Gavin, rubbing his head where he had been bruised in the vicious spoon attack.

"I don't think we've got much choice, mate."

"Oh get lost, Marco. We can't lose it again. Not after last time!"

"The way I see it, mate, we've got two options. One, you lay that crazy woman out and we do a runner. Two, you give her the bloody trophy and we come and get it back another time, once we've got everything sorted in town."

Gavin sighed, considering Marco's words. After what seemed like many minutes, he strode towards Kwei's wife, face red with anger. His friends watched in horror, convinced that he was going to take the first option, but as he reached the woman he slowed, taking her arm and shoving the trophy into her podgy fist. Turning away, he stormed over to the van and climbed into the passenger seat.

"Come on then, Marco", he said, his voice simmering with rage. "Are you gonna bloody well drive this thing or what?"

9

The companions stood around in the rain feeling lost once more. The previous day's driving had been slow going, and as the mileometer on the van was broken, they had no real way of knowing how far they had come. On the narrow and twisting jungle track they had rarely been able to travel faster than ten miles an hour, frequently less, and they had often needed to stop to clear wood or other debris from the track. Twice, the van had stalled and needed to be bump-started again. As darkness fell, Marco tried to keep driving, but after a near miss with a tree close to the track, they decided it would be better to kill the engine and stop for the night. It had begun to rain in the early hours of the morning, and many of the men had taken refuge under the van. When it finally became light, they spent some time trying to bump-start the vehicle on the now-muddy track, and by the time they set off they were thoroughly mud-covered and exhausted. Two hours into the morning's drive the engine had sputtered and died as they ran out of petrol.

"Anyone got any ideas then?" Gavin asked, his head drooping as he hunched his shoulders against the cold rain.

"Someone has got to fetch us some fuel", Joey said testily.

"Yeah mate, great idea, but I don't see any petrol stations around here", Marco replied with a sigh. "Anyway, how are you gonna pay for it? Sexual favours?"

"No, I will not do 'sexual favours'. This is not funny", Joey snapped back.

"I think we may be close to the road", Emil said, trying to calm the situation down. "I cannot be sure, but we have covered many miles since yesterday. It should not be far."

"So what, we just leave the van here and walk it?" Gavin asked.

"I thought that one or two of us could walk to the road and bring back some petrol. It looked like a big road on the map. There should be a fuel station close by."

"You reckon that's better than us all walking to the road and trying to hitch a lift?"

"Would you pick us up, mate?" Marco asked, looking down at his practically naked, mud-coated body.

"Yeah, right. Any volunteers for finding a garage then?"

The men stood silently, avoiding each other's eyes. Eventually Woody spoke up.

"We could draw lots. You know, that's fair to everyone."

Gavin glanced about at his friends, who each nodded in a resigned manner.

"Right, I'll get some sticks then. Give us a moment."

Gavin returned a few minutes later with ten twigs protruding from his hand.

"Whoever gets the shortest ones is walking", he said holding out his hand. "Take your pick."

One by one, the men approached Gavin and drew a twig from his hand. Comparing the length, it was clear that Woody and Damien had the shortest twigs, and they both sighed as they looked down the muddy and depressing track ahead of them.

"Okay, man. Are we gonna do this?" Damien said, turning to Woody with a forced grin.

"Yeah, I suppose", Woody replied.

"You can bring some food back, too", Joey suggested as they turned to leave.

"No problem, pal. Anything in particular?"

"I would like some chocolate."

"Gotcha. Anyone else?"

"Crisps. Salt and vinegar", Gavin requested.

"Perhaps if they have a selection of glasses. For my eyes. Bring a few different types, maybe one will be correct for me", Rudolph added.

"Will do, boss. I'll just put it all on the tab. Any more? Don't be shy."

"Okay, mate. Can you get us a cappuccino and one of those microwave burgers?" Marco asked.

"Anything for you, Marco. Tell you what; shall I get you an air freshener for the van? It's getting a bit stuffy in there."

Giving his friends the thumbs up, Damien turned and set off, Woody falling in beside him.

"You remembered your platinum card, right, Woody?" Damien asked when they were out of earshot of their friends.

"I wish, mate", Woody replied regretfully.

"It'll have to be the sexual favours then, superstar."

The twisty track widened gradually, and as Damien and Woody rounded a bend the main road came into view. The rain had died off an hour earlier, and the clouds had parted, bathing them in its hot glare.

Ahead, the road was made of tarmac, and the air above it shimmered as the sun evaporated the rain from its surface. With the sun behind them casting a dream-like deep orange glow on the clouds that still gathered above the road, it was an almost religious experience for the two men, and they cheered and jostled each other in relief and joy at finally having found evidence of civilisation.

Splashing through the puddles on the track in their bare feet as they sprinted the remaining distance to the road, they giggled as they ran. The road was at first glance deserted. No traffic was visible in either direction, and the tall palm trees leaned over the road on either side, as if menacing it. Shading his eyes against the sun, Woody pointed up the road to their left.

"Is that a hut, Damo?"

"Where's that, mate?"

"Over there. See that thatched bit? Looks like a roof."

"Yeah I see. Let's go and take a look then."

Wincing at the rough feeling of the tarmac on their unprotected soles, the two men limped down the road towards the hut. As they drew closer, they could see that the front of the tiny building was dominated by a large rusted billboard, the red and white logo clearly advertising Coca Cola.

"I think we're in luck, pal. Must be a shop", Damien said, turning to grin at Woody.

They quickened their pace, excited by the prospect of junk food and fizzy drinks. It wasn't until they were within fifty metres of the hut that they noticed the figure in the doorway. From the clothes it appeared to be a man, but a wide-brimmed hat was pulled down over his face, obscuring his features. He was slouched on a foldout chair, and his relaxed posture suggested that he was sleeping. Damien and Woody froze, watching the man for any movement.

"Do we wake him up?" Woody whispered

"No, mate", Damien whispered back after a moment's thought. "I mean, we've got no money have we?"

"You mean we should nick stuff off him?"

"Matter of life and death, isn't it?"

"Yeah, I suppose."

Damien and Woody crept closer to the stall, hoping that the road would remain quiet long enough for them to take what they needed. In front of the stall an assortment of bottles stood on a rickety table. None of the bottles had any label and they were all filled with a yellowish liquid. Damien looked questioningly at his friend.

"Whisky?" Woody whispered, shrugging.

Damien frowned, creeping up to the table and picking up one of the bottles. Unscrewing the metal cap, he put it to his nose and sniffed. Damien's reaction was instant, and he had to fight to stop himself coughing. With a drop of water in his eye and a grimace on his face, Damien turned to Woody and gave him a thumbs up.

"Petrol", Damien confirmed.

Screwing the top back on to the bottle, he gripped it under his arm, picking up another two bottles as Woody also helped himself. Amazed at their luck, the two men grinned at each other like mischievous schoolchildren. The turned away and had begun to creep back to the other side of the road when Damien stopped, looking back at the stall longingly.

"What?" Woody whispered.

"There's food in there."

"Yeah, but that bloke's in the way."

"We might be able to reach past him."

Woody nodded his agreement and the two men crept back to the stall, stopping right next to the sleeping owner. Stowing the bottle from his right hand alongside the one under his armpit, Damien leaned round the door and peered into the gloom.

The inside of the stall was as basic as the outside, with a few mismatched tables holding a meagre selection of goods. Immediately next to the door, a number of small polythene bags were piled together. Damien grabbed two of the bags, ducking back out of the door to examine them. They contained small pieces of what looked to be potato chips covered in a red powder. Shrugging, he handed the bags to Damien and poked his head back into the stall in search of something more appetising. Squinting in the semi-darkness, he made out a box containing individually wrapped bars. The writing on them meant nothing to Damien, but they looked about the right size and shape to be chocolate bars. Leaning in as far as he could without touching the owner, Damien reached out. His fingers only just reached the edges of the box, and he pinched the card between his fingers, dragging the box closer. With a thump, a bottle that had been leaning against the other side of the box fell over, and Damien recoiled in surprise.

Heart hammering, Damien and Woody glanced at the owner, making ready to run. The sleeping man was still motionless, and they were about to breathe a sigh of relief when a low growling came from within the stall. The two men looked at each other in fear as the growl became an angry bark.

"Run!" Damien hissed, and they sprinted away as fast as they were able to run with bottles clasped under their arms. A moment later, angry shouting came from the stall behind them, and the barking became more insistent. Glancing back, Woody saw a large Alsatian pursuing them, teeth bared threateningly.

The two men ran for a few seconds more before the dog caught up with them. It leaped up at Damien, its head brushing his elbow at it tried to bite him. Damien swerved away, dodging the dog as it landed and skidded to a stop ahead of him. The enraged animal turned its attention on Woody, who had halted to avoid running into it. Eyes wide and lips pulled back over its fangs, the dog snarled at Woody, forcing him to back away.

"Help us, Damo!" He panted, jerking back as the dog snapped at him.

Damien stopped and swung around, seeing his friend under attack by the slavering dog. Across the road, the stall owner was jogging over, a thick bamboo cane in his hand. Thinking quickly, Damien dashed back to the where the dog was menacing Woody, shouting to distract the animal.

As he drew close the dog whirled round, snarling and snapping at him. Damien raised his arm and hurled one of the bottles of petrol he was holding at the road between him and the dog. The glass shattered as it hit the hard surface of the road, splashing petrol into the air and over the dog's head. The animal shook its head and backed off, its angry snarls turning to yelps of distress.

"Come on, mate!" Damien yelled at Woody as he gawped in surprise. "Let's get moving!"

Woody snapped out of his shock and started running, steering a wide berth around the dog, which was now pawing at its head and sneezing. Damien turned and ran as Woody streamed past him, and the men ran on together, reaching the turning on to the jungle track and heading down it as fast as they could go. They glanced back as they went, but neither the man nor his dog was visible. For many minutes more they ran, until they were out of breath. Trying to pant quietly, they listened out for sounds of pursuit, but there was silence apart from the jungle noises.

"You alright there?" Damien asked, noticing that Woody's hands were shaking.

Woody nodded, grimacing. "Not keen on dogs."

"It was a feisty one, that", Damien agreed.

"Nice one throwing that bottle though, mate. Saved my life."

"Any time. I just hope we've got enough petrol left to get us out of here."

"It's pretty mad, you know. I mean, both of us've got enough money to buy any car we want. Jet planes, even. And we're stealing bottles of petrol from some poor bloke and his dog."

"Yeah I know, mate. I feel bad about it too. Tell you what; if – when – we get out of here, we'll buy the man a real petrol station, eh? What d'you reckon?"

Woody grinned. "Yeah, one with proper pumps and all."

"And one of them cappuccino machines, of course."

Many hours later, Damien and Woody were still making their way along the jungle track. It had been dark for most of the return journey, and with the moon regularly hiding behind clouds and plunging them into impenetrable blackness, they often found themselves veering off the track into the dense foliage which surrounded it.

The jungle itself had come alive with sound. An unending variety of animal calls serenaded them as they traipsed onward, while crashing and rustling noises seemed to stalk their progress. The two men, far more aware of their vulnerability than they had been when they were part of a larger group, had tried chatting to each other to keep their spirits up and their imaginations at bay, but the conversation had soon run dry. Stumbling forward in the dark, their only words were curses as they blundered into a tree or stepped on a piece of jungle debris.

When they did eventually reach the rest of the group, they almost tripped over their friends as they lay on the track sleeping.

"What the bloody hell's that?" Marco bellowed as Damien kicked his leg.

"Whoa!" Damien said, falling on to his elbows to protect his precious cargo of bottles. "Marco? Christ, you scared the crap out of me."

"Damo? You're back. Nice one, mate!"

"Yeah. What are you boys doing asleep?"

"We never thought you'd be getting back tonight, Damo", Gavin replied from somewhere nearby. "It's been dark for ages, so we thought we'd get some kip."

"Well thanks, lads", Damien replied sarcastically. "Don't worry about us."

"Well you're here now, mate, eh?" Marco said. "Any luck at all?"

""Yeah, actually", Woody replied eagerly. "We found a stall that had petrol. Managed to swipe a few bottles."

"Bottles?"

"Yeah, the bloke was selling it in bottles, like whisky or something."

"How many did you blag?"

"Five bottles."

"Okay, so that's almost four litres", Marco paused as he did some calculations in his head. "That's only gonna get us twenty miles, maybe twenty-five."

"It's all we could get!" Damien said defensively.

"Yeah, fair enough mate, I wasn't having a pop. I'm thinking it'll be enough to get us to the road. Maybe your stall-keeper bloke can be persuaded to part with a few more bottles."

"Good luck with that then, Marco. We'll be right behind you."

"Did you get chocolate?" The sleepy voice of Joey came from the darkness.

"Oh come on, Joey. You were joking, weren't you?" Damien replied, becoming agitated.

"No", Joey said after a moment.

"Well there's this stuff you grabbed, Damo", Woody suggested, rustling the two polythene bags he had hooked into the waist of his loincloth.

"What is it?" Joey asked, coming forward expectantly.

"No idea, Joey. Feels like bits of potato chip with some sort of powdered flavouring."

"Let me try."

The bags rustled again as Joey grabbed one from Woody and took a handful of the contents, first sniffing it and then pouring it into his mouth.

"Any good?" Damien asked.

"It is… how you say… 'dusty'. And very hot. Spicy."

"Like chilli crisps", Damien agreed, tasting a small handful himself. "A bit weird though. Maybe just very stale."

Some of the other men came forward at the prospect of food, each taking some until only half of one bag remained.

"Save some for breakfast, eh, lads?" Gavin suggested.

The mood was jolly as the companions settled down to sleep again, and all the talk was of their impending escape from the clutches of the jungle. They cheered as they compared ideas about what type of food or drink they would order when they reached civilisation and joked about how much they would embellish their story to their friends and to the press. In their jubilant mood they felt almost as if they were somewhere warm and safe rather than in a pitch-black wilderness. Gradually they dozed off, smiling to themselves in anticipation.

When dawn broke the next morning, the companions rose immediately, too excited to snooze. Even the grey, cloudy sky and chilly wind could not dampen their spirits as they stretched and gazed expectantly along the track ahead of them. Marco emptied the bottles of petrol carefully into the fuel tank and the other men got behind the van, ready to push. It fired into life at the third attempt and they cheered, jumping in to the open back of the vehicle.

As they drove along the bumpy track, Gavin shared out the remaining few handfuls of the unidentified food that Damien and Woody had procured the previous day.

"This tastes very bad today", Joey commented.

"What is it?" Samson asked.

"I think I know", Emil replied uncomfortably, holding the small pile of food close to his eyes.

"What?"

"Are you sure you want to know?"

"Go on, Emil – tell us!" Damien urged

"It is an insect. A cricket, I think you call it."

"Crickets?"

"Yes. Like a grasshopper. Do you know?"

"I know what a bloody cricket is, mate. What the hell are we doing eating them, though?"

Emil shrugged. "Maybe the people here like to eat them. They are covered in chilli, so they must be for eating."

Joey, who had munched through most of his handful, threw the rest of his away in disgust, swearing in Portuguese.

"Chilli crickets", Damien said, shaking his head in disbelief.

"Don't throw them away", Tommy requested. "I'll eat them!"

The men poured what remained of their portions into Tommy's cupped hands, and the boy crunched away at them happily.

"You're a sick man, Tommy!" Damien commented, grinning.

"They're alright, Damo", Tommy replied with his mouth full. "You've got no sense of adventure."

The men made good progress along the jungle track, and in less than two hours they had reached the main road. Marco stopped the van by the side of the road and they jumped out, laughing and congratulating each other on their success.

"Is that the place you got the petrol?" Marco asked Woody, pointing across to the hut on the opposite side of the road.

"Yeah, but there's a vicious dog, Marco", Woody replied. "I wouldn't go near it."

Marco shrugged off Woody's warning and set off across the road, leaving his friends to celebrate. After a few minutes he returned, smiling confidently.

"No-one there now, mate. It's shuttered up", he said, jumping into the driver's seat and revving the engine. "Jump in, lads, let's go shopping!"

Marco put the van in gear and steered it across the road towards the stall as his friends piled in to the back or hung on to the doors. Jumping off as they pulled level with the tiny building, a few of the men eagerly made for the door.

"It is locked!" Joey said, sighing.

"Yeah alright, mate. Give us a minute", Marco said as he rummaged around in a metal box under the driver's seat.

A moment later, Marco sauntered over, brandishing a long tyre spanner.

"Stand clear, lads!" He declared, levering the tool into the gap between the door and the frame.

With a sharp downward tug of the spanner, the metal plate holding the padlock broke off and the wooden door swung open with a creak. For a moment the men paused, looking at each other with a kind of amazed longing at the prospect of the food in the stall, then without a word they entered, jostling each other to get inside.

It was dark inside the stall, and after the brightness outside the companions found themselves almost blind, and they stumbled around in the tiny space, knocking into one another as their eyes adjusted to the darkness. Raphaël screamed as someone barged into his injured wrist, bringing a few apologies from the men around him, none of whom could tell if it was them who had hurt him, but pain and guilt were soon forgotten as they looked around them at the boxes and packets that covered the rickety tables that lined the walls.

Joey was the first to act, his hands darting out to take two chocolate bars from one of the boxes. This movement signalled a feeding frenzy as the other men burst into action, grabbing bars of chocolate, packets of crisps or banana chips, jars of pickled chillies, cans of fizzy drink and other convenience food that was stacked on the tables. Some of them started eating right away, spilling crisps on the floor in their haste to open the packets. Other men filled their arms full and went outside into the light to devour their plunder.

For many minutes the only sound was the ripping of paper and plastic as they opened packets, and crunching and slurping as they fed themselves. A communal sigh of contentment came from them, and a few began to laugh at their situation. Damien threw a pickled chilli at Emil, who retaliated by shaking up a can of drink and spraying it at Damien, half of it missing him and soaking Tommy. The chaos grew as more of the men joined the food fight, only Marco and Rudolph abstaining as Marco ducked into the stall and Rudolph carried on battering a tin of condensed milk with the tyre spanner in an attempt to open it.

When Marco emerged from the stall a minute later, the other men were lying or squatting on the dusty roadside in fits of giggles, crisps and banana chips littering the ground like blossom and floating on pools of spilt fizzy drink. Shaking his head and grinning at his friends, Marco crunched his way over the crisp-covered battleground with his arms full of bottles of petrol. He stashed most of them in the front of the van, holding on to four of them, which he proceeded to pour into the petrol tank. As he was half way through pouring the third bottle, Samson stood up, pointing down the road.

"Someone is coming. Over there"

"Where, Sams?" Damien asked, standing up and squinting. "Oh I see him."

"He is shouting, I think"

"Yes, mate. And I know why. It's the bloke who owns this place. We'd better get out of here."

"Come on then, lads", Marco said, jumping into the driving seat. "Get pushing!"

Tossing the remaining food into the van, all the men except for the injured Raphaël bent their backs and started to heave the van along the dusty track by the side of the road. Marco let the clutch out as soon as possible, wanting to avoid a confrontation with the stall owner, who was rapidly catching up with them. The van spluttered and shuddered, not wanting to start.

"Keep pushing!" Marco yelled out of the window.

Grunting with exertion, the men increased their efforts, pushing against the obstinate engine until with a loud bang it started up. Jogging to keep up with the moving vehicle, the men leaped on one by one, Damien and Gavin grabbing hold of Raphaël and helping him on.

Looking back, they saw the stall owner standing among the mess of spilt drink, crushed crisps and other wasted food. He appeared to be crying. A few of the men started laughing, but a wave of guilt suddenly filled Damien, and he felt tempted to get off the van to go and try to make amends with the man. They had stolen from him twice, in spite of the fact that he was clearly a poor man. Not only had they gorged themselves on his livelihood, they had pointlessly wasted much of it too, uncaringly throwing it at each other for the sake of a few moments of amusement.

"Shut up, you gits!" Damien said, turning angrily on his friends.

"Alright, Damo. Chill out!" Tommy replied.

Damien looked back at the man and his vandalised stall as it disappeared into the distance.

"I'm sorry, mate!" He shouted, but the sound of the beaten-up old van drowned his words out.

The road became wider and less rutted as other minor tracks joined it, and they passed a few vehicles travelling the other way, mostly scooters and dusty pickup trucks. The scenery became more mountainous as they progressed, the dense jungle giving way to lush hilly vistas. Scatterings of basic-looking dwellings appeared at various intervals, as did roadside stalls selling bottled petrol, very similar to the one they had stolen from. The road signs they passed had meant nothing to them, so they remained ignorant of the country they were in and the location they were heading to. Emil, who had seemed to understand Kwei's map, remained convinced that the road they were travelling led towards a major city, so they continued steadily onwards, stopping twice to tip more of the looted bottles of petrol into the van.

Some time around mid afternoon the houses and shops started to become more numerous, and the traffic in both directions more regular. The men were discussing whether or not to stop and try to ask directions to an embassy or other official building when they were startled by a loud siren sounding behind them. Almost jumping in shock, they looked round to see that they were being followed by a dusty, sand-coloured old jeep with a police light mounted on the roof. The siren sounded again and a man poked his head and arm out of the passenger window, pointing towards the side of the road.

"Pull over, Marco!" Gavin shouted.

"You what, mate?" Replied Marco who, what with the sound of the engine and his lack of a wing mirror, was unaware they were being followed.

"It's the five-oh. Pull over, can you?"

"Bloody hell, Gav. I don't like it, mate. We've got no driving license or anything. They might want us for ripping off that stall."

"I know, Marco. But what are we gonna do? Outrun them in this pile of crap?"

As if in agreement, the police siren sounded again.

150

"Yeah, right", Marco sighed, slowing the van and pulling over onto the dusty, hard earth by the side of the road.

The men remained huddled in the vehicle as the police jeep stopped behind them and its doors opened. From the passenger side, a short, stocky man with a gun and a baton in his belt stepped out, placing his grey peaked cap meticulously on his head. A moment later, a taller, skinny man with a barely-creditable moustache exited from the driver's door and gazed bemusedly at the van and its occupants.

Walking with his back held straight, as if to make up for his lack of height, the shorter man strutted around his vehicle towards the companions. With an expression of disgust, he examined each of them as he slowly made his way round to the driver's door. Drawing his baton, he rapped it sharply on the side of the door, barking some kind of order. Cursing, Marco opened the door and stepped out, holding his hands up in compliance. After studying Marco for a moment with a mixture of awe and distrust, he pointed back down the road with his baton, shouting again. Marco shrugged in confusion and moved in the direction of the policeman's baton, looking over his shoulder to keep one eye on the man as he followed. When they reached the back of the van, the policeman rapped on the windows, shouting at those in the rear of the vehicle.

A minute later, all of the companions were standing in a ragged group by the side of the road, squinting at the policeman and waiting to see what he would do. Keeping his baton in his hand, the man shouted an order at the other policeman, who had been staring gormlessly at the group. Startled, he hurried over and stood to attention. The stocky policeman spoke for a moment, inclining his head towards the van. Nodding vigorously, the other man scurried to the door Marco had just exited from and started rummaging around inside the van. Meanwhile, the stocky policeman fixed the companions with a steely glare, as if daring them to give him cause to use his baton.

After a tense few moments, the tall man returned, carrying two bottles, one full of petrol and one empty. Taking the full bottle, the short policeman held it up to the companions and shouted a few short phrases, obviously expecting an explanation.

"We can explain, mate", Gavin said, taking a step forward. "We're from England. You know? England? We got stranded in the jungle. We need to make a phone call. Can you take us to an embassy or something?"

His frown deepening, the policeman held his baton up to warn Gavin away. Gavin put his hands up in surrender, backing off slightly. Keeping his baton trained on Gavin, the policeman turned to his assistant and spoke for a moment. Looking bewildered, the taller man nodded and came forward.

"Pass. Port?" The man spoke in a high-pitched, almost apologetic way.

"No passport, mate. We were in a plane crash. All our stuff got lost", Gavin explained slowly.

The tall policeman stood with his mouth moving in silence for a moment, as if trying to understand Gavin's words. Then he turned to his superior and spoke, shaking his head. The shorter man glared at Gavin and his friends for a minute before stepping into the back of the van and poking around. A moment later he appeared again with an empty crisp packet hanging from his baton. Holding this up as if presenting evidence, he spoke to his assistant once more. Pausing for some time to think, the taller man approached Gavin with a pleading expression.

"You pay. Fine", he said, nodding hopefully.

"No money", Gavin explained even more slowly. "Take us to the embassy. We pay you if we make a phone call. Right?"

Taking a step away from his superior, the taller man spoke again in his own language, wringing his hands. The short policeman breathed in and out noisily a few times, as if controlling his rage, and then struck out with his baton, hitting and denting the rear of the van. Rudolph, who was standing right next to the man, jumped in shock and moved away warily. The policeman looked the companions up and down carefully once more before grunting disdainfully, as if finally deciding that there was no money to be made. He shouted an order to his assistant and then strode back to his vehicle, straightening his back and puffing out his chest theatrically.

"You follow", the taller policeman said, grinning nervously as he followed his superior to their jeep.

"What now then, Gav?" Marco asked, folding his arms.

"Not much choice really", Gavin replied. "If they're taking us to a police station at least we can make a call."

By now the police jeep had pulled alongside the van and was honking its horn impatiently.

"Pile in then, lads. Best not keep Mr. Angry waiting", Gavin said, nodding at the jeep.

The men climbed somewhat reluctantly into the van. As Marco drove off, falling in behind the police jeep, the men sat quietly in thought. A short while ago, the mood had been jubilant as they made their way towards civilisation and the certainty of rescue. Their run-in with the policeman, though, had potentially put that on hold. If the man was aware that they had stolen, they could be in some trouble, and with no proof of identity or money, they suddenly wondered whether they would be treated with any fairness. If the angry policeman was anything to go by, that seemed unlikely.

For almost half an hour they drove on, with the roadside becoming more and more populated. They followed the jeep as it turned off onto a smaller road that twisted and turned as it wove its way through the hilly terrain, passing through two small villages containing a mixture of modern-looking bungalows and more basic shacks. Driving over the crest of a hill, a town came in to view. It was difficult to tell the size of the town due to the fact that it sprawled, and disappeared here and there into the lush greenery. The most striking feature was a large pointed golden dome that flashed in the sun.

Reaching the bottom of the steep hill that led to the town, they joined a more major road and fell in behind some slow-moving traffic. Their side of the road was forced to pull over and stop so that an over-laden lorry carrying chickens and other caged livestock could pass the other way. Seeing that they would be stuck for a few minutes, Marco leaned over into the back of the van, handing over the last bottle of petrol to the nearest person.

"Tommy, stick the rest of this in the tank, can you? We must be nearly out."

"What, now?" The boy replied, looking surprised.

"Yeah, we're stopped for a bit. Hurry up, eh?"

Tommy clambered over the other men and climbed out of the van, moving round to the side of the vehicle to locate the tank. As he was un-screwing the cap, the short policeman leapt out of his jeep, slamming the door and shouting towards. Tommy, confused, continued to unscrew the bottle cap and pour the contents into the van. Stamping his feet as he advanced on Tommy, the policeman rapped his baton on the side of the vehicle, shouting at Tommy as if he required an answer. Shrugging and looking at the angry man warily, Tommy pointed at the bottle of petrol as the last drops emptied into the fuel tank. Pulling the neck of the bottle free, the boy held it up, grinning nervously. The policeman, hissing through his teeth, struck out with his baton, smashing the bottle from Tommy's hand. Tommy darted back, unharmed but shocked. Pointing towards the van, the policeman shouted again, shaking his head threateningly. Frowning, Tommy moved round to the back of the van and climbed on, rubbing his hand. Following him, the policeman looked in at the men through the open back of the van. He pulled his gun from his holster, holding it in his shaking fist as he barked some final words at them and then stood waiting for a reaction. Startled into silence by the policeman's rage, they nodded slowly. Breathing heavily and eyeballing the men for another moment, the policeman holstered his gun, stamped and strode back to his jeep.

As the two vehicles moved off in convoy once more, the men looked at each other with concern.

"Bloke's got a serious problem", Tommy complained, still shaken by the man's aggression.

"Yeah, right", Damien replied. "Bet he's a barrel of laughs on a Monday morning."

"Why's the man so bothered about making sure we're coming with him though?" Gavin said, brow furrowed in thought. "I get the felling he's not taking us for a feed up and a dip in the pool."

The companions' heads drooped and they fell silent, lost in thought as they imagined what the policeman might have in store for them.

As the livestock truck passed the van, Marco pulled out, joining the slow-moving traffic as it made its way along the dusty road towards town. Bicycles and scooters, some heavily laden with boxes or bags, weaved their way in and out of the vehicles, honking their tiny horns as they went. As they drew closer to the town, the roadside scenery changed. Where before it had been nothing but rough shacks built from scrap, gradually it became dominated by taller, brick and concrete-built structures. Narrow pavements carried a trickle of pedestrians, mostly dressed in the western style, while some of the women wore brightly coloured embroidered clothes. The concentration of people grew thicker as they approached what they judged to be the centre of town, and large groups clustered at the entrance to side streets where covered stalls suggested busy markets. The men put their faces to the van's windows and gawped at the exotic scenes, temporarily distracted from their worries about the policeman's intentions.

The scents of the town wafted into the van, rotten rubbish and sewage smells mingling with mouth-watering cooking smells and other unidentifiable odours which seemed magnified to the men who had been starved of all but natural smells for so long. For some time they followed the police jeep through the busy centre of the town, engrossed in the bustle and noise around them. It was only when the tall concrete buildings started to give way to palm trees and wooden houses that they realised they were heading out of town again. To their left, flat-roofed dwellings stretched away in tiers up a steep hillside while on their right the land fell away towards the river.

The road twisted sharply right and left, snaking its way down the steep hill until they were driving beside the river. It was a wide, straight river, and the rushing water had turned it a murky brown. The companions found themselves wondering whether it was the same river they had been travelling on up until a few days ago, and how much easier their journey might have been had they not become separated from the dinghy. Their musings were cut short as they approached a long road bridge and the police jeep began to slow and then turn towards a single-story building at the start of the bridge where a number of other vehicles were parked.

Pulling up in front of the building, the two policemen stepped out of the jeep, the stocky one taking his baton from his belt and glowering at the van as it stopped and the men stepped out. He waved them towards the entrance of the building with his baton, stopping them before they entered, and then barked a few words to his assistant, who stepped forward and faltered for a moment before speaking.

"You stay."

The stocky policeman looked the men up and down disgustedly once more before pushing open the door to the building and entered, slamming it behind him. The tall policeman grinned nervously at the companions, appearing out of his depth. Behind him, cycle rickshaws and motorised rickshaws passed at regular intervals, many bearing boxes or bags. Looking along the length of the bridge, they could see a narrow footpath along which a slow trickle of people passed alongside a tall green metal fence that ran the length of the bridge. White pillars divided the fence every few metres, and flags fluttered from poles that extended from the pillars. The flags alternated between a bright yellow one and a striped red, blue and white design. A few of the men peered at these flags, hoping for a clue as to their location.

"The striped one. I feel like I remember it", Emil said thoughtfully. "I am sure I have played with Holland a match against this country."

"I know what you mean, mate", Marco agreed. "Can't put my finger on it though."

As they were pondering the flags, the stocky policeman returned, followed by another man wearing a suit. The new man looked at Gavin and his friends with an expression of horror and then waved them inside the building, ushering them through a door beside a counter at which a pretty receptionist gawped at them. They continued down a short corridor and were shown into a tidy and featureless office. The man in the suit sat behind his desk and studied the men calculatingly. There was only one other chair across from the man's desk, and Tommy quickly sat on it. The stocky policeman, entering the room last, tapped Tommy sharply on the shoulder with his baton until the boy sat up, and then dragged the chair next to the door where he sat on it, hefting his baton menacingly.

The suited man cleared his throat, waiting for the companions to turn towards him, and then he spoke in confident, although heavily accented, English.

"Where are your passports, visas?"

"We've not got them, see?" Gavin said slowly as he stepped forward. "We had a plane crash. Landed in the jungle."

The man narrowed his eyes and sighed before continuing.

"Your nationality? Where you come from?"

"We're from England, mate. We were on a plane from Japan. We're a football team, right? Football?" Gavin made a kicking motion with his leg.

"You have money? Documents?" The man continued after a moment.

"Nothing. Look at us. This is all we've got."

The man made a few notes on a piece of paper before raising his head and looking accusingly at the companions.

"Where you get vehicle from? You steal?"

"No, mate. It's ours. We traded it with someone in the jungle."

The man grunted disbelievingly.

"You trade? For what?"

"We gave the guy our troph..." Gavin stopped himself, suddenly unwilling to let this suspicious man know about the treasure that they hoped to reclaim from Kwei at a later date. "We traded it for a shirt."

"Shirt? Trade for vehicle?"

"Well, not just a shirt. My match shirt. Worth a lot of money."

The man shook his head gravely and wrote on his pad of paper again, then turned his head to stare out of his window.

"Look, can you just hep us out here?" Gavin blurted out, becoming exasperated. "We've been in some bloody jungle for days. We were shot at by some terrorists or guerrillas, whatever it is you lot have here. They've still got some of our mates. Just take us to the British embassy, right?"

At the mention of terrorists and shooting, the man's head jerked back to attention. His eyes darted between the men, an angry frown forming on his face. Picking up his telephone receiver, he jabbed some numbers into the keypad. The telephone was answered almost immediately and the man spoke rapidly into it, sounding flustered. After a lengthy explanation, he sat in silence, listening to the reply and nodding occasionally. A tense few moments later, the man made a single-word response and placed the telephone receiver down, arching his fingers as he gave Gavin a cold glare.

"Was that the embassy then?" Damien asked, moving forward and placing his hands on the desk.

The man ignored Damien, turning instead to the policeman and speaking to him. The policeman reacted angrily, standing up and replying in an irritated voice, but the suited man simply shrugged and shook his head. Slapping his baton on his palm a few times, the policeman strutted over to the desk and glowered at the man behind the desk before swivelling round to face Damien and Gavin. Giving them a look of pure loathing, the policeman pointed his baton towards the door and waited, continuing to glare at them until they got the message and walked back out of the room and down the corridor.

Outside the building once more, the policeman directed the men into their van and climbed back into his jeep, leaning out of the window and shaking his head as the companions pushed the van to get it started. Revving the labouring engine, Marco turned round to follow the police jeep as it turned on to the riverside road travelling back the way they had driven a short time ago. A few minutes later they reached the turning that led up the hill back to the town, but the jeep drove past, continuing alongside the river.

A short while later, another bridge came in to view. It was much simpler than the previous bridge, and was in worse repair, its short concrete walls showing cracks in places. A guard post stood at the near end of the bridge, and as the two vehicles turned off the road and approached the bridge, a soldier emerged from the building, straightening the helmet on his head and hefting the machine gun that hung around his shoulder. The jeep stopped next to the guard post and the stocky policeman poked his head out of the window to speak to the soldier. There was a brief exchange of words before the soldier, seemingly reluctantly, unhooked a radio from his belt and spoke into it. After a crackling reply from the radio, the soldier stepped back and waved the jeep through with his gun.

The bridge was deserted other than the guard and his post, and small lumps of rubble littered the road where they had crumbled from the edges of the bridge walls. The two vehicles crossed the bridge at a crawl and made their way to the gravel-lined clearing that nestled between the tall palm trees by the river bank on the other side. Pulling over and stopping as soon as they reached the clearing, the policemen climbed out of their jeep and stood waiting for the companions to bring their van to a halt. Marco remained behind the wheel while the rest of the men climbed out of the van and made their way over to the police jeep. The stocky policeman, who now seemed calmer if no more friendly, spoke to his assistant for a while, who then took a tentative step forward and addressed the companions.

"You go. Not come back."

"Come back where?" Gavin asked, speaking slowly.

"My country", the man replied, pointing back across the bridge.

"Suits us!" Damien declared, folding his arms.

As they spoke, the stocky policeman paced over to the van, banging on the driver's door with his baton and waving Marco out of the van.

"What now?" Marco complained, climbing out of the van.

"You leave vehicle", the skinny policeman said after a prompt from his superior.

"Hold on. That's our van!" Gavin said, becoming agitated. "We were given it. You've got no right to take it!"

The skinny policeman wrinkled his brow for a moment, and then spoke haltingly.

"Licence from my country. Not leave country with no document."

"You've got to be kidding", Gavin exploded. "We've been stranded in a jungle for days. Had lads taking pot shots at us. Your boys haven't bothered to look for us. When we manage to get out, you want to steal our bloody van off us? Well, you can get stuffed!"

With these angry words, Gavin strode towards the van. After only a few steps, though, the stocky policeman reached out to hold his baton across Gavin's chest while he drew his gun with his other hand. Backing off, he pointed the gun at Gavin, motioning him back towards the rest of the group. Gavin stood his ground, glaring defiantly back at the man.

"Come on then, mate!" He said, waving the policeman forward with both hands. "Shoot us, then!"

Pointing his gun in the air, the policeman fired off a shot and then levelled the weapon once more at Gavin's head.

"Leave it, Gav", Damien said. "He might do it."

Gavin remained where he was, watching the policeman as he shouted some instructions to his assistant. The other man nodded, scurrying forward and climbing into the companions' van as the stocky policeman continued to keep his gun on Gavin. With a cough from the van's engine, he turned the vehicle around and set off across the bridge. Meanwhile, the stocky policeman backed away to his jeep, gun drawn menacingly, and opened the door. He gave the men one more disgusted stare before he cleared his throat, spat at them and jumped in the jeep, driving off in a cloud of dust. As the jeep reached the start of the bridge, Gavin picked up a stone from the ground and hurled it at the vehicle, receiving a satisfying metallic sound as he hit his target.

As the dust settled, the men found themselves staring forlornly after the departed vehicles. Gavin sat down on the gravely floor, hanging his head. After a moment, Rudolph cleared his throat noisily, glancing around to check that the other men were listening.

"We should be positive", he began, speaking deliberately. "Not too long ago we were lost in a jungle. Now we at least have roads to follow. With luck, we will meet kinder people."

Gavin took a deep breath, sighing it out before he spoke.

"The gaffer's right, lads. We should keep going. Follow the road. I don't want to spend another night out in the wild, do you?"

10

With their legs aching after sitting in the cramped van for so long, the companions gingerly made their way around the sharp stones of the wide dirt track that led away from the entrance to the bridge. The track curved very gently left and right, and tall palm trees towered over them on either side as they trudged onward. After a little over half an hour, the track led on to a rough tarmac road, and they peered left and right, unsure of which way to go. As they stood by the roadside, the sound of an engine grew louder and a vehicle came into view round a twist in the road to their right. As it drew closer, Tommy shouted excitedly.

"It's a taxi, lads!"

A moment later, all of them could see the bright paintwork and the roof sign that marked the car out as a taxi.

"We must stop it!" Samson exclaimed, moving into the road and waving his arms above his head.

The car slowed slightly as it approached the men, and a man poked his head out of the driver's window, studying the companions. In response, they rushed forward, waving their arms and shouting to the taxi. The driver's face changed to one of shock as ten bearded men wearing nothing but dirty loincloths raced towards his taxi, shouting hysterically and waving their arms. Hastily winding up his window, he revved the engine and raced away up the road.

"Bollocks!" Shouted Gavin in frustration as the taxi disappeared in the distance.

"That was not cool, guys!" Emil said, shaking his head. "We must be more careful."

"Look, at least we know there's traffic along this road", Damien replied more positively. "We can just wait for another taxi, eh, lads?"

"Well, we do not know how long that will be. Perhaps we were lucky this time", Emil narrowed his eyes. "But I have had a thought. The taxi had no passengers. So I am guessing that the driver is hoping to find some customers in that direction. Perhaps there is a town or some other destination that way."

"Good call, mate", Gavin agreed. "We'll head that way and keep our eyes peeled for more cars. And keep calm this time, right?"

Sighing and grumbling, they set off again, walking in the shade so that the aching soles of their feet didn't touch the hot tarmac. For some time they kept trudging onwards, encountering a truck and a scooter coming the other way. Both times they tried to hail the vehicle, but the drivers continued on in alarm. The heat and dryness of the road had exhausted them, and they became so dehydrated that they could barely speak. When a small shack came into sight on the opposite side, they braved the sunny side of the street and hopped over to the flimsy gate that led to the dwelling.

The shack was very basic, made from planks of wood and corrugated iron, and a long washing line stretched from the top of the building to the fence by the gate they had entered through. A few scrawny-looking chickens stopped scratching in the grass and stared at the men through beady eyes. Walking up to the door, Gavin knocked loudly on it. For a long moment, there was no reaction, but then the door opened a crack and a young woman peered out. She took a startled look at the men outside her house and then rapidly slammed the door, bolting it shut.

"We just need some water", Gavin said, trying not to sound threatening. "We're thirsty. Can you help us out?"

There was silence from within the house as they waited for a reply.

"What are we gonna do now, then?" Marco said, wiping sweat from his eyes.

Gavin shook his head tiredly, seriously considering whether he should try to force his way in to the house to locate some water and perhaps a telephone. As the men stood there awkwardly, a high-pitched voice piped up from the corner of the garden.

"Hello, mister."

Looking round, they saw a small boy of about eight or nine years of age standing with his hands behind his back and a serious expression on his face. He wore a stripy t-shirt which was a few sizes too large, a grubby pair of shorts and leather sandals. As the men stared at him, he walked forward.

"Where you from?" The boy asked.

"From England, kid", Damien replied. "Some of us, anyway."

"England. Best place". The boy walked forward confidently. "Play football?"

"Yes, mate", Damien chuckled. "You could say that."

"Can you get us some water?" Gavin asked, stooping down to the boy's level. "You'd be saving our lives."

"You will pay?"

"Yeah, no problem." Gavin replied, deciding that lying was better than dying of thirst.

"Wait outside gate", the boy said, grinning slightly. "I bring water."

"Good lad!" Damien called out after him as he sprinted away behind the house.

The men made their way back through the gate, sitting down in the shade on the verge by the road. After a few minutes the boy returned, carrying a plastic bucket of water and a small wooden bowl. He set the bucket down, floated the bowl in the water and folded his arms, looking at the men expectantly. One by one, they picked up the bowl, filling it with water and draining the contents. As they drunk, the boy approached Gavin, looking up at him almost insolently.

"My name Palat. You?" He asked.

"I'm Gavin."

"Mister Gubbin."

"Just Gavin."

"You want beer? Boxing?" The boy continued, affecting a businesslike expression. "I can show you. Only ten dollars, I take you to best places."

"No money now", Gavin replied guiltily. "If you take us to the British embassy, I'll give you plenty."

"British Embassy? How much you give me?"

"As much as you can count."

Palat wrinkled his brow in thought for a while, as if working out how much money he would be able to count. He looked Gavin up and down again and then held his hand out.

"Deal, Mister Gubbin. Shake."

Grinning at the boy's seriousness, Gavin took his hand and shook it enthusiastically.

"Okay, we walk", Palat declared, pointing down the road.

"Walk?" Joey said with a sigh. "Why walk? You can get us a car."

"I can get taxi", Palat replied patiently. "If you have money."

"We can pay later."

"Mister, you look bad", Palat wrinkled his nose. "And you smell bad. No taxi take you with no money."

"How far is it to walk?" Emil asked, sensing Joey's imminent wrath and changing the subject.

"Two hours", Palat answered, waggling his head from side to side. "Little more. I take you quick way."

"Okay, good lad", Damien said, patting the boy on the shoulder. "Lead on then, big man."

Palat grinned, stowed the bucket and bowl in his garden and then set off across the road, waving the men after him. They followed the verge on the shady side of the road for a few minutes before Palat stopped and pointed down a dappled footpath that wound through the palm trees and other plants that surrounded the road. It was cool and quiet beneath the palms, and the men were surprised to find that they were actually enjoying the walk. The soft, dusty earth beneath their feet and the gentle hum of the cicadas created a completely different atmosphere to that of the dense, daunting jungle that they had been stranded in up until the day before.

The path that Palat led them down wound gently upwards for quite some time, and the terrain became hillier, with moss-covered boulders poking their heads out of the earth and rope-like tree roots emerging from the ground. The men were panting with exertion by the time Palat halted and waited for them to catch up. He pointed ahead and the men followed the line of his arm to look out over a breathtaking panorama. They had obviously climbed a considerable height since leaving the road, because the land dropped away rapidly in front of them, the tops of the palm trees visible as they swept down to the flatter terrain roughly a mile ahead. The land at the bottom of the hills looked cultivated, with rough, uniformly shaded squares divided by narrow paths. The occasional coloured dots that moved lazily through these squares were obviously people working the land. Much further in the distance, they could just make out the white walls and terracotta roofs of a small town.

"British embassy. We go", Palat said, and then pointed ahead where the path down the hill became much steeper. "Walk slow. Very danger."

As the men began to descend, they saw exactly what Palat meant. No path was visible, perhaps due to the dry leaves which covered the slope, or perhaps because very few people attempted the descent that way. The men found themselves inching downward with their arms held out for balance. Palat was less concerned, and continued on at a reasonable pace, stopping to glance back every few minutes with a long-suffering expression.

They were making fair progress down the hillside when Marco, lifting his foot to avoid stepping on a knobbly stick, slipped and fell. On the steep hillside, his weight carried him downwards, and he began to slide uncontrollably on his back. Emil and Damien, a few metres in front of him, were also knocked off their feet as Marco careered into their legs, and the three of them slid down, unable to stop themselves on the slippery leaves. Samson reached his hand out to them as they slid past him, but their momentum was too much, and he got pulled down into the tangle of limbs. Joey was the final man to be knocked off his feet. As the four men sped towards him, he tried to jump out of the way and lost his balance in doing so. Palat, with time to react, deftly sidestepped the men as they gathered speed down the hillside. They grasped at roots as they sped on, but were unable to get a strong enough grip. A steep drop came upon them before they had a chance to do much more than yell in fear. As the rest of the men watched from above, Marco, Emil, Damien, Samson and Joey plunged over the edge and disappeared.

For some time, the remaining men held their breaths, listening to the silence from below and fearing the worst. Then a loud screaming started. Making their way down as fast as they could without risking another fall, Gavin, Palat and the others went to the aid of their friends. Palat was the first to reach the edge, and by that time, the screaming had changed to a whooping sound and then finally almost manic laughter.

Palat peered over the edge and then turned back to speak to Gavin, who was still picking his way down.

"They go crazy!" The boy called out, with an expression of concern.

When Gavin reached the edge a few moments later, he leaned over expecting blood and broken limbs. He breathed a sigh of relief when he saw that the men had fallen slightly less than two metres into a large bowl-shaped hole in the earth that was filled with dry leaves. They were still lying in a mess of limbs, and were in fits of laughter.

"You alright then, lads?" Gavin asked.

It took a moment for anyone to reply, but eventually Marco looked up at Gavin.

"What a ride!" He said, slapping Damien on the back.

"Let's go again, man!" Damien replied with a wide grin.

"They okay?" Palat asked Gavin.

"That's a matter of opinion, mate", Gavin said with an amused shake of his head.

Roughly fifteen minutes later, Palat had led the men out of the woods and on to the flat cultivated land. The men who had slid down the hillside sported a few scratches and bruises, but spirits were still high. They walked along a slim raised path that divided two paddy fields, and a middle-aged woman stopped her work in the field to stand straight and stare at the group as they passed. Palat nodded regally at her and continued on with his head held high, as if parading his companions.

It was humid in the paddy fields and the men sweated heavily with nowhere to escape the sun's rays. By the time they reached the cover of the palm trees on the other side of the cultivated land, they were exhausted, and were forced to sit down for a break. Palat, seemingly unaffected by the heat, stood around restlessly.

"Get up, Mister. Not very far", the boy said, frowning.

"Give us a break, kid", Damien replied with a grin. "You're worse than the fitness coach."

The thought of rescue, though, encouraged the men, and they heaved themselves up and stretched their cramped muscles before setting off once more after Palat. After a short stroll through a palm grove, they emerged onto a small, dusty road, on which a trickle of traffic passed. Palat led them by the side of the road and towards the town that they had spied from the hilltop earlier.

It was a quaint and pretty town, with mostly single-story buildings painted in white, and the traffic was mostly made up of taxis and motorised rickshaws. As they moved further into the town, they passed more and more people, some of who appeared to be western. These people stared openly at the companions, and they started to wonder if they'd been recognised. But glancing down at each other, they decided that with their beards and scruffy rags, it seemed more likely that it was their appearance rather than their celebrity that marked them out.

Palat turned a corner and led them past a covered market, where the smells of the food stalls made their stomachs rumble. Palat turned again down a smaller, deserted street and then stopped in front of a nondescript building. A small metal sign bolted to the wall marked it out as the British consulate.

"I wait here", Palat said, sitting himself down on the step outside the building.

The men stood staring at the building for some time. A part of them found it hard to believe that they had finally come to the end of their ordeal. Damien found himself choking back a tear, and instead put his arms around the two nearest men. They in turn embraced the men next to them and eventually the companions were locked in a tight group hug. None of them noticed the door of the consulate opening until someone spoke out.

"Can I help you?"

They turned to see a young man with cropped hair and a loose white shirt standing in the doorway. He looked slightly alarmed at the sight of ten bearded and rag-dressed men hugging each other on his doorstep.

"Yes you can, mate", Gavin said with a broad grin. "Can we come in?"

Gavin's accent and friendly manner clearly set the young man at ease, and he opened the door wider to admit the men.

"Yes, of course. Just through here, on the right."

"You don't know how pleased we are to see you, man", Damien, grasping the man's hand as he walked past.

When all of the companions had assembled in the young man's office, he closed the door and smiled hesitantly at them.

"I'm Allan. Administration officer", he said, and then squinted slightly at Gavin. "Do I know you? You look familiar."

"Don't think so, mate", Gavin replied. "Look, can you tell us where we are?"

"Where you are? Well, you're in Mae Sai. Is that what you mean?"

"No. Which country?"

"Country? Is this a joke?"

"No, serious!"

"You're in, ah, Thailand. How did you get here?"

"Across the bridge. Over that way." Gavin pointed in the general direction that they had travelled.

"The border bridge? The one with the blue arch and all the flags?"

"Sounds like the one, yeah."

"You came from Myanmar?"

"Where?"

"Myanmar. You know – Burma?" Allan looked quizzical, as if unsure whether he was making himself the victim of some kind of joke. "Were you robbed, then? Your clothes?"

"No, mate. We were in a plane crash. In the jungle."

Allan opened his mouth to speak and then seemed to make some sort of connection, looking at each of the men more closely. He then sat down on his chair, puffed his cheeks out with a sigh and smiled broadly.

"You're the footballers?"

"Yes, mate. How did you know?"

"You're famous!"

"Is that right?" Damien replied with a cheeky wink.

"I mean – you're famous for more than just the football."

"How d'you mean?" Gavin narrowed his eyes.

"You've been in the news. There's people searching for you. I've got to tell my mates about this one!"

"Hold on a bit. There were more of us. We got split up and they were taken away by some soldiers while we were in the jungle. We should let the authorities know. They're probably in danger."

"No, it's okay. They were rescued. You didn't know?

"Had no idea", Gavin said, breathing a sigh of relief. "You know what happened?"

"It's a great story actually. Like you said, they were captured. The soldiers you saw were actually part of a drug gang. They're very organised out there. So, this gang found out who your friends were and tried to ransom them. There was quite a debacle. Your management wanted to pay the gang. It wasn't much money compared to what your friends are worth to them, apparently. But the UN had already become involved with the initial rescue operation, and they wouldn't agree to letting your guys pay the ransom."

"Why?" Tommy piped up.

"Well, you know what the US/UN is like about that kind of thing."

"What, you mean 'never negotiate with terrorists'?" Damien asked. "I thought that was just in the films."

"Me too", Allan chuckled. "Well anyway, they sent in a group of soldiers. Special Forces or whatever it is they call them. These guys stormed the camp where your friends were being held. Fired off some sort of gas, shot off a few rounds. The drug gang fellows were caught completely off guard. Surrendered or ran away without firing back. They found your friends being held in a hut there. A helicopter rescue team too. Everyone was fine, I read. One guy a bit beaten up, but otherwise unharmed."

"Who, Kevin?" Woody asked

"Could be. I can dig out the article for you if you like."

"This is good", Joey interrupted. "But you have food? Something to eat?"

Allan thought for a moment. "Well, I could phone up and order something, I suppose. Or there's a vending machine in the hallway."

"Vending machine will be good."

"Yes, of course", Allan fished in his draw and produced a jar which was half-filled with coins. "Help yourselves, please", he said, tipping the coins out on to his desk.

As the other men took handfuls of coins and eagerly left the room to sample the delights of the vending machine, Gavin hung back.

"That reminds me", he said to Allan. "Can you lend us a bit of cash? I promised the lad outside I'd make him rich."

"How much do you want?" Allan replied, taking out a lock-box and unlocking it with a key that hung round his neck.

"About five hundred quid sound okay?"

Allan raised his eyebrows. "Five hundred is a lot of money here."

"It's fine, mate. You know I'm good for it."

"I'm sure", Allan said, flicking through the piles of banknotes in the lock-box. "It looks like we've got almost that much, but it's in small notes. We just use it for taxis and so on."

"Small notes is fine", Gavin said as he took the cash.

He could barely hold the thick wads of notes between both hands, and had to ask Allan to open the door to the street. Palat was still sitting on the step outside, and turned to see Gavin emerge with his hands hidden behind his back.

"You come back, Mister."

"Yeah, kid. Well, I promised you some money, didn't I?"

"As much as I can count."

"That's right. And here you go", Gavin said with a grin as he brought his cash-filled hands out from behind his back.

Palat stood, staring with wide eyes at the offered notes. "All for me?"

"If you can carry it!"

Palat burst into motion, grabbing one of the piles with both hands and cramming it into both of his shorts pockets. He then took the second pile and, finding he had no more room in his pockets, panicked for a few seconds before he stuffed the wad down his trousers and into his underwear. He backed off a few steps, looking at Gavin warily as if he feared the big man would change his mind. With a solemn expression, he brought his hands together above his face and bowed slightly.

"I never forget Mister Gubbin", he said before swivelling on his heel and dashing away up the alley and disappearing round the corner.

Gavin sighed and sat down on the step where Palat had waited. The sun was bright but it was cool in the shade, and the swarms of mosquitoes that had plagued him during their ordeal seemed to be absent from the town. The sounds of the market could just be heard from where he sat, and a faint repetitive metallic sound came from the building behind him. With a chuckle he recognised the sound as a vending machine in constant use.

Leaning against the warm exterior of the consulate office building, he closed his eyes and cast his mind back to the day they had become stranded. His face twitched with varying emotions as he remembered the panic and confusion of the crash, the fear of their encounter and flight from the drug gang soldiers, the hopelessness of their hunger and thirst, and the ever-present dread that they were lost in the middle of a wilderness that they would never find their way out of. The noise of the door beside him being opened shocked him out of his thoughts, and he found that his face had screwed up with tension and tears had begun to force their way from his tightly shut eyes.

"You want something, Gav?" Came the chirpy voice of Damien as he stepped out of the consulate door, chewing a chocolate bar. "They've got normal stuff in the machine, like back home."

"Left something for me, did you?" Gavin replied, surreptitiously wiping the tears from his eyes before turning around.

"You alright, skipper?" Damien asked, noticing Gavin's reddened eyes.

For a moment, Gavin wanted to grab Damien and jump up and down, screaming in relief at their salvation. But the man seemed relaxed and at ease, as if their recent trials had hardly affected him at all. Gavin took a deep breath through his nose and breathed it out gradually, feeling the smile return to his face.

"Yes, mate. Just got something in my eye", he said as he followed his friend through the door.

- Epilogue -

Two weeks later, the companions were back into their regular stride. The club's league games had been postponed while the players and staff were missing, and would have to be fitted into their schedule later in the season. It took a fair amount of feasting and retail therapy (and in Rudolph's case, psychotherapy), but all of them were surprised by how easily they resumed their normal lives. Some of the club's deeper thinkers had been worried that such desperate hardship would change their perspectives, but each of them seemed galvanised by their experience, and they were eager to return to the routine of training and, eventually, matches.

The trophy that they had been forced to trade for transport out of the jungle, however, was a different matter. FIFA, with directions and advice from Gavin and Emil, arranged for representatives to travel to Kwei's hut with the intention of buying the trophy back from the little man for what would be, to him, a very generous price. When the representatives eventually found Kwei's hut, though, it was deserted. It appeared that the man and his family had hastily moved out of the hut, taking all their possessions – including the trophy – with them. When this information was uncovered by a reporter for a tabloid newspaper, the story became huge. Various reporters and agents were sent in search of leads to the trophy's whereabouts, but nothing solid was ever learned. There were various unfounded reports than Kwei had arranged for the trophy to be sold on the black market and had then gone into hiding as a rich man. On two occasions, replicas of the trophy had been recovered after tip-offs from collectors, but both turned out to be fakes. It was rumoured that some people were making a good living from creating and selling replicas off the back of the missing trophy debacle. Many months later, FIFA decided that the trophy would never be found, and so commissioned the design and creation of a completely new trophy, consigning the lost trophy to legend.

Kwei halted, leaning against a banana tree to finish the last few puffs of his cigarette. It hadn't been a good day. For the second day running, he had failed to bring home any meat. No one could reasonably say that he hadn't tried – he'd been wandering the jungle for six hours now, but the few animals he had encountered had bolted before he could get a shot off - but his wife wasn't reasonable. She would say that he was lazy, and that he spent too much time dreaming. His daughters would agree, of course. As much as he loved them both, they took after their mother almost entirely. Ah well – they would have to eat rice again. It could be worse! Burning his fingers as he smoked the cigarette right down to the end, he tossed it to the floor, ground it out with his sandal and steeled himself for his return home.

The complaints began a few seconds after he shut the door behind himself. His wife's admonishments were swiftly echoed by his daughters, and he sunk down into a chair with a sigh. As much as he tried to prepare himself for these situations, and to convince himself he was not to blame, he never truly succeeded. After a few minutes of griping from the ladies in his life, he was sat with his head in his hands, holding back tears. Perhaps sensing that punishment had been aptly meted out, his wife and daughters ceased their lamentations and retreated into the building's only bedroom, slamming the door behind them.

It took some time for him to swallow away the tightness in his throat, but when he eventually raised his head, it was with purpose. Today, he would treat himself. He had been trying to do it as rarely as possible, always worried that the effect would no longer be so strong. But today he needed it. It was the only thing that kept him going. Glancing guiltily at the door, he padded over to his bookshelf, removing a few of the dog-eared books and retrieving a small silver-plated, patterned box that was hidden behind them. It was the box his father had given him. Two dragons curled around one another on the lid and his name was engraved in the oval space between them. He pressed the catch slowly, holding the box to his nose as he did so and enjoying the aroma of the precious contents. Standing up, he fished a small key from inside the box and inserted it into a cupboard on his wall. Closing his eyes and taking a few steady breaths, as was his ritual, he turned the key and opened the cupboard. Any worries he had about this experience losing its effect were instantly gone. His breath caught in his throat as he gazed at the gleaming treasure within, and a dizzy grin formed on his face. His mouth started to water in anticipation of the dreams to come as he donned the oversized football shirt he also kept in the cupboard and carefully lifted the trophy down, placing it reverently on the floor. Kneeling in front of it, he took the tin of aromatic metal polish from his silver box, along with a clean silk handkerchief that he used for polishing, and prepared to lose himself in pleasure.

Printed in the United Kingdom
by Lightning Source UK Ltd.
131516UK00001B/260/P